BURIED TROUBLES

A ROSARIA O'REILLY MYSTERY

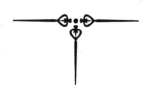

MARIAN McMAHON STANLEY

BARKING RAIN PRESS

Buried Troubles
Rosaria O'Reilly Mysteries, Book 2

Edited by Barbara Bailey (www.barkingrainpress.org/barbara-bailey/)

Proofread by Hannah Martine (www.portlandcopywriting.com)

Barking Rain Press
PO Box 822674
Vancouver, WA 98682 USA
www.BarkingRainPress.org

ISBN Trade Paperback: 978-1-941295-77-9
ISBN eBook: 978-1-941295-78-6
Library of Congress Control Number: 2018931551

First Edition: June 2018

Printed in the United States of America

DEDICATION

To the next generation. May they help
make the world a less troubled place.

———————

To Josie, Desmond, Johanna, Damian,
Nolan and Peter
With love from Nana

FOREWORD

LIBERTIES TAKEN

an Barry of *The New York Times* (and alumnus of Saint Bonaventure, the same Franciscan college in upstate New York that I attended) once commented in a column that the "chasm of presumption and misunderstanding between Irish America and Ireland is as deep as the Atlantic."

I have tried to be conscious of that thought while writing *Buried Troubles*. Still, as with any work of fiction set in real environs, I have taken liberties with historical events, persons, and places. These would include inventing an IRA conspiracy local to Connemara, imagining a dark institution at the end of the lovely, long road down the Errislannan Peninsula, rearranging the map between Clifden and Roundstone to better accommodate a chase scene down the bog road, creating entire edifices like the care home on the Galway Road, and proposing a fictional current Irish political scenario. These are deliberate fictions for purposes of story-telling.

As to any fictions and inaccuracies that were not deliberate, but were inserted for dramatic effect, I mean no offense and apologize for any errors in my research. This would especially apply around my mentions of the Gaelic Athletic Association, its competitive teams and matches, and the ancient Irish sport of hurling.

Likewise, my characters are an amalgam of different people, personality traits, and idiosyncrasies, and are not meant to represent any one person or family. Such is the case of Mossie O'Toole, as he blossomed from a cameo to a larger role. I hope the O'Tooles of Connemara are not offended by his earthy ways. Early readers seem to like Mossie, so that he will likely be featured in one of my next books, as will Sergeant Gerard Conneely of the local Garda.

All of the establishments mentioned are personal favorites from my travels in the area—in Clifden, the Buttermilk Lodge on the Westport Road, Cullen's Coffee Shop, Manion's Pub, the Clifden Bookshop, and in Galway City, the Quay Street Kitchen. I recommend them all highly.

Finally, to my long-lost and distant Burke and Conneely cousins, I have no doubt passed you on the streets and in the shops of Clifden or in Keough's Pub during our stays. Or, at least those of you who did not depart Ballyconneely years ago to London, Boston, New York or Sydney. All the best and God bless. Maybe one of these days...

CHAPTER 1

he hit came out of nowhere, a terrible, sudden bolt of pain at the back of his head. Gobsmacked. *Jesus. What the hell?* Patrick hit the cold water hard, the smell of brine and motor oil heavy as he gasped in shock. He went down fast but fought his way up. His head knocked away a couple of empty Bud Lite cans bobbing on the surface. Dazed, his arms flailing, he struggled to keep his head above the water. *Mother of God!* The pain was savage. He could see a figure up on the wharf watching him. Why wasn't he helping him? Was it that one smashed him on the head? Where was the guy he was supposed to meet? He needed help here.

Patrick tried to call out. The calls came from his mouth in frantic, hoarse whispers or watery gags. He strained to reach for the wharf pilings; just made it, but the surfaces were so slick that his hands kept slipping. Piece of luck, he found one irregularity in the wood sticking out that he could grasp—if only barely. Maybe enough for him to hang on. Everything was starting to look blurry. A tingling in his head. Had to stay with it. Had to keep his head out of the water. Had to stay with it.

The sound of wood against wood. He looked up to see a long oar hurtling down along the piling. The oar smashed against his hand, withdrew, and smashed it again. Patrick cried out and let go. As he sank, he could see the tall, shadowy figure on the wharf wielding the long oar like a giant dark archangel holding a fearsome staff. Patrick's kicks were feeble now. He could feel his blood warming the salt water around him. The scratch of the wharf barnacles on his cheek, the smell of seaweed under his chin. It all brought him—on the cusp of oblivion now—back to the cove near his parents' house in Ballyconneely. A cool, foggy, early summer evening there, heavy with the scent of the sea, his young black and white dog Fergus barking and chasing gulls across the sand and the rocks.

Better get going. Had to get to Clifden within the hour. Wind's coming up, water's getting rough and heavy, clouds gathering to the west. Getting darker now. Time to go.

CHAPTER 2

osaria O'Reilly turned a good-sized blackened bluefish on the grill and inhaled the heady scent of Cajun spices mixed with the smells of the harbor. Who could ask for more?

She took outsized pleasure from using her condo's tiny balcony in warm weather. Jutting over a glittering Boston Harbor, the balcony was one of the many benefits of living in Trinity Wharf, a refurbished granite warehouse on the waterfront.

"I'll take that glass of wine now," she called to the kitchen, pushing her silver hair away from her eyes. She ignored Archie, her West Highland White, who sat at her feet with his eyes pleading for just a little bit of that fish.

A few moments later, Rosaria was joined by Marguerite Fontaine. In her professional life Mother Superior of the Jeanne d'Arc order of teaching nuns, this day Marguerite wore jeans and a blue Boston Aquarium whale tee shirt. To Rosaria, Marguerite always looked stylish, no matter what she wore. Rosaria chalked it up to the nun's French heritage on one side, the other being Mohawk. Marguerite was genetically chic and she had those high cheekbones to boot. It just wasn't fair.

Now, the nun peered over Rosaria's shoulder, shooing Archie to the side with a stage-whispered "*Petit mediant*! Little beggar!"

"That's a good looking piece of fish," she said to Rosaria. "Sure you want all that seasoning on it? Might bury the taste."

Rosaria looked at her with elaborate surprise in her green eyes, brows arched. "And you, a Quebecois. Shocking, Mother Superior." She pointed to the fish in a dramatic gesture. "This, my dear, is the best of Cajun seasoning. Just the ticket for bluefish. A strong-flavored fish needs something with oomph"—here Rosaria made a fist and punched the air—"to balance it." She gave the nun another reproving glance. "Honestly, Marguerite. What do they feed you at the Motherhouse?"

"Gruel, dear. Nothing but gruel. No seasoning. I think we let too many Irish women into the order." Looking at the fish, she handed Rosaria a cold glass of Chardonnay. "Here. This will improve your temper. Well, this fish smells delicious. Point taken."

"You ever see a full bluefish?" Rosaria asked.

"Never had the pleasure."

"Ugly. A mouthful of vicious teeth. A school of them in a feeding frenzy is a sight to see. It'd give you nightmares for a week."

"Well, I'll be careful to avoid the experience if I can." The nun took a long look at Rosaria. "Glad to see you looking so well."

Rosaria nodded thoughtfully and took a sip of her wine. "Yep, feeling pretty good."

The winter before had been a tumultuous and violent one following the murder of an old nun in Marguerite's order. Rosaria had gotten involved in the search for answers and had barely survived that fateful winter. Now, she needed every moment of peace and physical recovery she could manage.

Invisible battle scars still kept her awake at night with disturbing dreams. The external battle scars—a broken nose that had healed slightly off-kilter and a damaged right eye—still had her avoiding the bathroom mirror.

The man in Rosaria's life, Boston Police Detective Solly Belkin, said that the crooked nose and the deep scar above her right eyebrow added a certain quirky and attractive interest to her face. And her hair—he loved her white hair now—a gorgeous color that had appeared almost overnight during that awful winter season. Rosaria appreciated Solly's gallantry, but personally agreed with another friend, cursed with a terrible candor, who said that she looked like an elderly boxer who'd lost a welterweight bout.

Rosaria shook her head and inhaled a deep breath of ocean air to clear those thoughts away. She took another sip of wine just before the sound of a blues riff from her cellphone on the granite kitchen counter reached the little balcony.

Rosaria handed Marguerite the grill fork and headed for the kitchen, the dog at her heels. "Have to get this. Don't let that burn. This might be Solly. Hope he doesn't have to cancel tonight."

But it wasn't Solly. After Rosaria punched the talk button and put the cellphone to her ear, she immediately began drowning in a cascade of disjointed words, sobs and tearful breaths. Rosaria held the phone away and closed her eyes for a few moments before gingerly putting the phone against her ear again, trying to figure out who was on the other end of the call. Through the sobs and broken sentences, she finally recognized that it was Bridie Callahan, an old friend from her hometown of Malford, now incoherent with despair for some reason.

"Bridie—is that you? What's wrong? Slow down. Take a deep breath."

Concentrating hard, Rosaria tried to listen again to the furious torrent of words and sobs, before she gave up. "I still can't understand you. Are you downstairs? Okay. Just calm down. Give the phone to George."

There was a fumbling at the other end of the line. Then, Rosaria heard the deep voice of the building's security guard.

"Hi George, it's okay," Rosaria said. "Let her up. Something's wrong. I'll take care of her."

———

Rosaria opened the door to a disheveled and sobbing Bridie Callahan, her storm of black hair loose and wild about her face, red and swollen with tears. From behind Rosaria, Archie charged Bridie with a frenzy of greeting, adding to the confusion until Rosaria pushed him away. She wrapped the younger woman in a hug. "Bridie, Bridie."

"Oh, my God." Bridie wiped her face with the palm of her hand. "Ro, oh my God."

"What's wrong?" She turned Bridie's face to hers.

Bridie couldn't talk for a few moments. Then, she choked out, "It's my sister's boy. The one from home you were helping with his project." Bridie stopped and stared at Rosaria in disbelief. "Padraig's dead. They found him in the water last night." She looked away. "Padraig's dead."

For a moment, Rosaria was confused. Bridie was using one of the Irish forms of Patrick—Padraig, pronounced *Paw-drig*, for her young nephew.

When she understood, she leaned her head against Bridie's. "Jesus, Bridie. I'm so sorry." Rosaria had never heard Bridie's Irish accent as heavy as it was tonight, the situation made worse as she began sobbing again and now hiccupping.

"What happened?" Rosaria asked, leading Bridie to a nearby couch. Exhausted, the young woman dropped heavily down onto the cushions and threw her head back. Rosaria slipped onto the couch beside her and Archie jumped up on the other side to join Bridie. Rosaria was about to push him down when she saw him wiggle close beside Bridie, pressing his body against her thigh and laying his head on her knee. Instinctively, Bridie reached down to stroke the little dog and she seemed to calm slightly.

Good dog. Good dog, thought Rosaria. *They just know.*

Bridie responded to Rosaria's question, her voice [in]terrupted by frequent hiccups. "They found him off the Lo[ng]... he was probably drinking and fell in and drowned." She [gave a] fierce shake of her head. "Ro, that couldn't have happened. [He doesn't] drink like that. He never takes more than a pint of an evening."

"Did you see the body, Bridie? You're sure it's Patrick?"

"Yes, yes. I saw him." Bridie put her face in her hands before looki[ng] again. "It was him."

"Oh, Bridie, Bridie." Rosaria reached over to stroke Bridie's arm. "You didn't go to identify him by yourself, did you?"

"I did. I was just at Assembly Square, picking up a few things when they called me. They found his Irish passport and a visitor visa on him. He had used my address and my cell as a local contact." Bridie rubbed the side of her face with her hand. "Jesus, Ro, I didn't know what to do. I couldn't reach anybody. I tried you."

Rosaria remembered with remorse now that she'd left her phone on the kitchen counter. They took only Marguerite's when they hired a small sailboat to explore the harbor islands that afternoon. "So," Bridie continued, "I took a cab over to that place. The morgue. And afterward, I just came here. "

"I'm glad you did," Rosaria said, feeling now her own frisson of shock and sadness at young Patrick Keenan's death.

Marguerite, who'd been standing quietly to the side, set a box of Kleenex and a glass of water on the coffee table in front of Bridie. "Drink some, Bridie. It will help," she said.

Bridie nodded. Her hand shook as, still hiccupping, she raised the glass to her lips. She looked up, noticing Marguerite for the first time. "Mother Superior? I didn't recognize you."

"In my civvies today, dear."

Bridie gave Marguerite a trembling smile before heaving a wet sigh and turning to face Rosaria. "I don't think he fell, Rosaria."

"Why not?"

"I told you," she said impatiently, rubbing the side of her face. "Patrick never drank that much. It just sounds convenient for them to say that's what happened when you have a young man, especially a young Irish man, out on the town."

"But it happens, Bridie, sad to say. It doesn't take much. A couple of drinks and a little stumble on the wharf." Rosaria concerned eyes met Bridie's. "It's tragic, but it happens."

No, Ro, no. When I saw him at that place. At the morgue." She stopped covered her face again for a moment before dropping her hands. "I saw . Oh, it was awful. He was all beat up. He had a terrible gash on his head." e reached her hand to the side of her head toward the back to show the spot. They said it was only because he'd been banging around under the wharf for a while."

Now, Bridie put her hand to her mouth. "Oh, Jesus, Mary and Joseph. Patrick banging around under the wharf . . ." Her voice tailed off in a low moan.

Rosaria let a few moments pass before asking, "Did you tell your sister yet?"

Bridie took a deep, wet breath and nodded. "I did. I did. She's destroyed. We're both destroyed." She stared into the distance, wiping her eyes. "So hard to believe. He was so much fun and such a bright boy. Maybe too bright sometimes. He was the package, wasn't he?"

Rosaria smiled and nodded.

"Oh, a wonderful boy, though I grant you that he could be full of himself," Bridie continued, patting the dog at her side with long, slow strokes. "You know how, when he had something in his mind, he'd keep going—dead set. But just young, you know. A good boy, just young."

"Right—a good kid, and he did have a head of steam on him sometimes," Rosaria said. "Not always a bad thing." She was relieved to see Bridie's blue eyes soften, and the hiccups seemed to have gone away. Maybe being with friends, maybe the talk, maybe the dog.

"Oh, he did, didn't he?" Bridie said. "God, he was just burning with that study thing you were helping him on." She turned to Rosaria, "but for the life of me I could never figure out what it was really about, could you? It seemed to change every time I talked to him."

"Well, maybe he was trying to figure it out as he learned more. That's sometimes how a project goes," Rosaria responded.

"Yes," Bridie said. "Well, it doesn't really matter now does it?" She dropped back on the couch and closed her eyes.

Rosaria put a comforting hand on Bridie's arm. She remembered how circumspect Patrick had been when she'd tried to help him with contacts for his independent research project at the National University at Galway. He'd remained coy about the shifting focus of the work, almost as if she were another student or an academic plotting to steal his idea for a thesis. *As if,* she thought. *Ridiculous*. Now, he was dead. Heartbreaking. She shook her head sadly.

"They'll probably need to do an autopsy." she said to Bridie.

"I don't know. Maybe we have to request one. I don't know anything about all this, Ro. I don't know what to do, what to ask for."

Bridie stopped and thought for a moment. Almost as if talking to herself, she continued, "I don't think he fell." She shook her head slowly, "No, he didn't fall. Patrick didn't fall."

Then, she faced Rosaria again, a plea in her eyes. "I thought maybe you and your friend Solly could help me. Maybe you could give him a call. See what's going on, what we should do and all. And just tell them, just *tell* them this was no accident. We have to..."

We? Did she say we? Rosaria caught her breath. *Just healing from a bad, rough time and now this on my doorstep so soon.* She glanced at Marguerite who was leaning, arms crossed, against the kitchen counter. Marguerite shook her head and closed her eyes briefly before shrugging her shoulders in sympathy. *What can you do? What can you do?*

She had to manage this, nip it in the bud. She had to say no. She wanted to help Bridie with the initial contact, but she didn't think she could handle more than that.

Too many emotions swept through in these few moments after a distraught Bridie asked her for help, including a sudden wave of fury. *Jesus Christ, how could Bridie have forgotten what I've just been through? Everyone thinks I'm so strong. I'm not. Dammit, I'm not.*

But it passed. It always passed.

In the end, without looking at Marguerite, Rosaria put her arm around Bridie's shoulder, pulled her close, kissed the top of her head and said, "Of course, honey, I'll call Solly. We can find out what the next steps are. Don't worry."

CHAPTER 3

osaria felt slightly off balance, a little dizzy, when she got up. She took a breath, straightened her shoulders and walked toward the kitchen. Bridie stayed on the couch, rhythmically stroking the small white dog and staring into the distance. Rosaria bit her lip as she passed Marguerite, who touched her shoulder briefly. Then, she picked up her cell from the counter and hit speed dial for Solly. He put her on hold for a couple of minutes while he finished another conversation.

"What's up?" he asked when he picked up her call again.

Rosaria told him about Patrick's death. Did he have any information on a drowning victim Patrick Keenan?

"Yeah, we got a drop-in off Long Wharf this morning. I caught it on rotation."

Rosaria knew that a *drop-in* was shorthand for people who'd fallen into the harbor. Usually young people who'd had too much to drink on the night-time cruises or at the harbor-side bars and took a tumble into the harbor. Sometimes they were fished out quickly. Sometimes no one noticed until it was too late.

"Solly."

"What?"

"This boy was someone's son, someone's nephew. Don't use that expression."

"Right. Sorry."

Rosaria also knew that casual, seemingly heartless terms like *drop-in* helped police distance themselves emotionally from the hard things society expected them to deal with every day. Having learned the details of his workaday life over the past year, Rosaria had a new respect for Solly's emotional stamina and that of his colleagues. But this time the use of the casual term *drop-in* was painful to hear.

"Anyway, what's the read on the situation so far?"

"Should I be talking to you about this, Ro? How are you involved? It's really a matter for his family."

Rosaria could almost see Solly rolling his eyes and running his big hand over his bald head, about to tell his buttinsky significant other that this affair was none of her business. "Hold on, Solly," Rosaria said as she walked over to the couch where Bridie sat watching her now, leaning forward, clasped hands on her knees.

"Putting you on speaker, Solly. This is Bridie Callahan, Patrick's aunt. She identified the body." Rosaria sat on the couch, Archie between her and Bridie, and placed the cellphone on the coffee table.

When Solly responded, Rosaria could hear the relief in his voice to have one of Patrick's family on the line.

"I'm sorry for your loss, Ms. Callahan."

"Thank you, Detective Belkin," Bridie whispered.

"You've met Bridie before," Rosaria inserted. "She's a waitress at the French Connection Bistro in Malford Square. We've known each other for a long time."

"Ah, I remember now. I thought the name sounded familiar. Again, I'm sorry for your loss, Ms. Callahan."

Bridie nodded as if the detective could see her acknowledgment of his condolences over the phone.

"So, Bridie asked me to help her get a sense of the situation so far. She has her own thoughts."

"I'll be interested to hear them."

Bridie started to respond, but Rosaria held her arm. "She'd like to hear what you have to say first."

"Okay." Solly started slowly. "Well, at the outset we thought this was a case of a misstep on the wharf. After—forgive me, Ms. Callahan—after a little too much to drink."

"But..." Rosaria prodded.

"I'm getting there, Ms. O'Reilly." Solly took a moment's pause. "The body had some wounds from being under the wharf and against the pilings when the tide came in."

Rosaria heard a small, strangled intake of breath beside her at Bridie's vision again of Patrick's body under Long Wharf. She leaned into Bridie for a moment in support.

"But there is a gash on the side of the head toward the back that we don't like."

Bridie sat up and came to life. "Right, Detective Belkin. I saw that too. Toward the back. I could see it even though Patrick was on his back when I saw him in that place."

Rosaria expected Bridie to break down at the thought of Patrick in the morgue. Instead she was suddenly animated to be confirmed in her suspicions.

"It looks like the blow that killed him came from the edge of a heavy object— wooden." Solly said. "We're checking out a heavy wooden oar we found floating in the channel."

Bridie nodded numbly.

"He had some bruises on his hand too, with a splinter. As if his hand had been hit with something like the oar." Solly said this last part gently.

"Mother of God," Bridie whispered.

"And, as for the drinking part," Solly continued, "your nephew's alcohol level was around .02%—about one beer. So, that's not really a factor here."

"I told you," Bridie said firmly, speaking directly to Rosaria, as if Rosaria had accused Patrick of being drunk and falling into the harbor. And maybe she sort of did, Rosaria thought, when she'd said earlier, *Well, it happens.*

"We'll know more after a full autopsy," Solly said, "but this doesn't look like an accident." He'd about finished when he added, "Oh, and he still had his wallet and passport—so we weren't thinking robbery. Did he have a cellphone, Ms. Callahan?"

"Oh yes. He was texting all the time."

"Wasn't on him, so we'll have to search for that—unless someone took it or it fell into the water."

"Okay," Bridie said softly, her mind elsewhere. Rosaria could see that the satisfaction of being validated in her reading of the situation that had buoyed Bridie originally was dissipating just as suddenly. She could sense that Bridie once again saw her young nephew on the morgue's stainless steel table, and her body slumped in despair.

"Ms. Callahan, under these circumstances, I'd like you to come down to the Tremont Street station for an in-depth interview. We need to know more about Patrick—his friends, where he was living, what he was doing with his time—all that."

Again, Bridie nodded as if Solly could see her. "She says okay," Rosaria inserted, nudging Bridie who was somewhere else in her mind.

"Do you think you'll be up to coming to the station in the morning, Ms. Callahan?" Solly clearly wanted a direct answer from Bridie.

Rosaria nudged Bridie again. "Yes, okay, okay," Bridie came to with a start and responded. "I have to change my shift." She shook her head, murmuring. "I'll have to take time off for this anyway. Maybe I should take a leave. I'll have to take the body home. This is so awful..." And then Bridie was lost in a well of deep grief again.

"How about 10:30, after the traffic clears up?" Solly soldiered on. Rosaria was relieved he hadn't said *after the traffic dies down*.

Bridie came to and remembered where she was in the conversation. "Yes. I'll be there," she responded slowly. "Could I bring Rosaria with me?"

Oh God, thought Rosaria, suddenly feeling a true wave of panic at getting involved further with another murder investigation. *I'm not ready for this. I'm still a mess. Jesus.*

"As a friend of the family?" Solly asked cautiously

"She's a friend of mine, Detective, and I'm all the real family Patrick had over here."

"I see. Do you feel comfortable coming to the station with Ms. Callahan, Ms. O'Reilly?" Solly asked in a very deliberate tone. Rosaria could feel his willing her over the phone. *You can't handle this right now, sweetheart. You're still a mess from everything that happened last year. Back out nicely, but back out now.*

Rosaria hesitated long enough that Bridie turned to her with a surprised, questioning look on her tear-streaked face.

Dammit. "No problem, no problem," Rosaria finally stuttered, giving Bridie a smile that was more wobbly than she would have liked. *What is it with me?* she thought. *This could push me over the edge. It's like I have an overdeveloped Get-Involved-in-Messy-Situations gene. I know where that comes from. My mentor—the old nun murdered last year. What a legacy.*

She heard Solly sigh at the other end of the phone. She may have heard a soft *"Shit"* under his breath and hoped Bridie hadn't caught it as well.

It took him a long time to respond. "Fine," he said slowly, "then we'll see you both in the morning. Thank you, Ms. Callahan."

"Thank you, Detective," Bridie responded. Rosaria closed the call while Bridie dropped back in the couch in exhaustion.

Rosaria had almost forgotten Marguerite was across the room, until the nun moved away from the kitchen counter and said, "Bridie, I'll walk you to the Haymarket T stop if you like. It's on my way. I have to catch the train at North Station to the Motherhouse in about an hour. Perhaps we can take the long way down the Greenway. Walking might help settle you a little."

Gathering her bag from a nearby chair, she added, "And maybe when you get home, Sister Josepha from The Immaculate in Everett might stop by, make a cup of tea, sit with you for a while. Would you like that? "

"Yes, I would, thank you," Bridie whispered before jerking herself into motion and responded in a firmer voice, "I'd like that. That would be good,

Mother." She turned to Rosaria before picking up her things and giving Archie a grateful goodbye squeeze. "Should I meet you here tomorrow and we'll go over together, Ro?"

Here we go. Rosaria gave her a slow, thoughtful smile before responding, "Okay. Here about 9:00? We'll have a chance to talk a little more and allow some time in case the T's not on schedule." Rosaria was still stunned at how fast the situation was moving, but starting to adjust. Maybe even getting into gear.

"What would I have done without you?" Bridie hugged Rosaria tightly before walking out the door the nun held open. Marguerite stopped briefly behind Bridie and gazed back at Rosaria, giving the same shrug to her that she had earlier. *What can you do? What can you do but help?*

A cup of untouched and cold coffee sat in front of Bridie in Rosaria's kitchen the next day. The morning sun showed no mercy on Bridie's face, ravaged by a sleepless, grief-drenched night.

Rosaria sat across from her friend at the granite island. "Patrick wasn't close to anyone here other than you, was he, Bridie? I know he was in a sublet for a few weeks, and he and his roommates were probably all just like ships in the night anyway."

"Well, you know, he did go out on the town with his roommates a few times. They all got along. But, no, no, he really knew no one to start with. We have only my cousin Claire in Chelsea, and she's off visiting her daughter in California for the summer. No one else to speak of."

She paused. "I wonder now if Patrick might have had words with someone at The Point, that bar he went to a few times down there on the waterfront. Maybe a person followed him to the wharf. Do you think that could have happened?"

"Well, it certainly does happen that people get into arguments at bars and the tiff gets carried outside. But, Patrick didn't seem like the kind of guy who'd look for conflict. I mean, he might go on for a bit, but he seemed like more of a..." Rosaria searched for a description here, "more of a just walk-away kind of guy, rather than a brawler."

"Yes, that's right. He'd say his piece but just walk away, you know, if there was some kind of fuss. He was friendly-like, good company." Bridie's eyes reddened. "He loved the *craic*, to chat and have a good laugh with people. Didn't matter if they were friends or strangers."

Rosaria glanced over at Archie, sleeping in the sun, and thought for a moment. "Anybody at home ever have an issue with him, Bridie?"

"God, no. Why would you think that? Everyone loved Patrick at home, not an enemy in the world. I'm sorry, Ro, I know you're a smart lady—worlds smarter than I am—but that's daft."

"Yeah, probably daft," Rosaria agreed as she looked at the time on her cell-phone and leaned over to pick up her bag. "Well, let's be going then. The Orange line to Ruggles is usually on time, but you never know."

Rosaria had prepared herself for a bare interview room with a metal table and chairs at Boston Police Headquarters for Solly's conversation with Bridie. Now, she mouthed an affectionate "thanks" to Solly as she and Bridie were ushered into a temporarily unused conference room with a wooden table, blue fabric-covered seats, and a window with full natural light looking out on Tremont Street.

Solly gave Rosaria a lift of his chin in acknowledgment and gestured to Bridie to take a seat. "Would you like a glass of water or a cup of coffee or tea, Ms. Callahan?"

"A glass of water would be great, Thanks."

Rosaria shook her head when Solly looked at her with the same question. He walked across the room and was pouring a glass of water from a pitcher on the sideboard when Bridie surprised them both. She suddenly exploded with a loud and aggressive, "He didn't just fall in, Detective, and he wasn't drunk. I just want to say that up front." Her eyes were wet and her trembling jaw thrust forward.

Rosaria moved her arm to embrace Bridie around the shoulders. "We know that, honey."

"Well, I want him to say it. I want him to say it." Bridie looked at Solly intently. "I want to tell my sister that." She wiped her eyes. "I want to tell my sister that," she repeated.

Solly put the glass of water in front of Bridie and leaned forward, his palms flat on the table. "No, Ms. Callahan, it doesn't look as if your nephew just fell into the harbor, and we know he wasn't drunk."

"That's good," Bridie responded shakily, not looking at Solly but at her hands clasped around the glass of water. "I wanted to hear you say that."

"Well, you just did." He sat down, pulled an iPad across the table in front of him, and posed it to take notes. Rosaria knew that Solly used small, black spiraled notebooks in the field, but was trying to adjust to electronic note-taking—at least when he was in the station. It was not an altogether comfortable transition for him. "Now, let's get to work. Let's start with who Patrick was, what he was doing over here, who he was seeing, where he lived."

And so it began. Patrick's parents' contact information and some history. An only child from the small village of Ballyconneely outside Clifden, County Galway. Excellent health, athletic, a football player, no substance abuse issues, a good student, a wide circle of friends. Matriculated student at the National University Galway due to get his degree this year, pending completion of his independent study project. Nice girlfriend, Sarah Glynn from Tuam, at university with him.

"How about his address here in Cambridge?"

"Off River Street, near Central Square." Bridie pushed an index card over the table to the detective with Patrick's address.

"You know the names of any other kids in the apartment?"

"I just remember one, Paul Malloy, I think." She frowned. "I don't have his phone number."

"That's okay, we'll find a way to be in touch with him," Solly assured her. "Any issues with his roommates?"

"No, no, they all got on like a house afire. Seemed like nice boys, though of course, I only met them the once or twice," Bridie responded.

"How did Patrick get around?"

"On the T. He had no car and I couldn't lend him mine. I need it for work."

Bridie had started to rock back and forth in her chair, as if she might fall apart any moment. Better cut to the chase before she did.

"What was Patrick working on here?"

"Just what I told you and Rosaria—American support for the Irish Republican Army during The Troubles in Northern Ireland. I can't tell you much more than that."

Bridie thought for a moment and slowed her rocking. "I do know that he was working hard on it. He told me he stayed up all night, just the night before he was killed, writing some kind of report or article."

Then Bridie slumped in the chair. "That's all I can tell you." She paused, "But maybe Rosaria can tell you about an appointment he had with the man at the homeless shelter—Saint Martin's. I don't know if that would help."

"Oh?" Solly turned to Rosaria.

"Yes, well." Rosaria shrugged. "I would really like to tell you about that, but I just set up the meeting. I wasn't there. And Patrick wasn't ready to tell me about what the subject matter was."

"You set up the meeting and he wouldn't tell you about what the topic was?" Solly raised his eyebrows.

"Yeah," said Rosaria ruefully. "He stonewalled me."

"Interesting," commented Solly.

"Rude, actually," replied Rosaria. "Sorry, Bridie."

"It's okay, Ro." Bridie shrugged.

And so, after an hour of questioning and information sharing, with Solly taking notes, Rosaria and Bridie Callahan walked back to the Orange Line at Ruggles Street station. Behind them, back at the Boston Police Department headquarters, a big city system clicked into gear to find out who murdered young Patrick Keenan last night on Long Wharf.

CHAPTER 4

ater that evening as she was cooking up a light dinner for herself, Rosaria looked out the big window facing the harbor, lost in thought. She considered Patrick Keenan's tragic end and remembered when she'd first met him over dinner at his Aunt Bridie's.

That soft, early summer night that Rosaria met Patrick, they'd had dinner at Bridie's house. Bridie had asked Rosaria to see if she might meet Patrick and perhaps suggest some contacts for his independent study at the university back home in Ireland. Rosaria was glad to agree, both to support her friend's nephew and—selfishly—to support herself during this time of her own healing. Rosaria wanted to fill these hard days with as many positive contributions as she could—a defense against the darkness that still threatened to engulf her.

Bridie lived on the second floor of one of those 1920's two-family houses in Malford with the gumwood molding, large windows, and high ceilings. Rosaria could remember thinking, *Why does anyone live in those new apartment buildings going up all over the suburbs when they could live here, close to the city, in a real house?*

She could see that Bridie had gone to great trouble with the meal—a well-cooked ham, smashed potatoes with a sweet turnip and carrots dish, and sautéed cabbage with garlic and bacon. The apartment smelled heavenly between the cooking and the fresh breezes coming through the open dining room windows.

Like any hungry young student on a limited budget, and still as thin as a rail, Patrick ate his fill and more of his aunt's meal.

"So, what have you seen now since you've been here, Patrick?" she had asked him.

"Oh, I have been out with these guys in my sublet a little—Fenway Park, Faneuil Hall Market, the North End. And last night I was at the Burren—we had a grand time."

"The Burren?" laughed Rosaria. "Now that's the place for spending an evening, for the *craic*." The bar in Davis Square in Somerville was legendary for Irish music and good times—or *craic* as the Irish said.

Bridie gave Patrick a wry smile. "But now, Ro, Patrick has to settle down to work on a project for his degree at the University. That's what he came over here to do. With all his partying around, I'm not so sure now."

"Oh, I haven't forgotten. I'll tell you that," Patrick assured his aunt. His dark hair fell over his forehead as he shook his head and applied himself to loading another forkful from his dinner plate.

"What's the focus of your project, Patrick?"

"Well, it's not as focused as it should be." He chuckled. "My advisor will tell you that." He closed his eyes with pleasure as he tucked the forkful of his aunt's good cooking into his mouth.

"I'm hoping to narrow it down on this visit," he said between bites, "but generally it's about Irish-American support of the IRA during The Troubles in Northern Ireland. Before the peace process and the Good Friday Agreement in 1998."

Rosaria had always marveled at the characterization of the stunning violence in Northern Ireland that went on for four decades and took over 3500 lives in a small country—essentially a long-running war—as The Troubles. It sounded like a tactful way to describe a contained family problem—perhaps an impending divorce, a child experimenting with drugs or a parent with a terminal cancer. Or all three. *The Donnellys have had some troubles, you know. Pity.* Not what you'd call an accurate description of bombs blowing up innocent people in the marketplace or the pub, not soldiers on Bloody Sunday mowing down unarmed protestors, not executions and torture, not bullet-ridden Mass cards left in mailboxes, not the shoveling up of body parts on the streets of Belfast.

"That's a pretty big topic," she said instead. "I suppose, for some, that support probably continues to this day."

Patrick put his fork down and wiped his mouth with his napkin. "Well, really not all that many. Everyone's pretty much moved on now to the political process. There was a transition period where some saw the path to power as 'the ballot paper in one hand and the assault rifle in the other.' Those days are gone except for a hardline fringe element. Those who never bought in, and still don't. But for most people today, it's the political process."

He shrugged, "I expect there are a few from here in the US who still support the Real IRA and the other splinter groups, the ones who don't denounce violence to bring the six northern counties under the Irish flag again. Not too many. Fewer every day. Still, they are a problem. And not just in the north—some of that ilk in the south, in the Republic too."

"Haven't a lot of those hardliners in the Real IRA kind of morphed into criminal gangs with drugs and robberies?" Rosaria asked before adding. "Still, I shouldn't say, I don't know who's who in the whole mess."

"Yeah, it's pretty complicated. They're not all thugs, you know, no matter what you read in the papers. One man's thug is another man's freedom fighter, as they say. Some highly educated people fancy themselves revolutionary nationalists and are active in surprising ways."

"Like how surprising?"

"Oh, maybe violent things they would never do in normal times."

Rosaria considered what *those things* might be, but decided she didn't need to hear the specifics over dinner.

Patrick resumed eating. He chewed slowly and thoughtfully for a few moments before saying. "But, you know, as I say, the truth is that many people, most of the country, certainly south of the border, they've moved on from those chapters. So much of all that feels like ancient history. We're part of the EU now. The world is much wider for our generation. We're Irish, of course, but we're Europeans too." He leaned back in his chair and took a sip of his beer.

"Still, that must have been a tough time," Rosaria commented.

"It was, it was. But, receding further and further into the past since the peace agreement. You know, the demographics are changing. Catholics were only twenty-two percent of the population in Northern Ireland in 1922, when we won our freedom in the South. Now—they're inching on up to the high forties. And suppose if England really wants to leave the EU—God knows where that will go, such a daft proposal—there may be more in Northern Ireland who'll want to stay part of the EU with the Republic. They get a good deal of funding from the EU for regional development and farming funds. They don't want a hard border with the South either."

He laughed. "That would be a nightmare for the non-Catholics in the North who want to stay on as British subjects. The Prods would probably start their own resistance movement. Just crazy there." Patrick kept smiling and shook his head with a low laugh as he reached for a second helping of the mashed turnip and carrot dish.

"Pretty dramatic changes," Rosaria commented.

"Oh yeah, now in the South, there are people already working on what a consolidation might look like—how it would work, and it's looking like the EU would accept Northern Ireland as part of the EU if people in the North voted for reunification. A poll shows over sixty-five percent of the population in the South would approve of reunification. I think that's likely to increase. Before, they were almost becoming indifferent as things got more complicated in the North. They didn't want all those troubles and that violence spilling over to the South, you know, even though they sympathized with and supported the Catholics in Northern Ireland. At heart, the fact is that many want the island to return to one nation. Can't get beyond that. It's an emotional thing, a heart thing. Lost sheep back into the fold, part of the real Irish nation—not some emotionally disengaged, shell of an empire."

Patrick raised his fork to make a point. "The UK would probably be glad to be rid of the headaches in Northern Ireland. They have enough on their hands. And now the Scots are making noises about independence. God bless them—it's about time, but it may be just noise." Patrick paused. "You know, there's even a politician in Ireland who was an exIRA leader—the big one— Cathal McKenna—who's a TD, that's a member of our parliament—the Dail. Anyway, I can't believe it, he's running for *Taoiseach*."

"Pardon me? Running for what?"

"For *Taoiseach*—our prime minister for the Irish Republic. *Taoiseach* is Irish for chieftain. It's pronounced Tea-shock."

"Well, that's a significant step."

"I'd say so," Patrick said. "He has some passionate support—especially among those who think he's the best one to bring the northern counties back under the Irish flag." Then, he added dryly, "Now, I don't know if he's got a good shot—since," he paused and took a careful drink of beer, not looking at her, "there are those who say he has a history. But, in any case, he certainly has the ambition."

"I imagine there are a lot of people from that time and that place that have a history. And didn't McKenna have a lead role in the peace process?"

"That's the truth, he did and you have to give him enormous credit for that, yet..." Patrick didn't finish that sentence. "Anyway, I'm not saying the struggle doesn't continue for some—over there and here—but I'm not focusing on those who are active right now. I'm interested in those active around the seventies." His blue eyes moved away from her. "A good many hard things happened in those days, much of it still coming to light. That's really what I'm looking at."

"Like what hard things?"

He avoided her eyes again. "Oh, I'd rather not go into it now, Rosaria—it's just something in my head. I don't know if I can even articulate it for you, so I'd rather not talk about it yet." Patrick straightened the silverware at his place setting before continuing. "But I think a big piece of the story I'm looking at is over here."

Bridie frowned at Rosaria before giving her nephew an annoyed glance. "Well, you know, Rosaria could help more if she knew what you're about, Patrick."

"Oh, I know, I know, Aunt Bridie. When I can work it out in my head, I'll let you know—really." He looked at them both apologetically. "In the meantime, there is so much else about the project to work on. Maybe we can come back to that piece later?" He gave Rosaria a winning smile.

"Okay." Rosaria drew the "Okay" out slowly and then leaned her elbows on the table. "How did you plan to go about getting information on this project of yours?" she said.

Patrick gave Rosaria a grateful look. "Well, I thought if I could just get to know the names of some of the supporters from those days over here. Maybe the people who organized and went to the fundraisers that supported the IRA and all. That would be a start, wouldn't it?"

"Yes, it would," replied Rosaria. "Those fundraisers were years ago and I was never involved in them, but I do have some contacts that are active in various Irish-American organizations. They'd probably be able to offer some guidance."

"Oh, I knew you were the right person, Ro." Bridie smiled across the table at her friend with affection. "Anyone for coffee with a touch of the Jay?"

CHAPTER 5

CONNEMARA, IRELAND—1974

he boy used to slip out of bed late in the evening and walk down the lane to the Home, watching for his father if he'd not been back for dinner. The boy was small enough that he could tuck himself between the rusty iron fence and a thick old oak with scratchy bark.

This night, he watched as a stocky nun carried a tiny bundle through a worn, heavy wooden door at the side of the hall, her gait uneven on the rough ground. A limp—perhaps a bad hip. She struggled slightly, but held the bundle with firm, practiced arms. Once, he saw a tiny hand fall out of the wrapped sheet and he thought he saw it move—a little twitch, then nothing more.

The nun maintained her balance and reached a hillock where his father stood waiting with another workman, both leaning on a large concrete slab pitched on its side. His father turned his face toward the iron fence for a moment as he took the small bundle from the nun. The boy quickly ducked behind the oak. But not quickly enough.

When he dared to lean out to look again, he saw the nun and the two men standing with their heads bowed. The men were holding their hats before them. Then, the nun crossed herself, and started back to the hall. The men crossed themselves as well and put on their hats. Each took a side of the concrete slab to replace it on the front of the vault. The boy saw his father's sidelong glance toward him as he lifted the earth-blackened concrete.

His father had never taken his hand to him. More than could be said for many fathers in the village. But he was a heavyset, quiet man with a dark stare when he was of a mind, and the boy could be afraid of him on the occasion. That night when he got home, he took his son outside by the back wall and spoke more words than the boy ever heard from him.

It was hard with the babies, all together like that. They caught things from each other. It could be the influenza or scarlet fever—or maybe they were born weak or things didn't go well at the birth. And the nuns at Saint Mary's were so overworked, and didn't have the money to give the poor babes the best of care. The Home was always cold and damp in the mountain bogs.

Others from the village never went down the long lane to the Home excepting the delivery men from the village. And they left as soon as they dropped their parcels. Cars came occasionally, usually with American visitors, people looking to adopt, but coming or going, they never stopped in the village. Not the nuns or, God forbid, the mothers ever came into the village. And people said the shadow of the place was warning enough to any local girls not to stray.

"I work at Saint Mary's every day to keep the roof over your head," he said. "Those girls at Saint Mary's now, the ones that got caught with babies. Didn't they deserve it? What could they expect for those poor little bairns? If they got lucky, the nuns found homes for them, but if they got sick or the birth didn't go well, now what could the nuns do?"

His father ended his speech with a warning not to say anything about the digging and the sad little bundles his father carried into the hole, to join the others in the old burial vault. Mounds of ancient bones and new rows of baby and child-sized bundles, occasionally punctuated by one or two that might be a little larger, some even adult-sized.

No, the boy must never say anything, sad enough business as it was. The nuns needed no further trouble. And so, the boy never did say anything about the tiny bundles.

CHAPTER 6

he Starbucks on Tremont Street in downtown Boston was buzzing, the smell of brewing coffee rich and heady as it wafted out the door into the early summer air.

Rosaria had agreed to see Patrick before his meeting with Liam Joyce, Executive Director at the Saint Martin de Porres Shelter for the Homeless by Boston Common. She was glad to have helped set up this meeting for Patrick, but also had a bone to pick on with him today. He'd missed a different meeting she'd set up for him—a high-profile contact. She'd had to use a good deal of social capital to get the man to talk to Patrick and was annoyed to find he had not kept the commitment.

While she looked around for two empty seats, Rosaria also mused that she wasn't quite sure how Liam Joyce at the homeless shelter fit into the scope of Patrick's project. As she recalled, his name wasn't on any list of donors or organizers in the Irish-American groups that supported community efforts in Northern Ireland at some point.

Community efforts in Northern Ireland, she mused. They were sometimes called such with a wink and a nod. Most really were, but there was no doubt that during The Troubles some or a good deal of money raised flowed to the Cause or the IRA. It was hard to believe that this fact was not known at some level to the organizations on this side of the Atlantic. Less direct contributions perhaps than the hats passed around at South Boston bars while songs of revolution played in the background, but money flowing to the Cause just the same.

Of course, she thought, coming back to today, *maybe Patrick had found a connection between Liam Joyce at the homeless shelter and those activities in Belfast during the '70s.* Unexpected connections did happen on projects. *Besides,* she reminded herself, *this is Patrick's project, not hers.*

Spotting two recently vacated seats by the window at Starbucks, Rosaria quickly claimed them by placing a few index cards and a pen from her bag in front of one chair and her scarf on the back of the other. Then, she headed for the coffee line, checking out the chocolate covered biscotti as she did so.

"Skim latte grande. Name's Rosaria," she said to the young woman when she got to the counter, scooping up the biscotti and paying with her phone. The young woman had just written her name on the paper cup when Rosaria felt a hand on her arm.

"You beat me here. The Red Line was flat out crawling. And I had to make a stop at the post office to mail something home first. Got a seat?"

Patrick's cheeks were flushed. He'd probably run the last few blocks. Rosaria could also see that he had a bad case of bed-head, as if he'd slept on his hair all wrong and hadn't had time to take a shower. But, with the grace of his years, this young man could carry off his dark brown hair sticking out at odd, almost lateral directions. Yes, it was his youth, she decided. If Patrick had been her age, the effect would have been that of an unappealing, disheveled waster. Instead, and although she was annoyed with him, Rosaria could barely resist a motherly inclination to ruffle that untidy hair.

"Right over there, by the window." She pointed. "I've already ordered. See you over there after you order."

Rosaria had taken her seat and was leisurely starting to unwrap her biscotti when she was jolted by a booming, operatic male voice calling her name. "*Rosaria, tu* deliciuso *café con leche desnatada esta listo*!" with a special emphasis on the *deliciuso*.

Rosaria smiled as she went back to the counter. "*Si, yo soy Rosaria, muchas gracias*," she said to the stocky, blond barista—looking beyond her for what he obviously assumed was his Latina customer. "Rosaria. I think you have my skim latte."

The young man turned a startled gaze to the tall, fair Irishwoman in front of him. "Sorry. The name, you know—Rosaria—just practicing my Spanish a little," he said with a sheepish grin.

"Not a problem. Happens all the time. It can be an Irish name too. Your Spanish is lovely. Made me feel more interesting."

They both laughed.

Patrick joined Rosaria in a few minutes at the window-side table, throwing his blue knapsack beside his chair and chuckling. "You know, at home we often use the Irish *Padraig,* instead of Patrick. But I decided that it's such a complication when you travel—Irish language names seem to befuddle people, even in Boston. I'm christened Padraig, but even my parents call me the English Patrick. Anyway, so, I told the barista my name was Pat. I can't imagine what that one would do with writing Padraig on my coffee cup."

Rosaria laughed, "Good move." *Damn. It is hard to stay angry at this young man.*

"Good to see you, Rosaria," Patrick said. Then, he looked around and commented, "Great city, this. Tons of energy and things going on. Young people." He smiled and looked-up. "Nicely left-wing politically. Reminds me of Galway City a little."

He moved his chair and settled in. "But not so old as Galway, you know." Patrick laughed. "Boston thinks it's old, but it's young. Galway City's been around for a while. Since the 13th or 14th century."

"Well, that's older," Rosaria replied. "But Boston's old for us in the States. You know, I'm familiar with Galway. I did a program there as a student and I've spent a number of holidays there. Great city."

"That's right. Bridie told me that. So, you know what I mean." He smiled.

"I do indeed," Rosaria replied before switching subjects. She leaned forward on her elbows and looked at him curiously. "Hey, I crossed paths with Jim O'Sullivan the other day. I was surprised to hear that you'd cancelled your appointment with him about his work with the Boston for Ireland group."

"Oh, right," the young man replied—not quite as embarrassed as she thought he should be. She hoped he wasn't one of those clueless young people who casually blew off commitments and appointments, after asking you to help them.

"Well, you know, I got involved researching another angle. One thing led to another and, you know..." He shrugged and gave her a sheepish smile.

"And you cancelled at the last minute. Jim is a very busy man, Patrick. That meeting was a favor to me. I was very upset to find out you cancelled."

"Oh, I am sorry, Rosaria. It won't happen again."

"I hope not," she replied curtly. "What about the meeting with Sean Fleming at Derry Aid? That one was tough to get too. I certainly hope you're not going to stand Mr. Fleming up."

"Yeah," Patrick said. "I think that's on the book for the beginning of next week. Don't worry, I'll be there."

Why does he seem so disinterested? Rosaria thought. These appointments were all right on target for what he'd said he was researching.

"But this one with Joyce is the best. Thanks loads for setting it up for me. Brilliant," he said. Rosaria noted a new energy in Patrick's voice.

"Glad to do it, Patrick," Rosaria replied, following with what she knew was a school-marmish comment. "So glad you aren't too busy to keep the appointment and be on time."

She was peeved again with herself for being charmed at Patrick's wry, boyish smile and his whispered reply, "Sorry, Rosaria. Sorry, sorry, sorry."

"Okay," she said shortly, but had to smile. Taking a sip of her latte, she asked, "Tell me, why is Liam Joyce of such high interest to your project, Patrick? Other than the fact that he's Irish—comes from Galway too, right?"

"Yes, outside Clifden, near where my family lives. He has a common last name there."

"Do you know his family?"

"My parents know of his people. Not him personally, except a glimpse when he came home for a visit or maybe they'd read about him now and again in the papers."

"Read about him for what? His work with the homeless?"

"Right. They call him Saint Liam. Do they call him that here?"

"Well, in some circles. He's very well respected—completely devoted to his work. Not married, no outside life, lives in a tiny room at Saint Martin's."

"I like the name of the shelter," Patrick said. "Martin dePorres, a South American saint, I think. Right?"

"Right," Rosaria replied. "Seventeenth century mixed-race Peruvian—a Dominican, if I recall. He's the patron saint of social justice. A good choice."

Patrick nodded.

Rosaria picked up the thread of the conversation again. "But, can we get back to Liam Joyce? How is he a terrific contact other than the fact that he's also a saint for social justice in Boston? I mean, he's not even on the list of donors you researched."

Patrick looked uncomfortable and moved back in his chair. "Right. But I think he may have some important information, even if he wasn't directly involved at the time."

"In Galway? Pretty far from operations in Northern Ireland."

"True, true. But it was an odd situation." He pulled back further from the table. "Not something I can talk about yet, but..." He looked at her with a plea in his eyes not to press him further. "I will. I will when I can. I promise."

Rosaria frowned and shook her head. "Okay. I don't get it, but okay. Let's go." She reached for her coat.

Patrick touched Rosaria's arm and met her eyes. "Ro, just to be clear, I'm going to take this meeting with Liam Joyce alone." Patrick's tone was firm and polite, if somewhat awkward. "I don't need you to be there. I can handle this one on my own." He gave her that damned charming smile.

Of course, Rosaria hadn't fully expected to be included in the meeting, but now she was surprised with how hurt and disappointed she was at being excluded. Patrick was being so mysterious about his project, her curiosity was being piqued. She was becoming increasingly interested in what exactly Patrick was looking to find. In addition, she was helping him set up these meetings with acquaintances from her business days, and she wanted some sense of what they were about. That was reasonable, wasn't it?

Maintaining her dignity at being put in her place by this very young man, Rosaria gave a careful, equally polite reply. "Right, Patrick. If that's the way you want to do it. It's your project."

He nodded, avoiding her eyes.

Their exchange came to an abrupt end as other customers pushed their way through the door to get their morning coffee. Her face set, Rosaria took a moment before tilting her chin upward, a signal for Patrick to move on.

Patrick could barely contain his excitement as they walked toward Saint Martin House. Though she was a tall woman with a long stride, Rosaria had to work to keep up with him. At the intersection of Boylston and Tremont, she'd held his arm back as he started to walk against the light in heavy traffic.

"Are you sure you're not from Boston?" she commented. "You act like a Boston pedestrian—worse than Boston drivers."

"Hey, we could have made it across easy, Ro."

"You can, I can't," The light turned and they started across the street with a clutch of other pedestrians. "I have this peripheral vision problem on my right side. I'm told that it's temporary, but right now I can't really see so clearly if there is an oncoming car."

Patrick stopped and turned to her. "Oh, sorry. The accident Aunt Bridie referred to?"

"Sort of," she replied with a smile, glad that Bridie had not given Patrick more details. How easily she'd said *sort of,* how smoothly it rolled off her tongue. *An accident? Sort of. A murderous assault more like it. On the Gloucester coast, her head smashed against a granite boulder by a psychopathic brute.*

The "insult to the brain," as the doctor called it, had impacted her vision. The loss of the peripheral vision on her right side, again temporary if she was lucky, and the occasional shimmering or flashing light just outside her field of sight. That too should go away in time, with work. And maybe it wouldn't. She'd just have to accommodate all that could be repaired—like her broken nose still waiting for more surgery—and be grateful she was alive.

Rosaria brought herself back from that time to this day—filled with a rush of gratitude to be alive and walking on a busy Boston street. A bright sun over the bustle of the sidewalks, its light cut in and out by the shadows of city buildings. She felt a random surge of pleasure just to be walking in a crowd of other able-bodied pedestrians, jostling against each other on the sidewalk.

The streets were still a mess of demolition and reconstruction. Did it ever end? Those infernal orange barrels with reflective tape strung between them. And the cones—meant to help guide pedestrians—cones that she often couldn't see until too late and frequently tripped over.

But still. Present and upright, with almost everything in her body working properly. Making her way in a crowd, accompanied by a slightly annoying but buoyant young Irishman on a mission.

Patrick continued to walk, far ahead of Rosaria, almost as if he'd wanted to lose her in the crowd. When he reached Saint Martin's, working his way through the milling street people lined up for a free breakfast near the entrance, he turned to her with a quick wave, really more a dismissal than a goodbye. He was obviously eager to enter the shelter and leave her behind.

Before he disappeared, Rosaria called to him over the crowd. "Meet you up at the corner of Tremont and Boylston after." She'd pointed toward the end of the street.

Reluctantly—had she seen a slight scowl on his face?—Patrick nodded.

What's this? She resolved to confront him about this whole business after he got out of this meeting. Frustrated, Rosaria turned from the shelter entrance toward the corner of Tremont and Boylston Street. As she did so, she bumped into a stocky man in a black Bruins tee shirt.

"Sorry," the man said. He continued to walk toward the Common without turning or looking at her.

Even though she'd just had a cup of coffee, Rosaria stopped to pick up an herbal tea at a corner shop near the Common, deciding she could use something to hold and settle her down a little. Maybe she just hadn't spent much time with young people these days. He wasn't a bad kid. She was becoming a curmudgeoness.

Rosaria was pleased to find an empty bench available. She balanced her cup of Lemon Lift on her knee after she sat down, enjoying the scent as she lifted the cover. She took a deep breath, beginning to regain her equilibrium, and she counted her good fortune to find a whole empty bench—until she noticed a thick ball of yellow spit at the base of the bench—just inches from her shoe. No wonder the damned bench had been available.

"Jesus, Mary and Joseph," she muttered shaking her head and picking up her bag to move to another bench. No way could she enjoy her cup of tea seeing that phlegmy thing staring up at her.

Rosaria settled into a nearby bench next to an older woman with a shopping cart of what looked like her life's belongings beside her. *Please, please don't be an angry, disturbed and talkative person,* thought Rosaria as she gave the woman a hopeful smile. The woman smiled back with dark intelligent eyes and looked away. *Thank God for that.*

Not for the first time, Rosaria wondered about what had brought people like this woman with the dark, lively eyes to living rough. The old children's board game Chutes and Ladders crossed Rosaria's mind—the chutes and ladders of life.

As she took a sip of the tea—so welcome and comforting—she looked around and saw again the man in the Bruins tee shirt she'd bumped into outside Saint Martin's. He was leaning against the wall by the subway entrance, not looking at her. Yet, she could somehow tell—in spite of all the other people around—that he was aware of, focused on her. *What's this?* When she was younger, she would have been on the alert for a strange man hanging about, perhaps following her, perhaps about to make an unwelcome advance. But she wasn't younger. She was older. *Stop it*, she said to herself, *probably just waiting for someone, as I am.* All the same, she pulled her bag closer. She thought she might have seen him give a crooked smile at that. *How aggravating.*

Rosaria's train of thought was broken sometime later when she saw Patrick crossing Tremont Street against the light. A broad grin on his face, he wove through the heavy traffic with high energy, deftly navigating between cars, trucks and taxis.

Patrick's breath was short and his cheeks flushed when he got to her park bench. The homeless woman got up and walked away through the crowd with her shopping cart to make room for him on the bench. He didn't sit down, but stood before Rosaria, smiling and looking everywhere but at her. He was shrugging his shoulders nervously. They almost jumped.

"Good meeting?" she asked after staring at him for a moment.

He looked at her directly for the first time, snapping and unsnapping the fasteners on the strap of his knapsack and laughed. "Oh, Jesus, yes, a really good meeting. It's done, I tell you, it's done."

"What's done? Rosaria asked, raising her hand palm outward to him. "And, please, Patrick, just stop the jumping around and fidgeting. Honestly."

"Sorry." He settled, but a triumphant smile remained on his face.

"What's done, Patrick?" Rosaria pressed, curious and impatient.

He shifted his stance again. "The meeting's done." He looked at her now with that fetching smile. "A good meeting done."

She cocked her head to give him a skeptical look. There was something more there and the irritating young charmer was not going to tell her.

"Really, I can't tell you more now, Rosaria. I'm sorry. Not now. You'll know soon enough." He looked past her toward the ballpark on the Common.

Rosaria absorbed that reply for a beat or two and stood up. Almost as tall as Patrick, she faced him with a frown, her head cocked to one side. "Listen, Patrick. I deserve to know what you're up to. I've been giving you a big assist. For crying out loud, I even set up this meeting with Joyce. These are my contacts I'm using to help you with your project. I can understand your wanting to take the meeting alone, but you can't even tell me what it's about? What is this?"

He closed his eyes against her in a childlike defense, suddenly serious, before opening them again and saying, "Look, it's better all-around for you not to know. For your own sake. Okay?"

"Better for me not to know? No, it's not okay. And for *my* sake? What's that supposed to mean?" Rosaria could feel her face reddening. She let out an exasperated sigh and looked around for a few moments to collect her thoughts. She was unsettled to see the man in the black tee shirt still leaning against the subway entrance wall and now watching them both closely. Shaking off that image, Rosaria took a deep breath and said, "Hey, Patrick. You're making me uncomfortable. I don't know what you're up to, but this is beginning to feel like something complicated. Something I may not want my name attached to."

She was surprised to hear him respond with a stubborn little nod, "Just as well, just as well."

"What the hell? You need to tell me just what that's supposed to mean."

Around them, people were milling and pushing in different directions as some rushed for the subway one way and students from Emerson College, headed to classes, pushed the other way. Patrick was jostled but the stubborn stare stayed on his face.

Her words rushed out, "And you'd damned well better not be getting your Aunt Bridie into anything messy, Patrick—or me, for Chrissakes, who's been helping you all along."

"I'm sorry, Ro."

She didn't think he looked sorry.

"This is big. Better you not know now. You'll hear about it soon enough."

She could feel herself starting to lose it. "Jesus Christ." She turned angrily to see the man in the Bruins shirt still watching them. Furious, she shouted to him over the crowd. "What are you looking at?"

The man gave her his small crooked smile and stayed where he was.

Distracted, Patrick looked over his shoulder before turning back to Rosaria. "He's looking at you because you're making a scene, Ro."

"Patrick Keenan, you are a piece of work," she said through tight lips, her jaw set, "Okay, I'm done. You're on your own now."

He nodded, screwing his mouth slightly. "Thank you for all your help, Ro," he said formally. "I hope in time you'll feel it was worth your while."

"I'll decide that."

Patrick gazed thoughtfully at Rosaria for a moment and then turned from her, hunching his shoulders as he walked briskly toward the Park Street station.

Rosaria watched the young man go, his blue knapsack bouncing behind him. She suddenly felt very tired and defeated. Maybe she could have handled that better.

The Bruins tee shirt moved away from his post at the Boylston Street stop. He glanced first at Rosaria with a look she couldn't decipher, then at Patrick's retreating back before he swung in Patrick's direction.

Rosaria felt a confused wave of concern, wondering if the man was following Patrick. But what would he be doing that for? She was probably being an alarmist. All the same, she usually trusted her instincts. Rosaria started in the same direction after them both. Walking at a fast clip, she dug her phone out of her purse so she could text Patrick and tell him to be careful.

Of what? Just a man in a Bruins tee shirt? How many of those were walking around Boston? Patrick would think she was an annoying, hovering middle-aged worrywart.

Maybe she was. Couldn't be helped.

A crowd of chatting, preoccupied students with large backpacks and bags rushed by her as she tried to text. She was lucky she didn't drop her cell phone as they surrounded her and held her back. *Dammit.* Then, she tried to remember whether Patrick could even get cell coverage if he'd already entered the station.

She tried to text anyway as she did a fast trot toward the station. *Patrick, Rosaria. There's a man following you into the station. Black Bruins tee shirt, wireless glasses.* She was having a hard time texting while plowing through the crowd of pedestrians. *Maybe nothing, but—*

"Do one goddamned thing or the other, lady. Walk or text" a man in a business suit muttered as he passed her.

Doggedly she finished the text. *"Just be careful, okay? Call me when you get this."* Finishing the text, Rosaria broke free and ran toward the Park Street station, feeling a sense of urgency—yet not sure about what. Maybe she was being ridiculous. Nevertheless, when she got to the entrance, she pushed her way down the stairs, rummaging in her bag to find her Charlie transit card. She found it just as she reached the turnstile.

But no sign of either Patrick or the mystery man. She raced through the crowd on the Green Line platform and down the steps to the Red Line, headed for Harvard Square and the end of the westbound Red Line train at Alewife station. She knew Patrick's sublet was somewhere near Central Square—the stop just before Harvard. But neither Patrick nor Mr. black Bruins tee shirt was on the Red Line platform bound for Harvard Square.

Stopping to consider her options, she decided to give Patrick enough time to reach home or get wherever he was going and call him again. She would make sure he was okay, tell him about the man in the dark tee shirt and tell him to be careful. That would be all she could do, right?

Patrick called her later, his voice light. "Hey, I'm fine. Back at the ranch with the guys in the apartment. Thanks for worrying about me."

"Did you happen to see that guy following you? The one who was hanging around the Boylston T stop while we were...talking?"

"You mean when you were...reaming me out, Rosaria?" He took a little dig. She could almost see his grin as he did so.

"Okay, I guess I was."

"No, no, I didn't see him on the T. And, honest to God, the Red Line to Cambridge is always so jammed, it would have been hard to. There must have been hundreds of people. If the guy was there, I missed him. And maybe he missed me if he was following me. And, Ro, why would anybody follow me, for Godsakes?"

"You're probably right," Rosaria replied, feeling slightly silly. "I usually trust my instincts, but sometimes I'm off. Anyway, glad to hear everything's okay." She paused. "And I just want you to know that I really do wish you well on your research project."

"Thanks, Rosaria. You know, things are kind of complicated right now. I'll be sharing everything with you after the next couple of weeks. I just need some time."

"I'll look forward to it, Patrick. But please be careful. I don't know what you're working on—but...But just be careful."

He laughed. "Stop worrying, Ro. Careful is my middle name. Padraig Francis Careful Keenan from Manin Bay, Ballyconneely, County Galway."

And that was the last time Rosaria ever spoke to Patrick Keenan. Many days afterward, she could see him in her mind's eye, moving away through the crowd with that happy, funny lope of his, blue knapsack bouncing as he strode away from her into the unknown.

CHAPTER 7

olly drove down Memorial Drive along the Charles River to the Central Square neighborhood where Patrick had been subletting with some other guys. He hadn't been able to get a phone number for the one roommate Bridie remembered—Paul Malloy. He decided to just take the ride over to the apartment.

He didn't expect to see a Cambridge patrol car parked outside the aged triple-decker on River Street. He pulled behind the CPD car and then got out to check the mailboxes beside the battered wooden front door. He could see multiple crossed out and added names on taped, ragged index cards beside the rusted mailboxes. Piles of uncollected mail lay underneath the boxes. All the signs of a young, transient student population. He hadn't thought Patrick Keenan's last name would be on a mailbox. The kid was, after all, only a summer sublet.

Bridie had mentioned a third floor apartment. Solly opened the door and headed up the worn staircase. The shabby corridors on the first and second floor were filled with bikes, skateboards and camping equipment leaning against dingy walls. He inhaled the musty, slightly garbagy smell of an old building filled with students for whom housekeeping and the hygiene of their surroundings are not a top priority.

Solly smiled as he climbed, remembering his own student days on Washington Street in Brighton. Days when he was young, flush with his first independence from his family home in Brookline. These old double and triple-decker apartment buildings teeming with young people looked like paradise to him then—exuberant freedom.

As he neared the third floor, Solly heard bits of conversation. He found the apartment door open when he arrived. A young, freckled-faced Cambridge patrol officer sat on a worn couch near the pyramid of beer bottles often found in students' first apartments.

Across from the patrolman, a young man perched, elbows on his knees, near the edge of a broken down armchair covered with a stained throw.

The patrolman looked up in surprise to see Solly standing at the door in a navy BPD golf shirt and chinos, his badge on his belt. He cocked his head in a question. "And you are?"

Solly walked forward, his hand outstretched. "Detective Solly Belkin, BPD."

The patrolman stood to greet Solly. "Officer Ron Delaney. Good to meet you, Detective Belkin."

Though the student also looked perplexed, he was well brought up and quickly took the initiative to stand and extend his hand as well. "Paul Malloy," he said—his firm, assured voice and handshake belying his baggy jeans and torn tee shirt.

Solly guessed Paul Malloy's executive dad taught him that handshake in... let's see, maybe Winchester or maybe Hingham. A solid white Colonial with a nice yard, tulips and lilacs in the spring, a few tasteful white lights at Christmas. A world left for now, but always there for the going back. This was merely a chapter with fond memories of youthful friends and grubby apartments.

"I'm here investigating a break-in, Detective Belkin. You?" Officer Delaney inquired.

"I'm investigating the murder of Patrick Keenan," Solly replied, watching closely the taut expression on young Paul Malloy's face and hearing a whispered "Fuck."

"You were not aware of Mr. Keenan's death, Mr. Malloy? It was in the news, on the front page of the Globe."

Officer Delaney, clearly taken aback himself, nodded slowly in agreement. "I saw that," he said. "But I didn't know he lived here."

Paul Malloy frowned, his face stunned, "What happened to him?"

Solly explained Patrick's murder and let the young man sit in shocked silence for a few more moments while he absorbed this news.

"No, no. I didn't hear about this," Malloy said. "None of us knew. After classes got out, we all took off on a rafting trip high up in the Adirondacks. No phone. No internet." He took a moment to collect himself and swallowed before responding further. "I'm the first one back. The others come from upstate and stayed to visit family for a few days..." He tailed off, looking suddenly like the boy he was.

"When did you get back, Paul?" Solly asked. He took a moment to look at Officer Delaney, acknowledging the fact that Solly was—appropriately—taking over the younger officer's conversation. Delaney waved his hand. "Go ahead. Go ahead."

Malloy jerked himself back and responded, "Just this morning. When I came up the stairs, the door was open, the locks all busted." He got up to show them the broken door locks.

Solly considered the ancient door locks, held on by rusted nails—now scattered over the floor.

"Wouldn't take much to knock these off. A nine-year-old could break in here through this door. You never thought to fix it?" Solly asked.

Malloy looked embarrassed. "Well, yeah. We just never had any problems."

"Everyone says that after a break-in," commented the patrolman. Solly turned to offer a knowing smile to Delaney and nodded.

"Well, anyway. What's taken?" Solly asked.

"You know, it's crazy. I've looked around and I just don't get it. The things you'd expect to be gone aren't." Paul Malloy pointed at a large, late model flat screen television sitting on a plank and cinder block bookcase. Seeing Solly's raised eyebrows, he reddened and shrugged. "The Pats games." Solly nodded. *Wonder if Mommy and Daddy knew this was part of the expense budget.*

"I even left my laptop here in my room. They didn't bother with that or the bikes or anything."

"What did they bother with?"

"Just Patrick's room."

"I see," said Solly.

"Come on, I'll show you his room. It looks like shit. A frigging disaster." He looked back. "Sorry."

Solly lifted his hand in a Jewish absolution. *Oh really. Why did some people feel they had to apologize for their language in front of cops, who had the worst mouths in the city?*

They turned the corner of the dark hallway, Officer Delaney bringing up the rear.

The room was indeed a frigging disaster. The mattress had been thrown to the floor and sliced open, the innards strewn from one side of the room to the other. All of the drawers had been emptied and turned over, the contents of the closet thrown about the room. Even the pages of books had been torn out and several floorboards removed.

Solly didn't comment. Motioning both the young man and Officer Delaney to stay in the hallway, he took a pair of latex gloves from his pocket and stretched them onto his hands, starting to walk slowly and carefully through the debris.

"Anything you think might be missing here?" he asked over his shoulder.

"Unless he had his computer with him, I'm pretty sure they took that. I think that's all."

"Sure?"

The young man looked around. "No, wait, there's something else. He used to keep a pile of notebooks over there." He gestured to a chipped painted window sill. "Those are gone. Again, if he didn't have them with him." He stared at the window sill. "I don't know why anyone would want those. Just his school project. This is crazy."

Solly inhaled deeply. "Okay. We're going to need crime techs in here. We'll work out the details with the CPD."

Officer Delaney nodded.

Solly looked at the young man. "You have somewhere else to stay? None of you will be able to stay here for a while."

"Yeah, I just live in Winchester," Malloy replied. "The other guys don't start work yet, so they can stay upstate for now."

Winchester. Boy, I can call them, thought Solly with some satisfaction. "Well, you'll all need to be available for questioning. Can they stay around here anywhere?"

"Yeah, yeah. I know my parents would be fine to have them at the house. Plenty of room."

I'll bet there is, thought Solly. "Good," he said as they walked down the hall to the living room. "You liked Patrick?" he asked over his shoulder.

"Oh, yeah. Sweet dude. One of the other guys went home for the summer. Patrick was just here for a few weeks as a sublet while he worked on his independent study. We didn't really know him well, but we liked him. Fun to have around."

"Know what he was working on?"

"Well, broadly. Something about Irish-American support of some political activities in Ireland—revolutionary activities against the Protestants and the Brits in Northern Ireland—but that's all I know. None of us here talked about our studies much. We all just finished a tough semester. We'd rather talk about anything else." He smiled.

"But he was pretty pumped up about it lately. Just kept saying he was 'getting closer, getting closer'. And we'd say 'Shut up. Getting closer to what, man?' and he'd say in a crazy, mysterious voice 'To the answer, boys.' By then, someone would throw a pillow at him. We didn't know what the hell he was talking about. Still don't."

"Know where he spent his time?"

"Really don't. We used to go out at night around here—to The Field and places like that. We took him to Davis Square to The Burren and Johnny D's one time. But during the day, he was off on his own."

"No idea?"

Paul shook his head. "Haven't a clue. Saw him on the Common one day—down near Boylston Street. Looking around a little, he said. Maybe he looked in the wrong places."

———

That night over a takeout pizza from Regina's with Rosaria at her condo, Solly said, with no preamble, "Yeah, so this case could be getting complicated. The sublet Patrick was staying in was broken into. Nothing taken in the other rooms, but his room was trashed. I don't know if it was before or after he was killed."

"Looking for something?" Rosaria asked. She picked up a slice of pizza and began carefully removing all the black olives from the topping.

"Oh, I'd say so. According to his roommate, whoever broke in took some of Patrick's notebooks and a laptop."

"Strange. Connected to whatever he was working on?"

"Feels like it." Solly took a swing of his Ipswich Ale. "Whoever did it wanted something like that from his apartment." Solly popped the black olives from Rosaria's pizza slice in his mouth as he talked.

"Wow. Interesting."

"Wow is right. I just wish we knew more about what that kid was working on."

"You know he was really secretive about it," Rosaria said.

Solly nodded.

"He said it was about one broad topic," she continued, "but it felt like he was taken with something very specific. Something very targeted that he wouldn't talk about."

"Any idea?"

"Honest to God, Solly, I haven't the slightest." *Yet,* Rosaria thought. *Yet.* She chewed thoughtfully on her pizza crust, then said, "You know, this may have been a random assault, but now with the break-in, it feels really different, doesn't it?"

"Uh-huh," Solly agreed, his mouth full.

"Solly?" she asked, wiping her fingers on a napkin, "Would you ever think a part of the answer may be over in Ireland?"

"Nah, too farfetched. Someone coming all the way over here to off the kid or arrange for someone else to do it? Sounds good in a book or a movie, but in real life? Nah."

"Yeah, unlikely," she agreed, "but, you know, from another perspective—he was so excited after he met with Liam Joyce at Saint Martin's, you could almost think what happened might have something to do with the conversation he had there. Might be a stretch, but..."

"We'll see. Talking to Joyce tomorrow."

CHAPTER 8

he next morning, Solly did interview Saint Liam or Liam Joyce, executive director of the Saint Martin de Porres House at the shelter. He'd timed his visit to avoid the height of the breakfast crowd, when the line might fill up the newly built atrium and spill out to the street, snaking down toward the Common.

The breakfast smells were still in the air when Solly walked into the lobby. It would have been unseemly for him to pick up a tray for a helping of asparagus and mushroom omelet with a side of hash browns, a breakfast biscuit and a cup of coffee. Inappropriate for him to sit down at one of the long tables with the other guys. Nevertheless, Solly found himself fantasizing about it for a few moments.

He was not in fact homeless, even if after his first marriage had collapsed and before he'd met Rosaria, there were days when he'd felt unmoored and homeless in a different way. Perhaps there should be a table at the shelter for lonely, recently divorced guys.

Solly came out of his reverie to show his badge to an imposing guard whose chest and arms stretched the fabric of a Peter Welch Boxing Gym tee shirt. The guard waved him past the metal detector and stopped him.

"What's up?" he asked Solly. "We got trouble?"

"Not from me," Solly replied. "Here to see Liam Joyce."

The man nodded, still not convinced trouble wasn't in the air. "Elevator and stairs over there." He pointed over his shoulder. "Third floor."

Solly could feel the guard watching after him as he started up the stairs.

The door on the third floor opened to a small corridor where Solly found himself looking directly into a cramped, paper-filled internal office.

Behind a battered metal desk stood a tall, slim man whose youthful build and features were at odds with a worn expression. *What was the right word?* thought Solly. *Used-up, maybe. A used-up man.* A heavyset Hispanic man with multiple tattoos stood leaning against a side wall, in conversation with the man behind the desk.

"*Reyerta*. Another line fight early this morning. Guys working on the condos next door bumped a client in line. Somebody shoved somebody else and then everybody got in."

The first man, who Solly took to be Liam Joyce, shook his head and responded in a rich Irish accent. "God knows we don't need this right now, Eduardo. Alpha is already complaining again. They'll be through the roof about this."

Solly knew that there was big time tension between Saint Martin House and Alpha Properties, the developer and manager of the pricey new condo complex expanding down the block. Alpha was not comfortable with the presence of Saint Martin House and its clients in its backyard, even though the House had been at its location for decades, well before the condos and before property values in the area shot into the stratosphere.

It was Alpha Properties in fact that gave the money for the House to build an atrium for people lining up to eat. Alpha hoped the addition would keep the clients off the sidewalks and out of the way of condo residents who didn't want to run a gauntlet of street people to get into their multi-million dollar homes.

At this point, Liam Joyce noticed Solly in the hall and held his hand up to wait a moment.

Solly saw Eduardo look at him with concern. "I can talk to you later," he said to Liam.

"Talk now, Eduardo. It's okay. No secrets." Liam said impatiently, glancing at Solly.

"BPD and Councilor Ross are supposed to come by this afternoon," said Eduardo, looking at Solly with a question in his eyes and some defiance. "No more lines unless we want to pay for a detail. We can't afford to pay cops to watch the clients. Besides, it sends the wrong message."

Joyce patted his hand in the air, looking to soothe Eduardo. "That I know. That I know."

He turned then to Solly. "I thought you were coming this afternoon with Councilor Ross, Officer. As you can see, we're not quite ready for you yet."

"Maybe you have me confused with someone else, Mister Joyce." Solly stepped forward and extended his hand. "Detective Solly Belkin, BPD. I called earlier."

Both men's faces went still.

Solly noticed a slight nervous tic in Joyce's left eye, and saw Eduardo's muscular body stiffen into a defensive posture.

Recovering quickly, Joyce waved his hand and said in a distracted voice. "Oh yes, yes. We have someone from the BPD coming in this afternoon about a little trouble we had here this morning."

"So I gather," Solly responded. "Not surprising. You have a lot of hungry, homeless people—mostly adult men—standing in a line. Didn't you just build an atrium?"

"You know, we've outgrown it already." Joyce dropped into a chair behind the desk wearily—like an old man, belying his adolescent looks. He gestured to Solly to take a seat.

"Call Mr. Twomey," urged Eduardo, forgetting Solly for the moment. "Ask him for money to expand the atrium."

"Oh, Jesus. I'm always calling Declan." Joyce put his hand over his eyes for a moment. "I don't know why he takes my calls anymore."

"Because he loves you and your *trabajo,* your *mision,* Saint Liam." Eduardo's face had softened briefly into a smile, his tone avuncular. "Have some coffee and a sweet. You'll feel better."

Still watchful of Solly, Eduardo turned to the window and retrieved a coffee and butternut doughnut for Joyce. Solly had thought that he'd smelled something fine like this, but figured that perhaps it was a kitchen smell coming up through the grate.

"Eduardo gets me a Dunkin latte and a butternut doughnut every morning. Is this man not a saint?" Liam lifted the lid off the coffee and inhaled deeply. "Mmmm."

Eduardo turned to Solly. "Would you like a coffee, Detective? I didn't realize we were having a guest." Solly thought he might have heard a hint of territorial reproach in Eduardo's voice. A subtle wave of wry amusement rippled across Joyce's face.

"No thanks. I'm good." Solly held up his hand in response.

Eduardo turned to Liam. "You've got someone from the Chancery coming in—maybe in an hour. The Cardinal wants to serve lunch sometime this month."

"Lovely." Liam looked at Solly. "Good man. Comes at least once a month. And *mirable dictu*, with no photographer."

Eduardo shuffled his feet slightly. "Would you like me to stay, Mr. Joyce?"

Liam looked at the bulky man with affection. "No, I'm okay."

Eduardo hesitated before responding, clearly reluctant to leave. "Okay, I'll go down and help with the signup for the training program." He held up his cell. "Just give me a call if you need anything." Solly was intrigued with the look of barely contained animosity directed at him from Eduardo as he lingered in the door.

"I'm okay, Eduardo. Thanks. I'm okay," Liam said. He waved his hand in dismissal with a small smile.

Eduardo nodded, holding up his cell and pointing at it before leaving the room and closing the door.

Solly dove right into it. "Mr. Joyce, you're aware of Patrick Keenan's death?"

Joyce nodded sadly, his eyes fixed on his cluttered desk. "Yes, yes. Sad business. I was shocked to hear about it."

"He came to see you the day before he died."

Joyce nodded again. "He did."

"Do you mind telling me about the purpose of that visit?"

"No, I don't mind at all, Detective." Joyce raised his head. "The boy was working on an independent study project at the University in Galway. He came to ask me some questions as part of his research."

"Questions about what?"

Joyce shifted in his seat, keenly aware of Solly's eyes on him. "Well, it was a pretty broad topic. Something about Irish-American support for community projects in Northern Ireland. And, of course, Saint Martin House here at home is an iconic institution supported by many people, but a particular favorite of the Irish-American community. He wanted to see if there had been any linkage."

"Really?" Solly was quiet for a few taut, still moments, staring at Saint Liam. "I thought Patrick's project was focused on Irish-American support for the IRA in the '70s."

The area around Liam Joyce's mouth went slightly white in a minuscule twitch, his body betraying him. "Maybe at the beginning, but I wouldn't know about that. He wanted to know about the House and how it came to be, where the support and financing came from—that sort of thing."

"I'm surprised, Mr. Joyce. That's quite different from what I understand about his research."

"Well, now, as I say, maybe the topic morphed. Yes, morphed, you know. To more about how the Irish-American community support for causes like Saint Martin's impacts civic society here and there. Maybe he shifted focus. Yes, maybe shifted focus." He looked hopefully at Solly.

Solly contemplated how an Irishman's accent, for some reason one of the most effective tools of persuasion known to man, became thicker while doing a sell. Saint Liam was doing a sell.

Solly didn't respond. Liam Joyce caught his bottom lip with his teeth, raised his brows and shook his head. "I can't tell you much more than that, Detective."

"I see, Mr. Joyce," Solly said slowly. He sighed before asking, "And how did Patrick seem when he was here?"

"Oh, enthusiastic, excited to be traveling, to be in Boston. You know, he was young." Joyce's voice trailed off and he looked momentarily stricken, staring into space. "Just so young."

The conversation flattened after that, with desultory answers from Liam Joyce that shed no light on the case. Solly left ten minutes later, feeling frustrated and intrigued.

It was clear to Solly that something complicated had happened during Patrick's visit to the House. Something Saint Liam was not being open about.

He was turning this thought over in his mind as he slowly descended the stairs. Distracted, he almost bumped into Eduardo on the second floor landing. *Waiting for him?*

"He's a good, good man, Detective. He's a saint." *That word again.* "Don't do nothing bad to him."

Solly was taken aback but curious. "I have to talk to everyone, Eduardo. A young man has been killed. I owe it to him and his family to make sure we get the answers here. Mr. Joyce is not being singled out."

Eduardo didn't respond immediately. He looked carefully at Solly and started to walk up toward the third floor. Partway up, he turned over his shoulder to say softly. "*Es un santo. Es un santo.*" before continuing up the stairs.

CHAPTER 9

osaria loved the way that Solly had developed the habit of walking to her right since her right eye became damaged. For the most part, she had learned to offset for this visual weakness. Yet, as Solly walked beside her and gave her arm a gentle touch when they approached a grate or an irregular piece of pavement on the right side, she realized how much energy it usually took her to compensate. He made everything so much easier.

Solly insisted on accompanying her to all her doctors' appointments. A good idea as she was not diligent about note-taking during the visits or writing down questions for the doctor in advance. This new kind of casualness was not like her. She'd always been an attentive, if occasionally unruly, student and had managed many projects successfully in her long career. Diving in and running things was her forte. Here, she was in some unfamiliar passive state about her injuries. Rosaria wondered if this new behavior was a form of denial about the damage to her eye. Or perhaps just a welcome collapse into Solly Belkin's care and competence. She wasn't used to collapsing, and the fact that she had was somewhat embarrassing to her personally. But every day, she was thankful for Solly.

Today, she'd flushed with this gratitude again when he'd pulled a small notebook out of his jeans pocket during the doctor visit. It was the same type of notebook he used for interviews and case notes at work. He must have bought dozens of these small black spiral notebooks that just fit into his jeans pocket. This particular notebook had a small sticker on the upper right corner that read *Rosie-Eye Appts*. In it were questions for the doctor (*"Exercises to strengthen the eye muscles?"*) and notes about medications and progress.

The doctor at Mass Eye and Ear had told Rosaria today that her eye seemed to be healing well on its own. He didn't see the need for surgery. Perhaps in about six months, she'd be back to normal, with the possible exception of an occasional flickering of light in the corner of her eye. They'd have to see about that.

"What would I do without you?" she asked Solly.

"You'd manage, you always do," he said, putting his arm around her shoulder. "But I'd be one lonesome guy without you, I'd tell you that."

"Oh, you'd never be lonesome. Good looking, macho cop who reads books, hikes, and has a vinyl jazz collection. Someone would snatch you up in no time."

Then, he looked into her eyes for a long time and said, "No one like you, Rosie. No one like you," and he kissed her.

Before they split up for Rosaria to go back to her condo and Solly to the Tremont Street station, they stopped for lunch at the Union Oyster House, down near the Faneuil Hall Market and not too far from Rosaria's condo. Popular with tourists and senior citizens, the old restaurant had first opened in 1826 in the Union Street Building. Earlier, King Louis Phillippe of France had taught French in an upstairs room to the young ladies of Boston while he was in exile after the French revolution.

The low-ceilinged and cramped rooms, filled with colonial and maritime paraphernalia, seemed to embrace Rosaria as she and Solly entered. How many meals had she had here as a child with her parents? Just being here gave her a sense of comfort and security, something she needed at this point in her life.

Rosaria felt so good that she was tempted to order a Blue Moon. But she decided that having a beer was not a good idea. Without Solly on her right hand side, she needed her wits about her to navigate the city streets.

"How's your friend Bridie?"

"Not so great. Terrible shock."

"Yeah. Patrick sounded like a good kid." Solly's brow furrowed over determined brown eyes. "We'll get whoever did it. Might take time, but we'll get him."

"I hope so, Solly, but—don't take this the wrong way, we have to try—it won't bring Patrick back."

"No, no, it won't." His big hand covered hers on the table. "It's okay to say that. I've been around a long time. I know the score."

"Sorry to be rude," Rosaria said to Solly as she took out her cellphone. "I forgot I have to text George at our building about letting the new dog walker in today." She keyed in her password and took a sharp breath as she saw an old text displayed on the screen. "Oh, my God, Solly. I totally forgot to tell you something important." She hit the side of her head with the flat of her hand.

Solly interrupted sprinkling oyster crackers into his chowder to look at her. "About your eye? About the case? About the Sox lineup? What?"

"I just saw a text I sent to Patrick the last time I saw him."

"Yeah?"

"Right after Patrick visited Liam Joyce at Saint Martin's, he and I met near the T stop on the Common. We...," Rosaria paused and reddened. "We had an argument."

"Oh?" Solly cocked his head.

"He just wouldn't tell me anything about what the real target of his research was or what his meeting with Liam Joyce was about. Patrick was driving me crazy. I wanted to strangle him." She stopped. "Sorry. That last part was not appropriate under the circumstances."

"Forget it. So—is that it? You had an argument? So what?"

"No, that's not the important part." She leaned heavily against the back of the wooden booth, and ran her hand through her white hair. "There was someone following us—a big guy in a black Bruins tee shirt. After we split up, he followed Patrick into the Park Square T-station."

"How could you forget something as important as that?" Solly's tone was more curious than angry.

"I don't know, I don't know." She shook her head. "Just so much going on." She gave Solly a helpless shrug. "I just...I just...forgot."

"Okay. So tell me now." He put his packet of crackers down and leaned forward on his elbows. Rosaria told him about that day and Patrick and the man and Patrick's return phone call to her telling her that all was well and not to worry.

"Might be nothing, a guy just headed home to Cambridge from work," Solly said. "But, it's possible he might have followed Patrick to see where he lived. And he could have been the one who broke in later to take Patrick's computer and notebooks. Never know." He sighed. "I wish we had gotten at least one good fingerprint from that break-in. And nobody saw or remembered anything. So many people coming and going in those multi-families in that area. If it turns out it's this guy with a Bruins tee shirt, you'd think that would maybe stand out." He stopped and shook his head. "What am I thinking? No, it wouldn't, not in this town. Anyway, go over it again and describe him to me. Everything you remember."

Solly took a small black spiral notebook out of his back pocket. This was a different notebook from the one he'd used earlier in the doctor's office. This notebook look well-used and had a small white sticker in the upper right hand corner that read *Homicide—Keenan*.

CHAPTER 10

osaria knew that Solly had been married before, as she had been. After he and Rosaria had been seeing each other for a few weeks, they'd shared their marital histories over a long dinner at Lucia's on Hanover Street.

"He was older," said Rosaria of her first husband Bronson. "Pretty traditional." She leaned back against the booth and took a deep breath. "I was probably too young to make a decision around marriage, not really fully formed, you know?"

"Oh yeah," commented Solly.

"He loved the fact that I was *spunky*—that was a word he used to describe me. *Spunky*. Anyway, he thought it was great to be married to a *spunky*, bright young thing."

"Probably was," Solly smiled.

"Well, for a while. Then I joined the workforce. Had some success, got a little too independent for his comfort level as I got older and had more world experience. And then not so great. He's a good man, but we were a really bad fit." Rosaria paused for a few moments, fingering the stem of her wineglass. "That's why I'm so jealous of my independence now. I couldn't breathe. It was such a relief to get out from under."

"I'll bet it was." Solly smiled and followed up with "I can handle independence."

"That's why I love you, Solly Belkin." She was surprised to find her eyes wet, and forged on. "He always seemed to have someone on the side, too, after I started to come into my own. And the worst part was that he kept telling me I was imagining things."

"Gaslighting."

"Yes, gaslighting. Of course, as it turned out, I wasn't imagining anything. He's good looking, and there always seem to be lots of available women, whether the men are married or not." She inhaled deeply. "Well, anyway, we ended it."

"Got it. Must have been tough." He reached over to cover her hand with his own. "You're safe with me, honey."

They were both quiet for a while before Solly asked. "Did he marry again?"

"Oh yeah, to one of the administrators he was seeing at the consulting company where he worked while he was married to me. She thought he walked on water, until they separated for some reason. Before then, though, they were very happy. One time I saw them together—they were going golfing, wearing matching pink golf shirts and green pants." Rosaria started to giggle and had to cover her mouth so as not to disturb the other diners. Solly joined in and they were lost in mirth for a minute or two.

"Oh, good grief, what a bad mistake," Rosaria gasped.

"The green pants or the pink golf shirt?" Solly asked. And they both broke out in laughter again. "No, no, my marriage, my marriage." Rosaria wiped the laughter tears from her eyes and took a big breath before saying. "Anyway, it didn't last. I think he's with someone else now. So, Solly, fair's fair. Tell me about Justine."

Then Solly told Rosaria about his own first marriage to the talented, beautiful and charming Justine. A talented, beautiful, charming woman who was apparently also "a little off"—whatever that meant.

Rosaria had taken this description with a grain of salt. She had always prided herself on a broad-band acceptance of those who were somewhat off-kilter. "I suppose we're all a little off in some way," she said.

Solly's mouth twisted slightly. "Maybe, but there's a range. Sometimes it's too much."

Rosaria didn't respond except to nod.

For whatever reason, perhaps because Solly had described her as "a little off", Rosaria hadn't expected to learn later in the conversation that Solly's first wife had a thriving practice as a therapist. She was also a little envious to know that Justine was an accomplished amateur photographer and further impressed in a different way to learn that Justine also volunteered one day a week counseling clients at Saint Martin's.

"Sounds like quite a mix," she said to Solly. "Complicated."

"You don't know the half of it, honey."

Rosaria squeezed his hand. "Let's take a walk on the harbor and get some fresh air. Blow all these old complicated memories away."

Now, in recent days, after some unexpected experiences with Justine, Rosaria's perspective on her capacity to absorb individuals who were a "little off" was shifting. There was off, and then there was *off*. Crazy-making off.

Justine had reached out to Rosaria shortly after she and Solly had started seeing each other. Distracted on a busy day early that spring, Rosaria had responded to an unknown number on her cell—something she rarely did—and instantly regretted her lapse.

"Hi, Rosie. This is Justine Perry calling."

Rosaria was startled and not pleasantly so. *What unknown person is calling her Rosie?*

"I'm sorry, I don't recognize the name, Ms. Perry."

She could hear the disappointment in the caller's voice. "Justine Perry, Solly Belkin's first wife."

Not ex-wife, but first wife. *Strange.* "Yes, what can I do for you, Ms. Perry?"

"Oh, please, call me Justine, Rosie."

The use of Rosaria's most private nickname by someone she'd never met aggravated Rosaria. Rosie as her nickname had only ever been used by her late father, an old boyfriend in the dim past, and now Solly.

"I just wanted to say hello," Justine continued, "and to see if you'd like to meet for coffee or dinner sometime. We have something in common."

"What would that be?"

"Well, Solly, of course."

"I see." Long silence. "I don't think that's a good idea."

"Why not? There's so much I could share with you that might help you understand him."

Rosaria held her cellphone away and looked at it for a moment, frowning—*Jesus. This woman is a little off all right*—before putting it back against her ear and responding. "I'll figure that out on my own, thanks. I need to go now."

"Please, just think about it. We could be friends. No reason why not. Open your mind a little. You might be missing out on a good experience, Rosie."

"I'll take that chance, Justine. The answer is no. And please don't call me Rosie. The name is Rosaria. I'm hanging up now."

Rosaria could hear Justine's flurry of objections before she pressed the End Call button. Then, she blocked the number.

Well, I hope that's the end of that. Good grief.

Except it wasn't the end of that.

Rosaria knew that Justine lived in a trust fund townhouse somewhere on Chestnut Street on Beacon Hill. Now, however, she was surprised to see Justine in the North End and in Rosaria's own waterfront neighborhood.

Rosaria had seen Justine in several pictures with Solly, taken when they were a couple. She remembered feeling a wave of jealousy looking at the long-haired blonde in the picture. Model slim and elfin Justine. Jesus, she was so, so... what? *Perky*. She was *perky*. What in the world did Solly see in Rosaria—tall, big boned, non-perky, independent and occasionally troublesome Rosaria O'Reilly—with her crooked nose and scars—after he had been married to someone who looked like Justine Perry? It was just depressing to think about.

When she'd first seen Justine's picture on a side bookcase in Solly's apart-ment, Rosaria had started to fall into an irrational black mood. Just then, coming up behind her, Solly had said casually, "Guess it's time to toss this. If I send it back to her, she'll think it's an overture and I sure as hell don't want her thinking *that*."

Rosaria had felt relieved at the time. Mostly.

Justine usually carried a camera when Rosaria started seeing her in the neighborhood. Rosaria remembered Justine's photographic pursuits. So, *per-haps* it was not *so* surprising that Solly's ex-wife was in Rosaria's neighborhood now, taking shots of picturesque Italian *caffes,* bocce games or boats along the wharves—images capturing the general ambiance of an interesting area of the city. If Justine caught Rosaria's eye, she'd wave cheerily between shots. "Photoshoot!" she'd call.

But why here? Why now? thought Rosaria with annoyance. She generally didn't respond to Justine on these occasions except for a cool nod.

Then, Rosaria had to stop going to her regular coffee hangout—Boston Bean on Salem Street—because of Justine. She'd looked up once or twice to see Justine entering the shop or already sitting at a table with her camera and her lens and accessory bag. Rosaria didn't acknowledge Justine when she saw her. This was starting to feel strange. The North End had a dozen coffee shops for Justine to hang out in. Why frequent Rosaria's regular stop?

Rosaria considered talking to Solly about Justine's increased presence in her life, but she felt she should be able to handle this little weirdness herself. Solly was so swamped and stretched to the limit with his demanding job. He didn't need any more complications to deal with. And, besides, while Justine clearly had issues, she didn't seem like a bad person. Just a little unbuttoned and—really—getting just so damned *annoying.*

Once, when she was jogging with Archie, Rosaria was sure that she saw Justine, positioned behind some parked cars, taking a photograph of her. Rosaria had swirled and, exasperated, hollered, "Stop it!" But Justine was nowhere to be seen. Passersby had looked at Rosaria curiously. She'd reddened and recommenced her jog.

Things came to a head with the picture in *The Boston Globe*. On the back of the Metro section, the Names page—as if people not included on the page had no names—tracked celebrities and high profile Bostonians at various galas and moneyed events. A large color photograph of Solly and Rosaria at a fundraiser for the Boys and Girls Club sat above the fold. Photo credit to Justine Perry. Rosaria hadn't even seen Justine and her damned telephoto lens at the event.

The worst part was the tagline. "Rosaria O'Reilly, heroine of Malford nun murder scandal and her Boston cop, Detective Solly Belkin." *Heroine? Her Boston Cop?* Could it get any worse?

Solly had gone ballistic. Rosaria didn't hear all the conversation when Solly had called Justine from Rosaria's kitchen. She heard just Solly's end which ran, in increasingly higher volume, along the lines of, "Thought I'd be pleased? No, Justine. I am not godamned pleased. I am pissed. I am frigging pissed. That's what I am."

While Solly spoke—or hollered—on the phone to Justine, Rosaria went out to her little balcony over the harbor, Archie trotting behind her. Settling in with a Jameson-laced cup of tea, she sat out much of the rest of the conversation in the fresh air with Archie nestled at her feet. Given how loud Solly's words were occasionally, she heard them anyway...and she imagined many of her neighbors did, too.

"Stay away, Justine. Stop. And don't give me that bullshit about a photoshoot down around here." Rosaria could not hear Justine's side of the conversation but she could imagine it. "Just stop or I'll take legal action. I swear to God I'll get a restraining order. Do you hear me?"

Then, the kitchen was very quiet, though Rosaria could hear Solly's pacing. She stood and reentered the kitchen. Solly had stopped to sit on one of the kitchen stools by the counter, holding his head as he listened on the phone.

Finally, his tone changed and he said softly into the cell. "Look, Justine honey." *Did he just call this lady honey?* thought Rosaria

"You have to stop this," he continued. "Get some help. This is not how a well person behaves." He listened to the response for a moment. "Don't cry, Justine. Don't cry," he soothed. "Listen to me. Just listen to me."

Rosaria heard subdued sobbing from the other end of the line.

"Promise me that you'll call Dr. Shaeffer right after I hang up?" he begged over the phone.

A question at the other end.

"No, I will not drive you. What about that guy you're seeing now?" Solly frowned. "Well, what kind of a guy is he that he wouldn't 'understand.' Of course, he'll understand if he cares about you. Give the guy a chance to step up. He sounds like he's really into you." Solly looked at Rosaria, shaking his head.

Finally, "Okay, I have to go now, Justine. I'm hanging up. Call Dr. Shaeffer. Take a cab to Brookline if you have to." Rosaria could hear Justine's voice continuing as Solly pressed the End Call button.

He looked at Rosaria again for a while before he said. "Why didn't you tell me this was going on before?" She started to respond before he raised his hand. "Never mind. I know you."

"*Honey?*" asked Rosaria.

Solly shrugged. "We were married, Rosie. I cared for her at some point. I still do—but differently. I don't want to see her go off the rails."

Rosaria nodded. She really did understand. *What can you do? What can you do?*

Solly looked out at the fading afternoon light on the harbor before standing up and putting his arm around her shoulders. He pulled her close and kissed her hair. "Your Boston cop is hungry. Let's go out and get something to eat."

CHAPTER 11

osaria saw it coming. She could feel Bridie Callahan leaning on her more and more in the days after the murder. So, she was not surprised when it came that evening.

The condo was smelling of an odd combination of air popped popcorn and leftover chicken piccata from Artu's. She and Solly sat with their long legs stretched onto the coffee table as they binge-watched *House of Cards* on Netflix. Archie crowded between them, Solly's arm over Rosaria's shoulders, her head on his. Three contented souls, thought Rosaria. This was how it was meant to be.

She almost didn't answer her cellphone when she heard it trilling in the kitchen. But, she decided a bathroom break was probably in order anyway.

"Want me to pause it?" Solly asked as she got up.

"Nope. That's okay. I'm not that into it, under present circumstances. You want another Ipswich?"

"Yeah, thanks."

Rosaria knew what the call would be about when she saw that it was Bridie. She'd already thought about her answer, though it was a hard decision.

"Ro, I have a favor to ask."

"Anything, Bridie."

"Would you ever be able to come with me when I bring Patrick's body back home, Ro?"

Rosaria glanced over at Solly's back as he sat on her couch watching Netflix. There might be her biggest problem with this decision. She tucked the phone under her chin and went to the refrigerator to get Solly's bottle of Ipswich Ale, clicking the top off with the bottle opener next to the fridge.

Bridie continued, "I just don't think I could handle it by myself. Bringing the boy home to Nora and Francis. I'm so ashamed."

With that, Rosaria was taken aback. "Why on earth would you be ashamed, Bridie? You are not to blame here."

"He came to visit me and I should have taken care of him."

"How can you say that? Patrick was not ten years old. He was not a child. He was old enough to be responsible for himself."

Nevertheless, Rosaria's heart broke for her friend when she realized she would have felt the same way—somehow responsible for the young man's death.

"Bridie, this could have happened in Galway City. It could have happened in Eyre Square or on the Long Walk by the harbor."

"Please come with me, Ro," Bridie said sadly.

Rosaria had already pretty much decided over the last few days to go to Ireland with Bridie if she asked. She was already involved in the aftermath of Patrick Keenan's murder. She could go deeper. She wanted to help her friend. And, in truth, she had to admit that she was getting intrigued—something felt a little off about Patrick's quest.

Rosaria looked over at Solly on the couch again. He would not be pleased. He'd had enough experience with her to know that she'd start nosing around about Patrick Keenan in Ireland. And sometimes her nosing around—or "butting in" as he sometimes called it—just made things...well, complicated. And then there was the basic fact, she thought tenderly, that he would miss her when she was gone. Besides her parents, she'd never had anyone miss her quite as much as he did when she was away. Rosaria wasn't sure how she felt about this since his missing her tethered her in unfamiliar ways, but she did love the man.

She held the cold bottle of ale against her forehead and looked again at Solly's back in the living room. *He'll get over it. We're solid, and I won't be gone that long. Besides, this is my decision.*

Then, she heard Bridie's tentative voice break through her thoughts. "Rosaria, are you there?" That lost, sad voice settled the decision in Rosaria's mind.

"Yeah, I'm here, honey. What flight should we go on?"

Rosaria didn't tell Solly about the Ireland trip that night. She needed more time to think about how to discuss the trip with him, and she had to admit to herself that she didn't want to ruin a sweet evening. When she did call the next day to tell Solly, she'd been spot on about his reaction. He was indeed not pleased she'd agreed to go to Ireland with Bridie. For all the reasons she'd anticipated.

Rosaria wasn't used to checking in with anyone when she made her decisions. She had to admit, she was not at all comfortable with it. A niggle of wistfulness for her previous independent life and decision-making worked its way through her mind as she listened to Solly go on. The longer he talked, the firmer her decision to go to Ireland with Bridie, and perhaps stay some extra time for good measure.

"Why you?" he fumed.

"Because I'm the only one who can do this for her. She's my friend and she needs me," Rosaria replied. "I won't be gone that long, Solly—a few days, maybe a little longer. Probably not more than a week." *Maybe a lot longer if you keep going on like this.* "Just for the services and some support for Bridie afterwards."

"Oh, no you won't, Rosaria." He used her full name. Never a good sign. "I know you. You'll be snooping around over there about Patrick Keenan and you'll get godamned *involved.*"

"Well, I could check on a few things while I'm over there," she ventured, the skin on her neck starting to prickle in annoyance.

"What few things, what few things? Just tell me that. I shouldn't have to tell you that if you plan on asking questions about Patrick Keenan over there—this is not your case. This is a police matter."

"I'm not going to intrude on your case, Solly. Besides, how strongly do you feel about the Irish angle in this case?"

"What's that supposed to mean?"

"I mean, really, do you think there's something over there that could explain why Patrick was killed, or do you think it's all on this side of the Atlantic?"

"I think it's a reach to think it's back in Ireland. I think we'll find the answer is a lot less complicated and that it's over here."

"Right. So, why is it a problem if I go and if I should check on a few things while I'm there?" Rosaria inhaled deeply and rolled her eyes.

"Look, I'm just telling you now that I don't like this. I don't like this at all." He went silent.

What am I doing with this guy? What business is it of his where I goddamned go and what I goddamned do?

"Well, I thought it was my business," Solly said. "But I guess I was wrong."

Oh, damn! She'd actually uttered that last thought aloud and Solly was responding. This was getting dangerous. "Look, Solly—"

But he'd already hung up on her.

———

Solly called back the next day. "What are you doing with the dog? I have a bad schedule, but I could get Justine's dog walker."

Rosaria saw that this was the closest she was going to get to acquiescence or, God forbid, an apology. Still, she was relieved and grateful, except for the

Justine's dog walker part. Rosaria's usual dog sitting option, her ex-husband Bronson, was at yet another economics conference to discuss grand things and sleep with as many charming young scholars as he could.

She had been stymied about what to do with Archie until Marguerite said, "Bring the little beggar up to the Motherhouse. God knows we could use a therapy dog for a while. And who knows, he might have a vocation."

CHAPTER 12

osaria wended her way through the crowd waiting for tables at the entrance to Al Dente on Salem Street. "Hi Amy," she called to the waitress hurrying by. "I have the vodka sauce tonight. I spoke to Dominic this afternoon for takeout."

"Hey, Ro. Right with you." Straightening the ballpoint pen holding her brown hair in a twist, the harried waitress headed for the kitchen before looking back to say, "But there's a lady at that table over there waiting for you. She said you might want to eat in." Amy cocked her head toward the corner of the restaurant.

Rosaria turned to a small side table tucked under a romantic scene of Lake Como. It was Justine. Rosaria tightened her lips. "No, that's okay. I'll pass. Just get me my takeout."

Amy looked over at Justine, who was raising her hand in a greeting, stolidly ignored by Rosaria. Amy turned back to Rosaria and shrugged. "Okay, suit yourself."

Rosaria steeled herself as she took her dinner from Amy and strode with purpose to the front door of the restaurant. She quickened her pace and went out the door even as she heard Justine calling her name.

Chattering groups of families and friends crowded Rosaria off the narrow sidewalk. She was forced to walk in the street. Her sweater brushed against the fender of a giant Lincoln Navigator, inching along and taking the breadth of the narrow one-way street. Jesus. *Why do people bring monster vehicles like this into dense city neighborhoods? There ought to be a law...*

"Rosaria. Rosaria." She heard Justine's heels clicking on the sidewalk behind her.

Oh God, what was the matter with this woman? She had almost reached Prince Street when Justine, still carrying a napkin from Al Dente, caught up with her and grabbed her arm. Rosaria roughly pulled away.

"Justine, what are you doing? You're stalking me and I'm sick of this."

"I know, I know, Rosie..."

"And don't call me Rosie. Jesus Christ."

"I need to talk to you."

"You don't need to talk to me. You need to leave me alone. That's what you need to do." Rosaria lowered her voice as a nearby couple stopped to stare. "Justine, I mean it," she hissed. "You need to leave me alone. Get some help, for God's sake."

"Rosaria, it's not about me. I have something about Patrick, that boy Patrick."

Rosaria stopped. "What do you know about Patrick?"

"When he came to the House."

"What house?"

"Saint Martin's."

Rosaria moved to the side to let a group pass. With her damaged right eye, she couldn't see a woman approaching alongside her, carrying several large white plastic CVS bags. In moving to the side, she knocked one of the big bags out of the woman's hands. "Sorry," Rosaria held her hand up in apology and picked up the bag for the woman, who pursed her mouth and hurried on.

"Come back to the restaurant and sit down," Justine pleaded. "It's important, but I'll make it short."

Justine turned to walk up the street. Rosaria hesitated only a moment before following her, weaving her way through the crowds.

Amy raised her eyebrows as Rosaria and Justine entered the restaurant again. Shortly after they sat at the small table, she brought a bottle of Rosaria's favorite Chianti and took her Styrofoam container away to arrange the still hot pasta on a heavy shallow white bowl.

"Tell me," Rosaria said to Justine.

Justine didn't reply immediately, but settled herself in and poured them each a glass of wine. Rosaria could tell she was enjoying this occasion.

"Let's just get on with it," Rosaria said

Justine leaned her elbows on the table. "Maybe Solly told you that I volunteer at Saint Martin House once a week, counseling some clients. He may have told you that I'm a therapist."

Yes, Saints preserve us, Rosaria thought. *How could such a woman be a competent therapist?*

Justine took a moment to enjoy the satisfaction of Solly's having had this conversation with Rosaria. "Anyway, a while ago when I was coming into work, there was a very pleasant young Irishman in the waiting room. A good looking young guy. We got to chatting while I got my coffee and set up for the day. He introduced himself as Patrick Keenan and said he was waiting for Mr. Joyce, the director of the House."

"Yes, I know about that meeting. I set it up for Patrick myself."

"Oh, really?" Justine looked at Rosaria with a sly curiosity. "I wonder what it might have been about."

Rosaria did not respond.

"So then my first appointment arrived. I told Patrick it was a pleasure to meet him, then I shut the office door. I didn't see the boy after that."

Rosaria hadn't touched the dinner Amy had set before her. "Is that it or is there more?" Rosaria asked.

Justine continued as if Rosaria had not spoken. "Later, when I had finished with my client and opened my office door again, Liam Joyce's door was closed, and a few minutes later, when I was in the workroom, I heard footsteps leaving. I walked back to my office and saw Liam's—Mr. Joyce's—door open a crack, just enough for me to see him at his desk with his face in his hands. I knocked and asked if I could help. He didn't answer and just stared into space. I repeated my question and he just said, 'No, Justine, you can't. There's no help for it.'"

"There's no help for it," Rosaria murmured. "No help for it?"

"So, I was going to stay with Liam to see if I could help in some way—maybe just get him a cup of tea, be with him."

Well, Rosaria thought, *Justine is certainly a mix. There's weird, stalking Justine and then there's compassionate caretaker Justine. Maybe the problem is that you never know which Justine is going to kick in.*

"But then I heard Declan Twomey," Justine continued. "You know, the big construction guy? He's on our Board."

Rosaria nodded.

"Anyway, I heard his voice as he got off the elevator, heading toward Liam's office, so I excused myself. Declan and Liam have a very close relationship, almost like father and son, and I thought Declan was in a better position to help. As I was leaving, I heard Mr. Twomey say, 'Well, what happened?'"

"Interesting."

"But there's more, Rosie."

Rosaria stiffened and stared at Justine.

She raised her palms and said, "Sorry, sorry. *Rosaria.*" She allowed herself a small smile before continuing. "So, later that day I was up on the fourth floor taking pictures—I do all their photos for the House newsletter. Anyway, I was taking pictures of the new training program graduates—all dressed up in their suits, you know. Liam is usually in the group shots, but I got a message that he was delayed and to go ahead without him, that he might be up later."

Justine took a sip of her Chianti. She was starting to seem almost normal. But Rosaria just had to remind herself in the midst of all this balance and helpfulness that Justine was not, in fact, always normal or balanced—at least in this chapter of her life.

"So I took the photos, but the thing is, when I was reviewing them, I could see that I had caught some background I hadn't meant to. Liam in the hall talking to Declan Twomey. Anyway, it looked like they were having words. I blew up the picture just to see. And it was strange."

"Strange?" asked Rosaria, her pasta with vodka sauce untouched before her.

"What should I say about it?" Justine responded. "Dramatic. That's what it was like...dramatic."

"Dramatic."

"Yes, I've never seen Liam like that. And Declan Twomey—he was just frightening looking." Justine slid an eight-by-ten black and white from a manila envelope at her side and lay it flat at the table. The picture was painful to look at. Joyce's face was anguished, like a picture Rosaria had once seen of the martyrdom of Saint Stephen, when he was pierced with many arrows. Joyce was a tall man but Twomey seemed to tower over him with an imposing bulk.

"I have another one," Justine said, as she placed a second photograph on the table. In this next one, Joyce looked about to weep, Twomey's protective arm around the younger man's shoulder, almost in a fatherly embrace.

"What's this about, Justine?"

"I just don't know, Rosaria, but it seemed important."

"It may be important." Rosaria looked away for a moment and when she turned to look at Justine again, she said, "You need to call Solly for this, Justine. He needs to know about this."

"Are you sure, Rosaria?" Justine cocked her head and said innocently. "He doesn't take my calls, you know."

"Call him at the station on the business line. I'll tell him he needs to hear this."

"Well, that would be very helpful."

A little sarcasm, thought Rosaria. *Unlike Justine.*

Later, as they stood and were preparing to leave the restaurant, Rosaria said, "Justine, I appreciate this very much, but that doesn't mean we're pals now."

"Perfectly clear, Rosaria," Justine replied with a quiet, satisfied smile. "Perfectly clear."

CHAPTER 13

CONNEMARA, IRELAND—1974

he boy hadn't been down to the Home after dark for a long time, but this night he decided to go. And this night was different. He saw an empty sheep transport truck, its lights low, creeping slowly into the cemetery, wheels thumping against the grassy hillocks and boulders of the roadless surface.

The boy heard someone call softly, "Over here, lads." Then, the boy could see a black car, which had been following the sheep transport with its headlights turned off, pull to the other side of the vault.

Several men, dressed in dark clothes and trainers, stepped out of the truck and the car. One stayed behind in the shadows, a tall, bespectacled and bearded man leaning against the black car and watching the rest. To the boy, this man looked like a priest or maybe what the boy imagined a poet might look like.

The men spoke in low voices, though the boy could hear what sounded like the hard, strange accents he'd heard on the Radio Eireann news about the war in the North.

"Where are we now?" said one. "I thought we was going to Westport."

"No Westport tonight. Change of plans," a broadly built man with a shock of ginger hair responded curtly. "Now, let's get over there and help open the vault."

The boy could hear grunts and soft curses as two of the men struggled to dislodge the massive, mold-covered slab in front of the burial vault. The tall man just watched, never moving from the car to help. It was then that the boy saw his father step out of the shadows. Shouldering the two other men aside, his father grabbed the edge of the heavy slab with his big hands and took a deep, noisy breath. Then, in one powerful movement, he swung the slab to the side and cleared the entrance to the vault.

"Good man," the boy heard the man beside the car say.

While the men and his father were opening the vault, another man had lifted up a false bottom of the sheep transport.

Once the vault was opened, a gust of dank and stale air escaped that even the boy, at his distance, could smell. Two of men entered the vault. He heard them cursing as they struggled inside.

"Jaysus. I can't breathe in here."

"Where's the frigging torch, I can't see a damned thing."

"Shite, hit my frigging knee."

"Och, use big torch. That's what it's for. No one will see it in there," the bearded man by the car called softly. "And keep your voices down. You'll be waking the sisters." The man lifted his chin towards his father. "Give the lads a hand again now, would you?"

The boy's father nodded and entered the vault, coming out shortly carrying one end of a long, heavy wooden crate while another of the men carried the other.

It was slow and heavy work. The boy could hear the men grunting and softly cursing. Ten long, wooden crates came out of the vault all marked North Atlantic Fishing Gear and Marine Supply Company.

"Open one," ordered the tall man with the beard as he walked closer to the boxes.

The ginger-haired man went over to the truck and returned with a crowbar. He quickly cracked open the top of one long crate. He lifted a long rubber fishing wader from the crate and reached inside.

"Aye. Aye," he whispered as he reverently lifted and kissed a long gun. The gun looked to the boy like the assault rifles he'd seen in the GI Joe comics his uncle had sent him from America, from Queens in New York.

"This is the ticket then, boys." The red-haired man grinned, holding up the assault rifle for the tall bearded man to see. "The Americans came through—finally."

"They took their sweet time about it" came a voice from behind him. "Thought they'd never stop with the planning and the talk. Jaysus." Then, the man went silent for a moment, surveying the crates. "But, but...they delivered."

"Right," said the bearded man, "Let's pack it up. We have a long ride tonight." He looked toward the boy's father. "You'll go in the truck to load the sheep?"

His father raised his hand in agreement.

"I'll help him with the sheep," said the man who thought they'd been headed to Westport. He started for the truck.

"You'll be going nowhere, sunshine," said the ginger-haired man. He now carried a snub-nosed black gun his hand.

The man turned in surprise, his face drained of color. "What're you talking about?"

The ginger-haired man came close and held the man's face in his big left hand, squeezing hard with his own face inches away. "End of the road for touts. How much did they pay you, Johnny?"

"What're you talking about, man?" the man called Johnny said again. He started to back up and stumbled over the hillocks of rough grass. "I'm no tout. You're crazy to talk like that."

"Jesus, how stupid do you think we are, ya bastard you?"

The redheaded man kept walking forward as Johnny pulled away and backed up, looking around for any support and finding none. "Tell him," he pleaded as he searched the faces of the other men, who all stared back expressionless. One spat to the side in contempt.

"Oh, Jesus. You've got it all wrong," Johnny beseeched in a high, strangled voice.

"Oh, no. We've got it all right, ya son of a bitch. Why do you think we told you the guns were going to Westport when they were coming here all along?" the ginger-haired man snickered. "I'll wager there are guards all over the Westport hills tonight."

Now the man with the beard spoke. "We could do much worse by you, Johnny—a much uglier ending than a bullet. You know that."

Johnny fell to his knews and began to weep.

"You've done that for us," the bearded man continued. "You've done worse and more to men who deserved it far less." His speech became faster and harder. "Deserved it far less than a traitor who would inform on this many men and this many guns here and the Americans supporting us on the other side. Stop your sniveling before we change our mind about how you end." His mouth twisted in disgust.

"How much was it worth to you?" asked the redheaded man. "The new car? The vacation to Majorca with the wife? That goddamned butch of a watch? Did you think we wouldn't notice?"

"I've got kids, I've got kids," Johnny sobbed.

"So do the men you sold out," the bearded man said. "Jesus, man! Stand up. This is a hell of a way to take it."

The ginger-haired man raised the small black gun and looked briefly at the bearded man, who gave the order with a curt nod before turning away and starting for his car.

Johnny stood up while the ginger-haired man was facing the bearded man. At first Johnny stood unsteadily, but he stood. He held a rock in his hand that he'd taken from the ground where he knelt. A jagged rock, a hard rock. With a roar, he threw the rock at the redheaded man. "Take that, ya murdering son of a bitch," he sobbed.

The rock's sharp edge hit the ginger-haired man in the right side of his face—giving him a savage gash along his cheek that drew blood—copious amounts of blood. "Jesus Christ," he hollered as he fell back a few steps and touched his bloody face with his hand. "Jesus fucking Christ." Then, he laughed. A big man's laugh. Through all the blood, he laughed. "Thanks be to God, Johnny. Jesu, I thought you were going to go down like a stuck pig, and not the man you used to be before you took your thirty pieces."

There was the crack of a gun and Johnny went down.

"Put him in the truck," the bearded man called over his shoulder as he opened the car door. "Get rid of it in one of the bogs."

The boy wondered when the dead man had become an *it*.

The bearded man looked around him then, speaking to no one in particular, his voice thick with the distaste of a city man for Connemara's barren landscape of mountains, rocks, and boggy moors, and followed with "God knows you've got enough of them out here."

"Right, lads, let's load up now. What say you?" the ginger-haired man said in a matter of fact, workaday voice, as if he had not just laid waste to the big man lying the length of a fence post away from him.

CHAPTER 14

olly had told Rosaria about his interview with Declan Twomey to find out what Twomey might have seen or heard at Saint Martin's the day of Patrick's visit. She knew too that they had discussed the conversation Declan had with Liam Joyce—the one captured in Justine's photo—in which Declan had appeared angry and Liam deeply distraught.

Twomey had explained to Solly that Joyce had just been upset—pressures of the job. On that day, Twomey said, Joyce had been distressed about the latest altercation in the breakfast line outside the House and had felt uncomfortable asking Twomey for more money to build out the Atrium to accommodate client overflow. Twomey was angry that Joyce was hesitant to ask for help. That's all there was to it.

Solly told Rosaria that he thought there was more there, but he couldn't get it out of Twomey. Rosaria was familiar enough with Solly's style to predict that he'd be back at Declan Twomey sooner rather than later with the same question. With his persistent, patient approach, Solly's track record showed that he usually had a good shot at breaking through if anything was to be had there.

Still, she wondered if it wouldn't be worthwhile for her to visit Twomey herself before she left for Ireland. Through Bridie, Patrick's family had asked her to see what she could find out that might help them understand Patrick's last few days. That was the rationale of the visit she'd explained to Twomey's admin, and that's how she had gotten this meeting. It was worth a shot. Too, perhaps Twomey might shed some background on Liam's reaction to Patrick's visit. He hadn't given Solly that, but maybe she might pick something up.

Rosaria gathered that Bridie had given the Keenan family details about Rosaria's work on a high profile murder last year—probably with a good deal of dramatic embellishment. She hoped the Keenans didn't think she was a superwoman on these types of things.

That had been an unusual situation. God knows she now felt like a shadow of her former self—the woman who'd leapt, at great personal risk, into a high profile murder investigation. Besides, the Boston Police Department in the person of the very competent Detective Solly Belkin was running the Patrick Keenan case.

This visit to Twomey, Rosaria had to admit, was as much to satisfy her own curiosity as to find out information that might help the Keenans understand how their precious only son lived his last days before being attacked and left to die in Boston Harbor. She was also intrigued about the look on Declan Twomey's face in the photos Justine had shown her. He said he was just angry at Joyce's reluctance to ask for help, but Rosaria didn't see concern in that look. She saw something darker. It might have been rage.

Rosaria left a message with Solly that she was going to talk to Declan Twomey for the Keenan family. She knew Solly would be angry—she was interfering with an investigation—but she also knew that he wouldn't stop her. Besides, he was already angry. How much more angry could he get?

She only had that morning before she was to leave for Ireland. She'd called Twomey's office and explained that she was representing Patrick Keenan's family—could she please have a few minutes of Mr. Twomey's time? Twomey's admin checked with her boss and came back to tell Rosaria she could see Mr. Twomey if she was over to his offices within the hour. Fair enough. She'd immediately picked up her keys and cellphone and headed over to Twomey's offices off of Melina Cass Boulevard, near the Southeast Expressway.

As she drove down Route 93, Rosaria reviewed in her mind the few things she knew about Declan Twomey. He'd made his considerable fortune on the Boston skyline. He was unfailingly generous over the years to Saint Martin's Shelter and other Boston philanthropies. He and his wife Carmella, childless, still lived in a modest home in the Dorchester section of Boston. He drove a ten-year old dark green Dodge Ram to work, and had a tuna on wheat sandwich with pickles and chips for lunch every day—either at his desk in the company offices near the expressway or with his workers at one of the construction sites.

She was not surprised then to see the character of his company headquarters. She arrived at an unadorned two-story red brick building at the end of a large gravel parking lot surrounded by a chain-link fence and a small Twomey Construction sign on the gate.

No receptionist staffed the entrance and Rosaria found nothing approximating a lobby when she entered. The hard-hatted worker she stopped on his way out the door looked vaguely familiar, with an appealing, crooked grin. But then, it was an Irish face and this was Boston.

"Declan Twomey's office?" she asked

He hesitated in his stride for a moment, gave her a curious, bemused glance and gestured with his thumb "Upstairs" over his shoulder as he hurried on.

Walking up a short flight of stairs, Rosaria entered a wide open area of metal desks covered with laptops, schematics and Dunkin Donuts Styrofoam cups. Jackets and vests were thrown on the backs of chairs. At the rear corner of the large room sat another metal desk, wider and more battered than the others.

An imposing heavyset man, mostly bald but for a scruff of gray hair with a tinge of red, and startling bushy eyebrows flecked with gray, was sitting there, intently studying a set of blueprints laid flat on the desk. His chin rested in his right palm and a big calloused hand covered half his face. Declan Twomey.

Twomey looked up to see Rosaria when she blocked the sunlight from the window beside his desk. He reached out a big hand. "Ms. O'Reilly." No question; he seemed to know who she was although she couldn't recall they'd ever met. *But,* thought Rosaria, *I'm probably the only stranger in the building and he was expecting me.*

"Thank you for your time, Mr. Twomey. I won't be very long."

"Good. I don't have very long," he said flatly and got right to the point. "You'll be wanting to talk about that poor young Irish student."

"Yes, Patrick Keenan." Rosaria wanted to put a name to Patrick. Not just *that poor young Irish student.*

Twomey looked annoyed. "I can't tell you anything about that, you know. I didn't really know the young man. And aren't the police investigating this? I just spoke to Detective Belkin yesterday." He stopped and looked at Rosaria. "You're not a reporter now or one of those parasites doing a book on someone else's troubles, are you? I think you're likely too good for that." A hint, a twitch of a smile. *How would he know I'm too good for that?*

"No, no. I'm not asking questions for publication. And the police are investigating. I'm just asking a few questions for the family."

Twomey's face eased slightly, though a shadow of suspicion remained in his eyes. "Well, my condolences to them. Horrible thing to lose a boy. I can give you a little time. We'll go to the conference room." Rosaria noticed his home accent was getting a little stronger as he talked.

Twomey started for a glass-walled conference room to the side of the larger room and gestured for Rosaria to follow him. He talked as he worked his way around the metal desks. "We don't have offices here. Hate offices. People start measuring whose is bigger. They put up pictures like they're in a family room. Jesus, sometimes rugs on the floor and sofas and easy chairs. Don't believe in that. Don't even like cubicles." He closed the door behind them after they entered a barren room with a wood veneer conference table and chairs. Over a chipped sideboard hung a print of a Cape Cod beach—a print that might be found at the Christmas Tree Shop. This one was apparently found at least a decade ago, judging by its worn and faded appearance.

"These guys are supposed to be out on the sites anyway, not in here," Twomey continued. "If anybody needs a private conversation or a meeting, they can go to Dunkie's. This room hardly ever gets used." He gave the dust on the sideboard an ineffectual swipe. They sat and he folded his hands on the table, waiting for her to get down to business—so she did.

"I was curious to know about Patrick's visit to Saint Martin's a few days before he died."

"I can't help you with that. I didn't know about his visit until Detective Belkin told me." Rosaria felt the impact of Twomey's flat tonality and the impassive, bored, withholding expression on his face. *So that's the way it's going to be*, she thought.

"You might even have seen him on his way out. One of the staff said you were coming in to see Liam Joyce just as Patrick was leaving."

"Well, there's a staff member without enough to do," he replied curtly. "Anyway, I wouldn't have known who it was, would I?"

"Of course not." Rosaria paused. "I heard Mr. Joyce was quite upset after Patrick's visit. You must have seen that as you were in his office just after Patrick left."

Twomey, too big for his chair, shifted in his seat impatiently. "You are asking the same questions the police did. I don't know why you don't just let them do their jobs. I'm sorry for the family, but this is not going to give them anything useful." Then, he relented, "Like I told Detective Belkin, Liam had other things on his mind than the boy when I went to his office. I don't know what this staff person saw, but they got it all wrong." Defiant eyes, purposeful and direct. Rosaria's instincts told her that she had just been told an aggressive lie. *Well. Well.*

Taking a risk, she pushed a little further. "Mister Joyce remained quite upset later as well. He was delayed for the training program graduation. There is a photo with you both in the background showing an animated conversation in which Mr. Joyce looks distressed and in one you look quite angry."

"I've already explained that. I often look angry, Ms. O'Reilly. That's how I get things done, don't I? I get angry with things that don't go well, like fights in the breakfast line. But, I get angrier with people who waste my time asking questions I've already answered—questions from the authorities. I've spoken to Detective Belkin about all this. You, Ms. O'Reilly, nice as you are, are just wasting my time."

Twomey moved to get up from the table, but apparently thought better of it and dropped heavily back in the chair. "What else?" he growled. Rosaria could almost see the steam coming out of the man's ears. Lowered black bushy brows, red face, hard green eyes with an unusual yellowish tint and a scowling mouth—yes, angry indeed. "I'm only doing this for the boy's family back home. But, Jesus, they are going to hear from me what a hash you're making of this..."

Time for another tack.

"How long have you been in the US, Mr. Twomey?"

"Is this part of the investigation? What's that got to do with anything?"

"No, just curious."

She could see Twomey's face and shoulders relax. "Oh, I'd visited often enough, but I came to stay about thirty years ago. Worked in construction—under the table, of course, totally illegal—just like all those immigrants today that everybody is hollering about, God bless them." Rosaria was relieved to see the big man smile. Almost smile—not quite, but almost. "But it all ended up okay. The American Dream. And here we are." He waved his hand in the direction of his kingdom in the squat red brick building and the Boston skyline.

"And you've been generous in the city. We're lucky to have you."

The big man warmed. "I try. I've had my day when I needed a wee bit of help. I don't forget. No, I never forget. Sometimes people need a hand. I give to a lot of causes, but Saint Martin's is closest to my heart."

"Liam Joyce does great work. You're very good to him."

Now, Twomey smiled a real smile. "Oh, the man does wonderful work. He does. Saint Liam, everyone calls him." He laughed again before turning serious. He leaned forward, hands clasped, arms flat on the table and looked directly into her face. "And I have his back. He's soft. He's like Saint Francis himself. The man needs watching out for, and that's what I do." *Was there a threat in there?*

"And what would he need watching out for, Mr. Twomey?"

He pulled back. "The world is a complicated place, Ms. O'Reilly. Let's just say that saints can get hurt."

She could feel him starting to close down now. "Where in Ireland are you from Mr. Twomey?"

"Oh, up north." A brief, telling pause. "Derry. Belfast".

Rosaria paused a moment herself. "West Belfast? I thought I recognized the accent. Must have been tough days when you left."

"Been tough days for hundreds of years in Derry."

She nodded and then took a risk. "Were you active?"

A cold look. "Everyone was active." Twomey's mind was somewhere else—perhaps in West Belfast for a few moments. "They did what they thought had to be done, didn't they?" he said. "And we did what we thought had to be done. It was war." He turned to face her. "But it's all over now except for some and they're crazed. For most people it's over. Still tension, not a walk in the park, but people aren't killing each other anymore."

It had started to rain. Rosaria could hear the summer rain beating on the window of the conference room now, and see the puddles forming on the far side of the parking lot. She thought the old man was talking more to himself than to her as he continued in a low voice. She was mesmerized.

"There are those who say that people have amnesia about some people involved in the struggle that went on to take positions of power in the government—both in the North and the South. Not pretty, but that's the way liberation usually plays out. That's the way the Republic's struggle for independence was too. Hard things were done."

Here, Rosaria knew he was talking not about his adopted Republic of the United States, but about the Republic of Ireland in the South. The Republic broke away from Britain in 1922, but was unable to make the northern six counties part of the deal.

Twomey turned to gaze out the window, now looking his age—the looseness of the jowls, the deeply creased cheeks, and the puffiness under the eyes. "And then the Republic left us behind when they broke free. Left the North behind. With the Brits. Maybe they didn't really have a choice, but still...they left us behind. And some say they didn't look back." He turned to her, his jaw set. "So, we had to fend for ourselves as best we could. But we'll be under the Irish flag again, mark my words." He nodded to himself. "No question. And it might not be too long before it happens."

A light knock on the door. An admin opened the door a crack and leaned in. "Just wanted to remind you that you're expected over in Allston in twenty, Mr. Twomey."

"Right, thank you, Anne Marie."

She left the door open when she walked back down the hall.

A prearranged interruption after the allotted time was up? Rosaria thought. Apparently her allotted time was thrifty—just half an hour. *Maybe he's wanted over in Allston in twenty minutes, maybe he's not.*

Twomey turned back to Rosaria. "Nothing more to tell, Ms. O'Reilly. I'm not a good source on this. Again, my condolences to the family. I think you know your way out." He rose and walked to the door.

Rosaria got up from her chair and followed him. Then he paused in the doorway, swinging his broad shoulders and body so smoothly, so quickly to face her that she almost bumped into him. She was only inches from his face when he spoke. The words came out silken and amiable, his mouth in a slow, joyless smile on a heavily lined face with its marks and scars of a hardworking life, and his eyes—yellow-green, wolfish eyes, almost loving. Rosaria found the effect terrifying. She was conscious of his big, callused hand poised on the door frame.

"O'Reilly's the last name now, is it? From Malford, by any chance?"

Rosaria nodded cautiously. "How did you know that?"

"Oh, I used to know an O'Reilly from Malford. Jimmy O'Reilly."

On alert in some strange way, she frowned and cocked her head. "Well, that would have been my late father."

"Worked in a big shoe factory, did he?"

"Yes, that's right. How did you know him?" Rosaria tried to respond casually, but felt an odd tingling in her chest.

"Oh, he used to be *active* on some projects with us." Twomey lingered on the word *active*. "Helped us with packaging and some logistics, transportation. He was good at that. A good man, a solid man, and good company, too. Could always count on Jimmy O'Reilly."

Rosaria was too stunned to respond.

"Good day to you, Ms. O'Reilly. Mind yourself out there."

Twomey turned and left, pulling all the air in the room after him.

CHAPTER 15

osaria and Bridie left for Shannon on the 7:20 PM Aer Lingus flight from Terminal C at Logan Airport the next day on an aircraft named the Saint Columba. Rosaria dimly remembered a 6th century monk and patron saint of Cork who might have been astonished at having his name on this silver machine flying over the great Western Sea back to Ireland—but then saints probably anticipate all kinds of miracles.

The flight was uneventful, though both women were keenly aware that young Patrick Keenan's body lay in a mahogany coffin with the cargo below them. O'Gorman's Funeral Home in South Boston had done the arrangement, long being the go-to funeral service for transporting bodies to Ireland.

Bridie told Rosaria that the owner of the funeral home referred to himself as the Lord Mayor—fashioned after the Lord Mayor of Dublin. She wasn't sure what Mr. O'Gorman was Lord Mayor of, perhaps of South Boston. In any case, Bridie said Mr. O'Gorman and his staff were very accommodating.

There were some that said O'Gorman's transported other things with the bodies in the old days—guns that found their way to the IRA. Perhaps a legend from back in the day. A joke suggested over drinks—"Who's going to check a coffin at customs, I ask you?"—that just persisted as fact. Then again, some of those improbable stories from past and more complicated times turned out later to be true. Hard to tell fact from colorful fiction.

A hearse from Clifden met the flight at the airport. While paperwork was exchanged and the sad cargo loaded into the hearse, Rosaria picked up a rental car so that she and Bridie could follow the hearse back to Clifden, a drive of a good three hours with a stop for coffee and perhaps a breakfast on the way. Rosaria took an odd comfort in noticing the same craggy, cranky man at the car rental return booth who'd given her such a hard time about a dented wheel rim on another visit she'd made to Connemara—home of many rocky roads and dented wheel rims.

Though she didn't feel confident of her own left-side of the road driving skills, given Bridie's state of nerves, Rosaria took the wheel.

Along the way, they and the funeral home staff stopped for coffee and a breakfast at a place improbably called Mother Hubbard's. Rosaria got a take-out coffee and stood near the car, checking the messages on her cell. She saw one from Solly and, although it was the middle of the night in Boston, she expected he'd still be awake, maybe working. Sure enough, he answered her return call on first ring.

"How're you doing, Ro?" he asked. Solly's tone, uncharacteristically soft and almost wistful, threw Rosaria off balance for a moment. Perhaps he was feeling some late night loneliness.

"Better if you were with me," she ventured. "It could be like a holiday for you to come over. Pretty over here."

"Honey, I'm sure it is, but you know I just can't take off in the middle of this case and everything else."

"I know. I know. Anything new?"

"Not much. Asking questions at the bars down at the waterfront and by Faneuil Hall. At The Point and the Purple Shamrock and all those to see if anyone remembers the kid from that night."

"Any luck?"

"Nada. Not yet. Coming up dry. If he was in any of them that night, he wasn't very memorable."

"Well, lots of young people in those places and they're always so packed."

"Yeah. And, oh, we're checking out Eduardo Mendez, a guy at the shelter who's Joyce's right-hand man. He and Joyce are each other's alibis the night of the murder. They were still working together upstairs. Best I can figure, they never stop working. Anyway, we're just checking them both out with the security cameras there and all that."

"I don't understand. I suppose there is some connection between Joyce and Patrick, but why in the world would Eduardo want to kill Patrick?"

"Beats me. Maybe for whatever got his boss so upset the day the kid visited him."

"Could make sense. I guess," Rosaria replied, sounding unconvinced.

"Mendez could have a little edge to him. Something about him for me—not just the tats—says he could be capable."

Rosaria knew that the word *capable* meant capable of killing someone, of doing a hit, an execution. "Why would you think that?"

"He's got paper—a few months at Middlesex for assault. Looks like he was in some kind of street fight. Said he was protecting someone. Could have been.

Court must have sympathized. Let him off light. He started at Saint Martin's as a client and moved up the ladder."

"Well, I'd hate to think that he's involved after being a solid employee at the House."

"Yeah," Solly replied. "And I like the guy. He's tough, but I don't think he's the type. I have to check him out anyway." Solly stopped for a moment. "Of course, none of this is appropriate to share with the family yet."

"I understand."

"Miss you," Solly said.

"Me too."

"Makes more sense for you to come home as soon as you can than for me to go over there now, anyway."

"You're probably right, but you never know—I might find something helpful over here."

She heard a deep sigh over the line. "Right. Yeah, okay. Just remember you're not a cop and this is not your case. I'll let you know what's happening when it's appropriate for the sake of the family—but you are not to take the lead on anything. Anything."

"I know, I know. I really do."

"Do you? I'm not sure."

"Yes, I do."

She was about to sign off when Solly said, "Rosie, honey?"

"What, Solly?"

"You really don't know at all that you are not to take the lead. I'm pissed that you went to talk with Twomey yesterday. He called this morning to complain."

"Oh."

"Nearly took my head off. He's absolutely right. Cool it. Seriously, cool it. You're not making my job any easier by screwing around."

"Right, Solly. Sorry. Got it. I really do."

She heard him sigh at the other end of the line. "Night, Rosie. Behave yourself."

CHAPTER 16

Saint Joseph's church in Clifden was filled with students and Patrick's friends. The young women clung to each other, arms intertwined. The young men—vulnerable with their brave, stunned, self-conscious faces, stood a little closer than normal together—shoulders touching. All still in a cocoon of shock—that one of their own should go so young and in such a violent manner.

Rosaria sat toward the back of the church some distance from the statue of Saint Theresa. Damp breezes carrying the sweet scent of bogs and water wafted through the open rear doors. Another soft day, as they called it here, a light mist and a moist, refreshing feel to the air in the lungs. She heard movement at the rear of the church as Patrick's parents, his girlfriend Sarah Glynn, and his Aunt Brigid gathered in the church's entryway—white-faced, moving slowly. Bridie supported her sister Nora, Patrick's mother, on one side. On the other, Patrick's father, Francis, heartbreakingly ramrod straight and stolid, stood with his chin up and eyes red, arm around his wife's waist.

Mrs. Keenan stood tall, mute and frozen in the center of the small group, a light quiver to her angry, set jaw. The fierce blue eyes told it all. Nora Keenan's eyes were fixed accusingly up the long aisle, not on the coffin, but on the altar and the crucifix. *How could He let this happen to her boy?*

Sarah Glynn stood to the side—tall, willowy, with long dark hair—very still and dense with sadness, a dazed, confused expression on her face. Just before the family pulled itself together to walk up to where the coffin waited at the altar, Mrs. Keenan reached her hand out to the girl.

Bridie dropped back and followed the trio, Sarah in the center of the Keenans. They walked toward Patrick's coffin and the altar, joining an extended family of cousins, other aunts and uncles standing at the front of the church, and sat in the first pew. A cluster of palpable grief, the ancient mother's rage of Mrs. Nora Keenan burning at the center.

The Mass was familiar to Rosaria in many ways, unfamiliar in others. While the older people stood at the lectern to read their liturgical passages in English, the young people, slim and stylish, read theirs in fluent school Gaelic. The priest, Father Roche, spoke of the strangeness, pain, confusion—and yes, anger, he said, glancing at Mrs. Keenan—in a world where a loved one is lost so young to violence. He had a low, soft voice and the gift of giving solace.

After Mass, six young men in dark suits lifted and carried the coffin down the aisle and into the church parking lot. Looking at them, Rosaria was reminded of the faces of the boy-men who carried their fallen comrades lost in Afghanistan and Iraq. So young, so very, very young.

The coffin and its bearers led the procession of family and friends from the parking lot down Bridge Street. All processing toward the cemetery where a dark mouth in the earth awaited young Patrick Keenan, the boy who thought his trip to America would be the making of him.

The Keenan's house in Ballyconnelly was too small for the crowd after services. The mourners joined together instead at Manion's Pub, closed for the day for Patrick's funeral. With hushed, contained movements fitting the occasion, servers laid out the funeral meal of seafood chowder with brown bread, a good ham and salmon on long tables beside an open bar. A handle of Jameson sat at the end. Beside the bar, a fiddler played a soft tune.

The crowd was subdued. The Keenans stood near the stone fireplace, greeting the mourners and accepting condolences. Rosaria thought about these grieving parents of a dead child, meeting a line of young people. Young people who would most likely live out healthy lives, be a source of pride, comfort and support to their parents, maybe have children of their own, come to Sunday dinner now and then, return home for the holidays and other visits. How could that not be passing through the Keenans' minds, causing wave after wave of new pain as each young person approached them?

Rosaria joined the line behind a crowd of students, silently inching forward. She was almost startled when she reached Mrs. Keenan. Before Rosaria could murmur her sympathies, Nora Keenan grasped her hand tightly in her own two.

"Ms. O'Reilly, so good of you to come with Bridie to bring Patrick home." There was a catch in Mrs. Keenan's voice at the end of the sentence. She paused to take a deep breath. Rosaria could feel a crackle of energy and an urgency in her eyes. "Would you ever stay for a few minutes after the line goes down? I have something I need to discuss with you."

"Of course, of course, Mrs. Keenan. I'll stay 'til you're done. As long as you like."

Nora Keenan nodded and whispered "Thank you." She held Rosaria's eye, nodding again even as another mourner approached.

Later, sitting at a side table with a cup of tea and an untouched plate of food someone had placed before her, Nora Keenan asked for Rosaria's help.

"Ms. O'Reilly..." she started.

"Please, Rosaria, or Ro. Or even Rosie, if you like."

"Rosaria—a lovely name. I went to school with a Rosaria." The first, tentative smile Rosaria had seen on Nora Keenan's face since she arrived in Ireland. "I'm sure you're a much nicer person than *that* Rosaria. She was a wild one."

Rosaria returned the smile. "Maybe I am, maybe I'm not."

"Fair play." The smile lingered for a moment before it faded and she got down to what she wanted to talk about. "Anyway, Rosaria. I'd like you to stay here a little longer, to do some work for us. Maybe even a few weeks. We could find you a place to stay. Could you ever manage that?"

"I'm scheduled to fly home day after tomorrow. Why would you want me to stay, Nora? What would you have me do?"

Mrs. Keenan leaned forward, forearms on the table. Her straight gray hair, cut in what used to be called a bob, swung forward to frame her face. Rosaria sensed her energy again. This was a formidable woman. Patrick had had that energy, but young, unformed, not careful.

"I just have this feeling, Rosaria. It's only a feeling, mind you, that whatever Patrick was working on, that independent study project or whatever it was, had something to do with what happened to him."

Rosaria didn't respond directly but her eyes met Nora Keenan's in tacit agreement. "And why would you think that?"

"Whatever it was, I think it started over here. It finished over there, but I think it started over here. Something he found out here made him fly over to Boston." She sat back in her chair, straightening her shoulders and neck, chewing her lower lip. "Now, I know the police in Boston are investigating and all, but I don't know if they'd really look closely from this angle."

Right you are, thought Rosaria.

"They might think it too...fanciful."

Indeed.

"We'd be willing to pay you for your time—"

Before Mrs. Keenan finished with her sentence about payment, Rosaria had held up her hand, palm out, "No, no. Forget that. Don't talk about that."

She took a deep breath and looked around Manion's, noticing that the crowd was more relaxed now, and that the fiddler was starting to play livelier tunes. She heard the first low laughs from clutches of young people, reminiscing about times with Patrick. Children darted in and out like small birds among the mourners. A full Irish wake in progress.

"Let me think about it, Nora."

Mrs. Keenan continued as if Rosaria had not spoken. "The Garda—the police here—wouldn't have the time to look into things—all the budget cuts, you know—unless there was something concrete—like to work on a request from Boston. And I don't think that will be coming soon."

"No, I don't think it will."

"So, if you could stay, just talk to a few people here—like you did in Boston about that poor old nun..."

Almost on cue, a tall young man in a guard uniform approached. Straight brown hair, the moss green eyes and handsome features of many of the local Connemara families. He nodded at Rosaria and touched Nora Keenan's arm.

"I'm so sorry I missed the service, Mrs. Keenan. A bad accident up in Letterfrack."

"Oh, but you're here now, Gerard. Thank you."

The young man lifted his chin toward Rosaria. "I don't want to be disturbing you. I just wanted to give you my sympathies. Patrick was a fine young man."

"He was, he was, Gerard." Nora Keenan was lost for a moment in thought and then brought her mind back to the table. "Where are my manners? Gerard Conneely, this is Rosaria O'Reilly from Boston—a friend of my sister Bridie. She helped Bridie bring Patrick home."

Nora put her hand on the young man's arm, looking at Rosaria. "Gerard is a local boy, in the guards now, a sergeant, mind you. He keeps us all safe and in line." She smiled.

"Well, that's a comfort," Rosaria said. "Good to know you, Gerard."

"And Rosaria," Nora continued, "is going to help us figure some things out about what happened to Patrick."

Good gravy, thought Rosaria. *Just what a cop wants to hear. Off to a dicey start.*

"Oh, is she now?" Rosaria felt a chill in Sergeant Conneely's response. "Are you a private detective, Ms. O'Reilly?"

"No, no. Just a friend of the family helping out. Nothing formal. The investigation's in good hands with the Boston Police Department."

"I expect it is," he replied, giving her a glance she couldn't interpret.

"Well, I'd better leave you to it, Mrs. Keenan." He knelt down to be at eye level with her. "You know I'm here to help you in any way I can."

"That's a comfort in itself, Gerard."

He stood. "Pleasure to meet you, Ms. O'Reilly. I'd be happy to be of assistance to you as well."

"Good to know, Sergeant Conneely."

After Sergeant Conneely left the table and joined the group at the fireplace, Rosaria thought about Nora's request. Conneely's reaction to her was a minor version of Solly's. Amateurs getting involved in police business, nothing but trouble and complication.

Solly would be more than aggravated at knowing that she'd be staying *to help the Keenan family out a little bit*. Just as he'd predicted. She'd get involved here, get in his business, and complicate things for him in his new job. Rosaria felt a sudden wave of anger run through her. *Well, too bad for Solly and Sergeant Conneely too. Who do they think they are? It's not just their call. It's the Keenans' call too.*

"I'd be glad to help, Nora."

The wake was in full swing while Nora Keenan and Rosaria talked quietly in the corner.

"I hope I can deliver something for you, Nora. I wouldn't know where to start in finding out the details of Patrick's project. He must have talked about it when he came home on visits."

"Yes, yes, but only very general-like, you know. Something about American support for the IRA in the '70s up Nordie—up North. Now, I hate to think what happened to him had to do with digging around that old bad business—but you never know." She closed her eyes. "Jaysus."

She shook herself out of her thoughts and turned to the bar to call for her husband. "Get Sean to pull me a pint of Bridewell, would you, Francis? Find Sarah and bring her over here now? We want to talk to her."

Mr. Keenan nodded.

"Anyway," she continued with Rosaria, "I think it would be better for you to talk to Sarah about what he was working on. They were always together. Two peas in a pod, they were, always yammering at each other about this, that, and the other thing." After a sad clip of silence, Nora looked up at Rosaria and then at her husband. "You know, if he'd just cry or rage or something, it would be better. He doesn't really talk. Just sits there, maybe walks down to the bay with the dog. And even the dog makes him sad. Reminds him of the boy." She shook her head. "I'm afraid he's going to break if he doesn't get it out."

Rosaria watched Francis Keenan wade through the crowd to where Sarah was standing beside a group, a fixed smile on her face, holding a glass of wine she wasn't drinking. She started when Francis Keenan took her arm, looked over to where Nora and Rosaria were seated and came toward them across the floor. Rosaria had expected Francis Keenan to join them, but he resumed his position near a group of equally taciturn older countrymen at the far end of the bar. They greeted Francis's re-entry with wordless nods as he was absorbed into the silent comfort of his own ones.

Nora pulled a chair out for the young woman. When she was seated, Nora put a hand on her arm. "Sarah, I'm only after wondering if you'd take some time to talk to Ms. O'Reilly here about Patrick's project at the university?"

A flicker of panic ran over the girl's face.

"Oh, not now, not now, dear, but maybe this coming week? Ms. O'Reilly's going to help us out a little in finding some answers that might help the police with the investigation."

"Sure, sure. But I have to go back to Galway in the morning to see about my classes and my new apartment." Sara looked at Nora with anxious, distracted eyes, lost to grief.

"That's good, Sarah." Nora placed her hand on Sarah's. "I'm glad you're moving places. It would be so hard to move back into the Corrib Village where you and Patrick were."

"Right." The three women sat together in silence for a moment.

"Anyway, I have a ride back. So, I'm not sure when..."

"Not a problem, Sarah. I have business in Galway City. I could rearrange it to meet your schedule," Rosaria said. A white lie, but she was sure she could find something to do in the city. "If you have time, we could meet for coffee or a lunch and talk then."

 meeting of the Board at Saint Martin House had apparently just finished when Solly entered the lobby for a follow-up visit with Liam Joyce. He recognized some of the board members coming off the elevator from the meeting—well-known lawyers, bankers and business people who gave time and money, clergy and social workers who gave expertise. All doing their best to alleviate the long-running chronic problem of urban homelessness. No complaints about these do-gooders, and Liam Joyce was probably indeed *un santos*, as Eduardo insisted. Solly only wished he was *un santos* who was more forthcoming about his meeting with Patrick Keenan just before the young student was murdered.

Another elevator arrived in the lobby as Solly was headed for the stairs. The doors opened to the formidable bulk of Declan Twomey. Twomey's face darkened at the sight of Solly. "Aren't you done here, Detective?" he asked.

"Need a follow-up visit with Mr. Joyce," Solly responded.

"What for? I'm sure Liam has told you all he knows, as I have."

"Oh, I'll be coming by to see you again too, Mr. Twomey, to see if you might remember more than you thought."

"I'm not going to remember anything else and neither is Liam. People are busy, you know. They have things to do without going over the same ground again and again."

Solly walked back to face Twomey directly. He wasn't quite as tall as the big man, but he didn't have to look up at him when he spoke and he had a solid build himself. "You know, Mr. Twomey, I have a job to do. Sometimes people remember things after the first or the second or even the third time you talk to them. A young man has been murdered, and it's my job to find out who did it."

Twomey snorted in response and pivoted away toward the front door of the lobby.

"I'll be coming to see you again too, Mr. Twomey," called Solly before he walked toward the stairs.

Liam Joyce's eyes were closed when Solly entered his office. Perhaps in meditation, perhaps in exhaustion. Solly waited until Joyce opened his eyes.

Solly had expected Liam Joyce to be flush with irritation and anxiety when he saw Solly standing at the door to his office. But he was neither. As he opened his eyes, Joyce's manner seemed gentle, peaceful, perhaps resigned.

"Hello, Detective. What can I do for you?"

"Hello, Mr. Joyce. I'd just like to go over a few things with you again about your meeting with Patrick Keenan. Sometimes we find people remember things as time goes on—even small points—that might be important to the investigation."

Joyce nodded slowly. "Yes, I can see that."

"I sense that Patrick talked to you about more than the Irish-American community support of Saint Martin House and similar shelters in Ireland."

Joyce was silent for a few beats before he said, "The time period that Patrick was researching was a complicated one in Ireland."

Solly didn't respond, didn't push.

"People here, Irish-American people here, wanted to help the Cause in some way, whatever their understanding of the Cause was. They didn't have a very nuanced sense of events and everyone had a bitter distrust of the Brits bred into them—for good reason given our history. They never considered the Protestants in Northern Ireland as Irish, and don't to this day. They saw them as intruders that came and took Catholic lands. These are long, centuries-old memories in a small country. So, you see, some people here thought the Cause was just and, yes, they wanted to help."

He picked up a pen, one of a number of cheap Bic pens standing in a Dunkin Donuts paper cup on the desk, and played with it mindlessly as he talked. "You know, from far away, from over here, you just hear stories like something in a heroic movie or video. You don't really know it or understand it—the horror, the cruelty. On our side to our own too." He looked somewhere near a file cabinet in the corner, his mind very far away from Boylston Street in Boston.

"Is that what you talked about with Patrick, Mr. Joyce?" If this was the truth, it wasn't all of it.

Solly heard a deep intake of breath and saw Joyce rearranging his face, preparing to tell a lie. Perhaps not a complete lie, but maybe a half-truth. Or the Catholic sin of omission, an interesting sin which Rosaria had once explained to him, her Jewish significant other. Lying by omitting or leaving something out.

Perhaps the most important something, the most critical, the most damning something. He was certainly familiar with that form of lying from his experience as a cop over the years. He just had never heard it given a category name before.

"Yes, that's what we talked about," said Saint Liam.

Right, thought Solly. "Is that all you talked about, Mr. Joyce? Was there any specific event or person you touched on in your conversation with Patrick?"

"No, no. Just the general lack of understanding of what the war in Belfast was like and what the money and the support was really going for."

"I see," Solly said. He let the silence settle in.

After some time, Solly left his card on the desk. "Well, if you think of anything else or if you want to talk, Mr. Joyce, give me a call. I'll probably swing by again soon."

Liam nodded and closed his eyes.

CHAPTER 18

 brisk breeze was coursing off the water the day Rosaria drove out the Sky Road, headed for the short-term rental cottage that friends of the Keenans had found for her.

She'd been content staying in the Buttermilk Lodge on the Westport Road with Cathriona's full Irish breakfast and the peat fires that Pat had started to make in the cooler evenings. But Nora Keenan had taken the initiative to sign and pay for the cottage rental.

Rosaria was bemused that the cottage owner's name was Burke, one of her family names. But the Burke grandfather who had emigrated to Massachusetts left so long ago that she couldn't imagine making the connection with anyone in Clifden or Ballyconneely now. And she was not sure she had the energy to try. Not where her head was at the moment.

On this day, Rosaria was concentrating on staying on the correct side of the gorgeous Sky Road with its breathtaking vistas around every corner. Patrick's border collie Fergus occupied the passenger seat beside her, his head stuck out the window, greedily breathing in the fresh ocean air.

Somehow, through unspoken agreement, Rosaria had become Fergus's foster parent during her stay. The Keenans had a hard time having Fergus around after Patrick's death. On the one hand, the dog was a well-loved, living reminder of their son. On the other hand, because Fergus was a well-loved, living reminder of her son, Mrs. Keenan often burst into tears when the dog came bounding through the door. "Fergus is always hoping to see Patrick standing here," she said. "Just like us."

Everyone could see that the yearning, confused dog missed his young master and needed attention. So, when Fergus had attached himself to Rosaria, she was happy for it. She'd be living alone in an isolated cottage for several weeks and could use the company.

She had hoped Solly might find time to visit, but she saw now that it was impossible for him. He was so tightly tied to Patrick's case and others in Boston right now. Nothing to be done about it.

Despite the affectionate tone to their call when Rosaria had first arrived in Ireland, she and Solly were both still subdued and careful in conversation. His calls recently were disappointingly businesslike and brief. Their clash over her coming to and now staying in Ireland had surprised them both. They both had considered their relationship strong and loving enough to withstand these perturbations.

Yet, in retrospect, Rosaria thought the clash should have been expected. Two strong-willed people who were used to operating independently and, to a certain extent, calling the shots, were trying to build a partnership without losing the core of themselves. Solly's brief marriage to the needy, dependent Justine and his past relationships, from what she knew of them, had certainly not prepared him for the likes of Rosaria, no matter what he said. Independent, challenging Rosaria. She couldn't be different. She was too old to change.

This particular decision, to come to Ireland in the middle of Solly's investigation into Patrick Keenan's death—when Rosaria thought there may have been something relevant to the case on this side of the Atlantic and Solly did not—was tailor-made for igniting a fiery debate. She was not ready to give up on their making it together as a couple, and she had hopes that Solly would come to terms with her staying here and working with the Keenans.

Still, Rosaria knew she was not the only one in the relationship who wondered if this partnership would work out over the long term.

Now, it was toward the end of summer in Connemara. The strange and wonderful half-light of the long Irish summer evenings would be gone soon. The days would be getting shorter and the air chillier. Summer visitors were even now heading back to Dublin or Munich, London, New York or Boston. She knew she'd be glad of having Fergus around as it got quieter on the Sky Road. Enthusiastic and inquisitive, he was good company and it was never a bad idea for a woman living on her own to have a watchdog around.

Entering through a break in a low stone wall along a narrow dirt driveway, Rosaria pulled beside the Burke house. The house sat on a lonesome stretch off the main road along the sea. But it was not too far from town and, it came with a precious WiFi connection. This last at the insistence of Mr. Burke's only child—a daughter in Seattle, who with her husband and children Skyped with the old man every week.

The estate agent hinted that the house might be on the market when Mr. Burke came back. He'd likely be moving to be with his daughter—what with getting on in years and his wife being gone since two Christmases ago. What was there here for him?

Rosaria looked over the expanse of open water behind the house for a few minutes, listening to the ocean rolling and murmuring like a watery, restless, gray blue beast. She inhaled a deep breath of the fresh, chilly air heavy with the smell of brine and seaweed. Then, braced by the sounds and smells, she took out a key and walked to the side door to enter the cottage.

She turned when she heard and then saw an ancient dark Renault van coming around the bend from the direction of Clifden. The van had signage on the side, too far away to read, and a piece of cloth flying from its side window. Rosaria wondered if, like so many country people, she'd get in the habit of stopping whatever she was doing to watch a car go by on a quiet day. This one was certainly interesting enough.

She raised her hand to the driver—a heavy man with an angular face and a shock of dark hair. The man stared at her for a moment and returned a shy wave before driving on. Rosaria reminded herself that people in the Gaeltacht, the Gaelic-speaking regions, had a reputation for being clannish and shy.

"Ah well," she whispered as she turned the key in the lock and called to Fergus, who was chasing seagulls over the seaweed and sand. "Let's go, Fergus," she called. "You're wasting your time. You'll never catch those guys." Forgetting all about his chase, Fergus came racing to Rosaria and they entered the house together, the dog pushing his way through the half opened door first.

It was an old man's house, living inside the shell of another time when he was long-married to a loving, attentive and fussy homemaker. A tattered dark green reading chair and ottoman sat squarely in front of a small television. On top of the set, a plastic statue of the Blessed Mother. A stack of dusty books held up one corner of the chair where the fourth leg should have been. Beside the chair, a cluttered end table covered with a plastic blue doily held a large ashtray, a pipe stand, a laminated card with a novena to Saint Jude, a racing form for the Galway Races and a solitary photograph in a silver frame. What she took to be the late Mrs. Burke smiled gaily out of the frame—a sweet-faced, tight-curled woman in a blue ruffled dress, apparently enjoying a party or a wedding.

An animated Fergus poked and sniffed around the room, delighted with the new and different scents of a strange house. He occasionally interrupted his explorations by standing on his hind legs to look out the large window at the rocks and the gulls, to let them know he was still on the watch. Rosaria smiled and lowered herself gently into the big green chair, feeling that she was entering someone else's life. Over the next few minutes, she just breathed—inhaling the smell of pipe smoke, wool, and the scent of an old man. Gradually, Rosaria sensed that she was being introduced to James Burke and that they would like each other.

Looking around the living room, Rosaria saw touches of Mrs. Burke—a floral settee with lace doilies in the corner. A rose-covered china teapot on a small tea table. On one corner of the wall, a portrait of Pope John Paul II with a palm cross from some long ago Palm Sunday tucked behind the picture. On the other wall, John F. Kennedy with rosary beads hanging from the corner of the picture frame.

She reached into her side pocket for her cellphone to call Solly. She was calling in part to hear his voice, but also to get an update on his conversations with Eduardo Mendez and the other staff at Saint Martin House regarding Patrick's visit just before he was killed.

Rosaria knew that this part of the investigation would require an interview with the ever-present Justine. Rosaria just hoped that the interview would happen with another officer present and at the Boston Police Department headquarters. She didn't want to think about the interview happening with just Justine and Detective Belkin in some cozy coffee shop on Beacon Hill or, God forbid, in Justine's apartment.

Rosaria's spirits lifted when she opened her phone to find a photo sent from Marguerite—Archie on a couch with three elderly nuns at the Motherhouse. Archie was sitting up and on alert, staring straight ahead intently. One nun's wrinkled hand lay affectionately on his back. They were all apparently watching television. Rosaria knew how much Archie liked watching mysteries and dramas. Sure enough, the text from Marguerite read *"Monday night, watching Midsomer Murders. This was the best idea. Archie is everyone's darling."*

Rosaria smiled and wondered about the wisdom of leaving Archie at the Motherhouse. Now she hoped she could get the nuns to release him. She blew a kiss at the photo and then hit Solly on speed dial.

Not for the first time lately, she had to be content with hearing Solly's voicemail greeting. "Detective Belkin, Homicide Division, Boston Police Department. Leave a message. Back as soon as I can."

Rosaria suppressed her irrational fear that Solly couldn't answer the phone because he was locked in conversation—or other activity—with Justine. "Stop it, just stop it," she whispered to herself before Solly's greeting finished and she left her message. "Hi, just calling to say hello and see what's going on. I'm in a little cottage the Keenans found for me. I have a watchdog, sort of. Call me when you have a chance. Miss you."

Rosaria stared into the distance for a few thoughtful and melancholy moments after leaving her message. Then, she shook herself and punched the number for Sarah Glynn, Patrick's girlfriend—to confirm she would meet her in Galway City the next day. No answer there, either.

"Sarah here. I'll call you back."

Rosaria knew from seeing Sarah at Patrick's services that the distraught young woman was still in a hard shell of shock and grief. It had only been two weeks since Patrick's murder. Nevertheless, Sarah was trying to rally—heading back from her parents' home in Tuam to the University in Galway. She had rented a new apartment, to reduce the number of memories of Patrick that she would have to face every day. She'd be stopping by her department at the university, visiting friends and generally trying to pick up the pieces of her life. Hard work.

Rosaria had been surprised and grateful when Sarah had agreed to meet and talk with her. Now, as she left a message on Sarah's cell, she wondered if the young woman had been so numb and distracted that the commitment to meet never really registered. She could only hope for the best.

As she ended her message to Sarah, Rosaria reflected for a moment on her email exchange the previous day with Patrick's faculty advisor at the university— now on sabbatical in Germany. The conversation, a sad one as the professor had been fond of Patrick and believed he had a bright future, had turned up nothing new, but overall confirmed her sense of the situation with Patrick's independent study project. The topic—Irish-American support for the IRA in Northern Ireland—was worrisomely broad and unfocused and Patrick had not been turning in his status reports. The advisor had to warn him several times, just before Patrick had gone to America, that he was in danger of falling behind. Being awarded his degree with the rest of his class might be in jeopardy.

Rosaria frowned and shook her head. What in the world had happened to this bright boy in the middle of an independent research project—perhaps gone all wrong?

Then, trying to energize herself, Rosaria put her cell back in her pocket, slapped her thigh and said to herself loudly, "Enough muddling around. Get moving!" She got up from the green chair to retrieve her bags from the car. Calling Fergus, she walked through the kitchen, noting the single place setting

neatly stacked on the wooden counter and the pictures of American grandchildren in Little League and soccer uniforms beaming from the front of
the refrigerator.

Fergus beat her through the door again and ran joyfully once more toward
the seaweed-covered rocks on the shore. He resumed his great display of ener-
getic sniffing around the rocks and his fearsome barking at the gulls, who
continued to ignore him disdainfully.

As she stood on the low concrete step outside the front door, Rosaria pulled
her sweater closer against the chill. The ocean had turned a metallic gray and
the waves choppy. She opened the back door of her car, reaching for one of
her travel bags, when she heard the hum of a motor again. She thought it was
a boat and looked toward the cove, but then realized it was a car on the road.

The dark Renault van she had seen earlier drove slowly by again. She still
couldn't make out the printing on the side of the van but she could see that the
odd little piece of cloth fluttering out a side windows was some kind of red and
white flag. The same heavyset man with the dark hair and eyes was driving the
van and staring at her—not friendly, not curious, not menacing—just a flat stare.

A gust of air off the rocks made Rosaria shiver. She did not wave at the
driver this time, but called the dog and hurried with her bags into the house.

CHAPTER 19

he next day, Nora Keenan called, asking Rosaria to join her for lunch at Cullen's Coffee Shop on Market Street in Clifden. Rosaria's confidence about driving in Ireland was still somewhat fragile. After accepting Nora's invitation, she took the Sky Road to Clifden and pulled into the parking lot of Saint Joseph's Church on the Westport Road. She couldn't face trying to find a parking place and then maneuvering the car into a space on a busy Main or Market Street. She'd leave the rental car here and walk the few blocks to Cullen's.

Rosaria was surprised at what a timid driver she'd become on this visit to Ireland. A veteran Boston driver and parallel parker par excellence, she somehow couldn't adjust to the left side of the road driving, especially at the roundabouts. She wondered if the *"insult to her brain"* that the doctor had diagnosed last winter had given her some kind of driving dyslexia. And her healing, but still damaged, right eye was truly a liability in navigating the narrow roads here.

A pale sun caught on the steeple of Saint Joseph's as she headed toward her appointment with Nora Keenan. Main Street was busy with shoppers. Except for the SuperValu market, which was not really that big, there were no large stores in Clifden. You had to drive to Galway City for that, to find a Boots or a Tedesco's. As a result, small shops—pharmacies, clothiers, stationers and probably the best bookstore in the west of Ireland, the Clifden Bookshop, survived and prospered in a fashion Rosaria hadn't seen since her childhood decades ago. Some rural towns in Ireland had been left behind. It was as if they were places missing a spine or vertebrae with their empty shops and storefronts on the High Street. But not Clifden.

She turned the corner of Market Street and walked down the slight incline to Cullen's. The tables were filled and the shop crowded. Nora Kennan sat in the rear of the shop near a small fireplace. She raised her hand in greeting as Rosaria came through the door.

Rosaria made her way through the diners to join Mrs. Keenan. Rosaria was a natural hugger, but she had learned over time that many people were not. So, she held back until Nora Keenan opened her arms and said. "Good to see you, Rosaria."

Rosaria leaned in for a hug. "And you, Nora."

"Welcome to one of my favorite haunts," Nora said as Rosaria took a seat and surveyed the coffee shop. Really, more of a tea shop despite its name. Normally, this amount of bric-a-brac, old photos, pictures and lace would have given her hives, but today Rosaria felt embraced and comforted—like being in a grandmother's parlor. Rosaria's own Nana O'Reilly had, in fact, been more given to bling in her decorating and played the dogs at the Wonderland track—but Rosaria knew there were other nanas, if not her own, with parlors like this one.

"I always get the soup and sandwich special here. Never disappoints. Hello, Mary," she said, turning to greet the waitress.

The waitress's eyes were moist. "My heart goes out to you, Mrs. Keenan."

"Thank you, Mary." She reached for the waitress's hand and squeezed it tightly. "It means the world to us, all the kindness."

Mary nodded and, after a moment, asked Rosaria, "Coffee today?"

"Yes please."

"Would you want the soup and sandwich special with Nora? Today, it's a potato leek soup and salmon salad on a brown bread."

"Yes, thank you. That would be perfect."

Nora Keenan lost no time when Mary left. After a perfunctory "How are you settling in?" she got right down to business. "I know you'll be talking to our Sarah. Is there anything else we can help you with?"

"Sarah is probably my best start at getting an overview. I'd hoped to talk to Patrick's advisor, but I understand he's on sabbatical in Germany. My email exchange wasn't perfect, but it will have to do for now."

Nora nodded. Mary brought their soups and sandwiches. As they ate, Rosaria hungrily—enjoying every bite—and Nora sparingly, Rosaria sketched out her general plans at the moment. "I'll stay on top of what's happening with the investigation in Boston and keep you posted with whatever they are at liberty to share with the family. What's the best way to do that, Nora?"

They agreed for the short term to meet every few days or as necessary at Cullen's for a face-to-face update if they could. If not, then a phone update would do.

"Fine, that's good, Rosaria," Nora Keenan said when they had finished, briskly pulling her bags together. "I'm going to walk up to visit Patrick now. Would you keep me company as far as Bridge Street?"

"Of course, I'd be pleased to, Nora."

As they walked up the main street, Nora took Rosaria's arm. Walking arm and arm with another woman was not something that Rosaria had experienced since Catholic school, though she'd often observed older Italian women in Boston's North End, near her condo, amiably strolling arm and arm down Hanover Street. She often envied them. Now, she was surprised at how comforting it felt to face the world with another human's touch.

As they passed the news agent, Rosaria caught a glimpse of Cathal McKenna's bearded face on the front page of one of the national newspapers. The photo of the ex-IRA leader Patrick had mentioned to her, the one with ambitions to be the prime minister or Taoiseach of Ireland, sat over a headline about his party's opposition to certain social service cuts. She thought she saw a line underneath about the "Man of the People". The Cathal McKenna in the picture looked dynamic, hirsute and vaguely academic—perhaps a classics professor. She couldn't imagine his having a *history*, as Patrick had said, whatever having a *history* meant.

She and Nora approached where Bridge Street, leading to the cemetery, veered off Main Street. "Well, I won't keep you now," Nora said, in the polite Irish form of dismissal. "I like to go there by myself, you know."

Rosaria nodded. She could imagine Nora Keenan as the kind of woman who would prefer to give vent to her deepest grief and anger in private. She could see her getting up from her bed at night, too restless in her body, too wracked with grief and rage to sleep or even to stay still. Trying not to wake Francis as she walks to the darkened kitchen, and once there sits with the cat at her feet, a cup of tea growing cold on the table. Moaning in physical pain, weeping. Always with the door closed.

"Talk to you soon, Nora."

Nora raised her hand in goodbye. Before she moved away, she said, "You know, sometimes I feel so strongly that he's here. Just out of my sight. But here. I feel his presence. My darling boy."

Rosaria met Nora's eyes for a few moments, but didn't respond.

Later, as she walked toward her car, Rosaria turned to watch Nora walking down the Bridge Street hill to visit the grave of her only son. She had lifted a blue patterned kerchief over her head against the light mist that had begun. Her pace was now slow and meditative, her straight spine slightly stooped. With a melancholy heart, Rosaria saw the old woman that Nora Keenan was fast on her way to becoming.

CHAPTER 20

olly had called ahead for a follow-up appointment with Declan Twomey. He didn't think he could trust the possibility of catching him in his office with all his comings and goings.

In his conversation with Declan Twomey's administrator, Anne-Marie, Solly made it clear that Mr. Twomey had no choice as to whether he'd have an interview with Detective Belkin. His choice was either in his office or at the station.

Now, as he climbed the stairs to Twomey's office, he passed a burly construction worker in a light vest over a black Bruins tee shirt.

"Nice shirt. Big fan?"

"Oh yeah. Thanks."

Solly stretched out his hand. "Solly Belkin, Boston PD."

"Frank O'Brien. Good to meet you." The man shook Solly's hand briefly and then raised his hand in goodbye as he headed down the stairs and out the front door at a good clip.

Solly took out his little black spiral notebook and made a note. *Frank O'Brien. Bruins tee shirt. Paper?*

Solly was rarely intimidated by an irate interviewee. He'd tirelessly come back to the same questions again and again and wait out long, surly silences.

Now, he wouldn't say that he was intimidated by Declan Twomey, but he had to admit that he found the man chilling in some way. There were the eyes, such an odd color, staring out from under those massive black and gray brows. And, of course, his bulk.

The image that came to Solly's mind when he looked at Declan Twomey's person was that of a destroyer. A massive destroyer on the high seas, coming right at him. And he was about as personable as a destroyer, not giving an inch.

"I have nothing to say about that boy. I never met him."

"Of course I looked angry in that picture with Liam Joyce. I look angry half the time. Look at my eyebrows, man. I look angry even when I'm smiling." A hint of a real smile on Twomey's face. But that was the only break in the wall. After thirty minutes of impenetrable blocking, Solly had to admit defeat. On this day, anyway.

As Solly was leaving Twomey's office, he heard him thunder from behind him, "From this point on, you can talk to my lawyer, Detective Belkin."

"I'll look forward to talking to both of you, Mr. Twomey," Solly responded without looking back. His mind was already on checking whether there was paper in the system on one Francis O'Brien of the black Bruins tee shirt.

CHAPTER 21

t wasn't that serious an accident. Rosaria couldn't calculate how close she was to the farm truck on the other side of the road. The scrape along the side of the rental car would have to be fixed, but wouldn't be a big job. She thought her credit card might cover the deductible.

Back in the US, the Massachusetts Department of Motor Vehicles allowed Rosaria to drive with her damaged right eye because she demonstrated she had learned to compensate with her left eye. She had passed the road test on the streets around the Watertown Registry offices outside of Boston easily.

But that was driving on the right side of the road and on wider streets, even though they were busy and congested with notoriously unpredictable Boston drivers.

In Connemara, the roads were often so narrow that one car had to pull off the road into farm gateways to let another vehicle creep by. Impossibly winding, with gorgeous fuchsia hedge rows so close and lush that the branches reached through the car window to greet you. Perhaps also to obstruct your field of view so that you might never see a car coming the opposite way until it was ten feet in front of you. Not to mention the sheep and the occasional cow being led from one pasture to another. Or, in the case of her incident, large farm equipment.

Rosaria knew when she was beaten. Later that day, she stopped into Cullen's Coffee Shop and Bakery and asked Mary whether she knew of a good driver who'd be willing to cart her around for a few weeks. They could use her car, but she really couldn't drive here.

Mary called to the back of the shop, "Peg, does Mossie the Yank still take people around?"

Peg came out of the kitchen, wiping her floured hands on her apron. "Yes, yes, he does. Now, I don't know if he's available and he does like to drive his own car if that would suit you as well."

Rosaria shrugged. "All the same to me. I just need someone to get me from here to there."

"Well, he'd be your man then, I'd say. And he knows this area like the back of his hand."

She looked at Rosaria closely with a smile. "Did the roads here defeat you?"

Rosaria laughed. "I'm not equal to them yet."

"Not surprised at all. Here, let me see if I have Mossie's card somewhere here." Peg shuffled through cards for various local services that were stacked near the cash register. "There we are. Mossie's Livery Service."

Maurice Ignatius O'Toole or Mossie the Yank of Clifden by way of Adams Corner in Dorchester, Massachusetts pulled up beside the Burke cottage the next morning. He drove an ancient, battered Renault panel van with a TACSA sign on the top, Mossie's Livery Service sign on the side and a maroon and white flag for the Gaelic Athletic Association Galway hurling team on a side window. Rosaria recognized the mysterious car that had twice driven by the Burke cottage when she'd first arrived.

From the living room she could see a big rumpled man heave himself out of the van with surprising agility given his size. He reached one meaty hand down to tousle Fergus's head and threw his head back to give a laugh as big as himself as the dog danced around him, thrilled with this new company. *My watchdog,* sighed Rosaria. *Hopeless.*

Mossie raised his head to look at the sea, now a deep blue gray with white-caps under an overcast sky. He paused a moment, breathing in deeply before he turned and headed for the kitchen door.

He filled the doorframe as Rosaria opened the wooden door. "You must be Mossie."

"At your service, Miss O'Reilly." He removed his cap and smiled.

Rosaria had made the tea. She poured them both a cup and, over the tea and yesterday's scones from Cullen's, she broached the subject of Mossie's cruising past the Burke cottage twice on the day she moved in. "You know, you had me scared half to death—a big man like you riding by the house twice. What were you thinking?"

Mossie's face was flush with embarrassment even as he tried to explain himself. "Forgive me, Miss O'Reilly. I wasn't thinking. I was only curious, you know, about who might be renting Burkie's cottage for a few weeks. I meant no harm."

The big man looked as if he wanted to drop through the floor. Rosaria knew what she was doing when she stared at him for a few moments before she showed mercy by moving on to other subjects. They talked about Boston and changes since Mossie was last there.

Rosaria learned that Mossie's mother had returned to Galway from Dorchester with her boy after she'd been left a young widow. Mossie was only five when he returned and soon had no trace of an American accent, but all his life, he'd been called the "Yank".

"They always had a time with it, you know. Even if your parents are from here and you're just a little kid," he explained. "But that's okay. They're just having fun and I don't mind. The name stuck, though, didn't it?"

They talked about new development plans in Clifden, about how long it took Ireland to recover from the banking crisis. There seemed to be no end of interesting topics to discuss with her new driver. She could see that it would be a pleasure to ride the roads with this chatty and intelligent man. An unexpected added benefit.

As the conversation wound down, Mossie put his hands on both knees. "So, where are we off to first, ma'am?"

"Galway City, tomorrow. You can drop me off near the quay at the Spanish Arch. I'm meeting someone for coffee at a café off Cross Street. Maybe I can meet you back at the quay—I'll text when I'm done."

"Brilliant. What do you say? Pick you up after first Mass tomorrow?"

Rosaria cocked her head and looked at Mossie with a frown. "And when would that be?"

"Ah. About half nine—half past nine. You do your business there and whatever errands. We'll leave Galway half past two or three. God willing, we'll be home with the cows."

"Perfect."

Mossie rose to go. "See you in the morning."

"After first Mass," Rosaria smiled.

"Will I see you there?" he asked.

"Sorry, Mossie, no."

"Pity. Well, I'll pick you up here then."

As he got to the door, he turned and said, "Lovely name to this cottage. Did you see the plaque on the side wall?"

"No, I missed it. What would it be?"

"*Beannacht*. Irish for Blessing. I hope it brings some to you, ma'am." He tipped his flat cap. "I hope it does."

After Mossie left, Rosaria made a quick call to Solly and was happy with it. The tone felt more like old times between them.

She caught Solly up on her move to Sky Road and other details. He was especially relieved that she now had a driver. "I'd have a hard enough time driving on those roads, and I don't have one damaged eye," he said.

For her part, Rosaria was relieved he sounded like her Solly in the call. She asked him about Eduardo Mendez as a potential suspect—not knowing if Solly would take this opportunity to remind her once again that this was not her case or if he'd feel comfortable talking.

He felt comfortable talking. Maybe he was just tired and relaxed.

"How about Eduardo?"

"Well, you know, we looked at his history and he certainly is somebody who could take a guy out without a second thought if he felt like it."

"And?"

"And he's somebody who could take a guy out without a second thought, but who also has an alibi."

"Which is?"

"The security guard for the House was on duty the whole relevant time. Neither Joyce or Eduardo went out by him during that time and all the security cameras for the other exits are clear."

"How inconvenient for one of your hypotheses." Rosaria chuckled softly.

"Yeah, blows that theory apart."

"Is he the success story he seems?"

"Oh yeah, big time. Even going to night school at UMass Boston, scheduled to get his degree next year. Will probably succeed Joyce as Director of the House. Could take over now if Liam were to leave."

"Disappointed?"

"Nah, I told you I liked him. He's solid. Maybe too loyal by my book, but a good guy. You'd want him in your corner."

"Liam Joyce certainly does inspire loyalty."

"You know, you can see how he would, can't you? He's been dedicated to the homeless population for years, working himself to exhaustion sometimes so that he had to be hospitalized. I'm told he takes only enough of his salary to meet some minimal living expenses and turns the rest back into the operating budget of the House. And there's something about him that's..." Rosaria waited while Solly searched for the right word. "Something that's broken."

"Broken?"

"Yeah. Like he needs taking care of somehow. You could see how a big, smart, tough guy like Eduardo might want to protect a person like Joyce."

"Everybody wants to protect Liam Joyce," Rosaria commented.

"Hell, even I want to protect him." Solly responded.

"What's his major?"

"Liam's?"

"No," Rosaria laughed. "Wake up. Eduardo's".

"Right. Major in social work with a minor in Latin American Studies. Dean's list every semester."

"Well, wrong profile for whoever did Patrick in. How disappointingly outstanding of Eduardo."

"Yeah, the country has another immigrant success story and I have no suspect."

Just before Solly ended the call, their conversation took a different turn, a difficult one for Rosaria.

"From the beginning, Justine had told me that Eduardo was not the kind of guy that could do this. She was right."

Rosaria couldn't help it. "Justine's your advisor now? You trust Justine's judgement?"

She could almost see Solly's neck stiffen in irritation. "Justine has some good observations about people."

"You two have good conversations about the case together?"

"Stop it, Rosaria. Justine's on the staff of Saint Martin House. She knows everyone at the House and she was there the day Patrick visited."

"Right."

"She has good observations and..." Rosaria could feel the windup for the fast ball, "she doesn't try to run my case."

Ouch. "Okay, I got it. You probably have some other things to do right now."

"I do, as a matter of fact."

"Bye, Solly."

"Bye, Rosaria."

Rosaria closed her phone and looked at the dog. "Shit, Fergus. Shit, shit, shit."

CHAPTER 22

osaria and Mossie listened to Jimmy Norman on Galway Bay FM during the ride to Galway City, while Rosaria got a tutorial on hurling from Mossie. She was glad for the distraction of both.

As best she could determine, hurling was played with an airborne small hard leather ball called a sliotar, hit with a curved stick called a hurley that was made out of a special cut of the ash tree. Mossie's hurley looked a little like a long and curved field hockey stick to her.

"When the sticks of the opposing teams hit, it's called the *clash of the ash*", Mossie explained as he made an unauthorized turn around a large sheep transport on the road. "Great sound—gets your heart going, it does."

"You ever play, Mossie?"

"Oh, I did when I was younger. I wasn't the best, but I had a great time. Around here people mostly follow the football." Rosaria knew Mossie referred not to American football, but to the other, fast wild sport popular in Ireland—unpadded, uncompensated, and unfettered GAA football. "But I'm partial to the hurling. It's more popular around the City—Galway City, I mean."

"I'll bet football clubs tried to recruit you."

"Oh, right you are. And the rugby clubs. That's really what I'm built for. But I'm partial to the hurling. The first time I picked up a hurley stick and whacked that little ball, there was no other sport for me." He turned to her with a wide grin. To Rosaria at that moment, he looked like a large, happy brown bear.

A happy bear, a happy man, thought Rosaria. His little cabin in the mountains up in the Inagh Pass that he'd told her about, his old van, and his hurling passion. What man could ask for more than Mossie O'Toole?

The smell of low tide infused the air as Mossie and Rosaria pulled up to the Spanish Arch on the harbor in Galway City. Rosaria sighed with pleasure. How she loved this well-preserved medieval city. No place like it.

She remembered the sturdy Arch—part of a fortification built in the fifteenth century to guard the unloading of wine from Spain—from her student days and recent trips. When fourteen Anglo-Norman families established Galway City on the wild west coast of Ireland in the 13th century, the city at the time was surrounded by marauding native Irish clans. Thus, the fortifications to protect a prize any chieftain would aspire to—crates of fine Spanish wine. The founders of Galway City were disparagingly called the Fourteen Tribes by their nemesis, Oliver Cromwell. Today, the Galway football and hurling teams proudly carried The Tribesmen as their team names.

Mossie was lucky enough to find parking near the Arch. He hauled himself out of the van and surveyed the scene with satisfaction. "A grand sight," he said as he rocked back and forth on the balls of his feet.

Rosaria exited the passenger side while Fergus, who'd somehow insinuated himself into the journey, jumped joyfully from the back seat. He sniffed the air before relieving himself on the back tire of Mossie's van.

"Marking his territory—my old wreck," commented Mossie, pulling Fergus in. "Anyway, we're a little early. If you like, I'll just wait with you for a few minutes, ma'am. Stretch my legs."

"Sure, glad of your company, Mossie," Rosaria replied.

The pedestrian traffic was heavy down the narrow cobblestone streets through the blocks of medieval buildings to the harbor and across the Wolftone Bridge over the River Corrib. The Salmon Tower—where in the old days men would watch for the avalanche of salmon storming downstream to the open water and call to the fisherman near the mouth of the harbor to cast their nets—stood bright and still watchful in the morning sun.

Rosaria had always understood why Irish banks and companies called lively and interesting Galway City the "graveyard of ambition". Once posted here, staff often refused to leave, even for lucrative promotions.

"Rosaria!" Suddenly, Rosaria was interrupted in her reverie when she heard her name called. "Rosaria!" came a booming voice again, emphazing and lengthening her name like a sporting event cheer—"R-O-O-saria!"

She swirled around once or twice to see the source of that distinctive voice, a voice she remembered from a long time ago. And then her heartbeat quickened when she saw a vision from her past striding down the cobblestoned Quay Street. Hugh Moran, a long-ago friend and old flame from student days. Hugh's youthful mass of black hair was now an aureole of the early snowy white that marks so many Irish, but she would have recognized him anywhere.

There he stood, with his arms outstretched for a welcoming hug and a wide smile "Is it really you? Oh, Jesus wept. It's really you."

She had forgotten he had that lethal cleft in his chin. Were his eyes always that deep hazel color? *Oh goodness,* she thought, *why did I ever let the connection with him go?*

Rosaria laughed in disbelief and walked into his embrace. "Incredible. I can't believe it, Hugh." She felt a surge of pure joy as he rocked her in those long arms.

"God, I was just thinking of you this past week," Hugh said. Rosaria considered briefly the fact that Hugh had been wondering about her the past week—*why would that be? I'm not that unforgettable. But, but...we did have something special.*

Hugh held her at arm's length to look at her damaged face. "Jesus, Rosie. What did the other guy look like?" He turned her head to the side to see the area around her right eye a little better. Then, he looked at Mossie. "I hope your big man here is going to get whoever did this to you. I'll bet from his club flag that he has a hurley stick right in the back seat." Mossie flushed and turned his eyes to the water in confusion.

"Long story, the new map of my face. Some other time," Rosaria said. "And the guy that did it is in a place beyond retribution."

Hugh stared at her seriously, clearly wanting more.

"Not now," she said, as she turned to Mossie. "And this is Mossie O'Toole, who's driving me around while I'm here, since I can't seem to get the hang of the roads anymore."

Hugh extended his hand to Mossie. "Ah, and here I was thinking he was your latest beau."

Mossie again flushed with embarrassment at being mistaken for Rosaria's "big man" or "beau". He shook Hugh's hand wordlessly and nodded.

"Well, then, if he's not your man, let's go somewhere and catch up on the years," Hugh said enthusiastically as he put his arm around her shoulder.

"Oh, Hugh, I'd love to, but I have to meet someone now. Would you be free in a couple of hours?"

He looked disappointed, but smiled. "Okay, I'll try to be patient. How about in two hours at the Quay Bar—just up the way?"

"Oh, I remember," Rosaria laughed. She did remember many the night there with Hugh Moran and friends during her year at the university in Galway. Happy days.

Rosaria looked over her shoulder at Mossie to say, "It looks like the afternoon will be a little longer. That okay?"

"Just fine," Mossie replied, with one eye still on Hugh. "We can meet back here. What time?"

"Late afternoon. Maybe about 4:30? I'll text."

Hugh put his hands on his hips and gestured to the maroon and white Galway United hurling flag on Mossie's car. "They looked weak at the last match against Kilkenny—just not the same caliber as the black and gold. Good old County Kilkenny. Now, that's a club with a proud history. No comparison." He stuck his chin out in a mock challenge.

Not amused and in no way ready to be teased about his beloved hurling team, Mossie flushed and his jaw tightened. "Yes, Mr. Moran, I would have a hurley stick in the back of my car, as a matter of fact."

Clearly taken aback that Mossie had not responded in a similar teasing manner, but had taken him seriously. Hugh said, "Ah good. You can never know when you might need a good solid piece of ash to do your business."

"Hugh, stop it. Rude, rude, rude." Rosaria said sharply before turning to Mossie. "Sorry for my friend, Mossie. I think he hasn't grown up after all these years."

"I guess I haven't. Sorry, man, just kidding," Hugh said cheerfully as he raised his hand in apology to Mossie. "Anyway," he said to Rosaria, "I won't have to be worrying about you now, will I? What with this big one and his hurley at your side?"

Hugh held his hand out to Fergus and gave him a rough caress. "And this fearsome watch dog." Fergus shivered with delight in attention from a new admirer.

Mossie didn't smile. Rosaria thought she might have heard him call Fergus a "treacherous canine" under his breath as he pulled the dog in, but she couldn't be sure. His face had turned a dark red. For a terrible moment Rosaria thought he might indeed reach for his hurley stick to take a swing at Hugh.

Men and their sports, Rosaria rued. She had forgotten that Hugh was from County Kilkenny, apparently County Galway's arch-rival in GAA hurling and one of the best clubs in the country.

"Behave yourself, Hugh," she said with a helpless look at Mossie. "The only thing Mossie'll be protecting me from is totaling my car on these crazy roads. I'm sorry that I have such a rude friend, Mossie." She checked her watch. "I have to get a move on. I'll be late. See you at the quay in two hours."

She started to walk up Quay Street before turning around. "And leave Mossie alone."

"Never changes," Hugh complained to Mossie. "Just the same as always. Pushy American. She was this way even when she was young. I can see she's even worse now."

Mossie, his face still dark and angry, his mouth flinching in distaste, didn't respond.

"Okay, I'll do a few things and then to Quay Bar and oysters it is," Hugh said brightly.

Without turning back, Rosaria waved in mute apology at Mossie as she walked away. Unsmiling, he raised his own hand and turned back to the car, yanking Fergus's leash as he went.

CHAPTER 23

arah Glynn, the late Patrick Keenan's girlfriend, puffed nervously on a cigarette as she walked down the secluded lane behind Cross and Quay Streets in Galway City to the Cobblestone Café.

Over a black coffee inside the café, Rosaria waited by the window, surrounded by a crowd of young people and the birdsong of their cellphones. She watched Sarah Glynn approach. The girl had one of those pale, soulful, lightly freckled Irish faces, framed by a sweep of dark hair. Beautiful in an ethereal way. The folds of her light scarf lifted beside her like wings in the wind from the harbor.

Rosaria was relieved. She had half-expected the girl to be a no-show. But here she was.

At the café entrance, Sarah sighed a last, thin stream of smoke from her mouth before dropping her cigarette into the sand receptacle by the door.

Sarah nodded at Rosaria as she entered the café. Murmuring a brief hello, she sat quickly, dropping a heavy messenger bag on an empty chair at the table and taking off her long, light scarf. Rosaria could smell the cigarette smoke on Sarah's clothing. It was not only smoke but clouds of grief that seemed to eddy up from the girl.

"Thank you for coming, Sarah. I know this is a hard time."

"Yes, it is," the girl replied, her eyes shifting from the window to Rosaria to the crowd in the coffee shop and back to Rosaria. The waitress approached the table. Looking up, Sarah said, "Latte, skim milk." It seemed like an effort for her to talk.

"Nothing else?" Rosaria asked. "A sandwich, a salad. Maybe a scone?"

Sarah shook her head.

Rosaria let a few moments pass before speaking again. "I'm so sorry about Patrick, Sarah. I appreciate your talking to me. Maybe it will help."

"Maybe." Fingering the row of silver piercings along the side of one ear, Sarah glanced across the table with a look that Rosaria was surprised to see—anger. Perhaps at her. At Patrick. At the world. "Not that it matters. He's gone, isn't he?"

Rosaria didn't respond. Sarah took a deep breath and looked at Rosaria again. "Sorry. I'm usually a very nice person. Maybe I wasn't ready to come back to Galway and the university."

"It's okay. I understand. Had you been going together long?"

The girl took a sip of a glass of water before responding. "A year or so. We were in the same department."

"Journalism? Same year?"

Sarah nodded and murmured a thank you to the waitress who brought her latte.

"Working on the same project?"

"No, I'm working on something different."

"Related to Patrick's in any way?"

"Mine is on the Garda—you know, the police." Sarah's voice picked up some energy. "I'm working on the budget cuts—the closing of so many stations, especially in the country. Leaves some areas with scant coverage."

Sarah stopped and waved her hand. She had forgotten her grief for just a moment. Now, she'd remembered and sank back against the seat.

"I'd like to hear about that some time. So, nothing to do with Patrick's project?"

"No, no."

Rosaria let some time pass. "What was Patrick's project, Sarah?"

"I'm not sure I should really talk about that. Patrick was very private about his project."

"Patrick's dead. You can't hurt him by talking about it now."

"Right." Sarah bit her lower lip and thought for a moment. "It was a history project."

"Recent history?"

"Yes." She fiddled with the wooden buttons on her sweater several times. Then, she inhaled deeply and closed her eyes. She opened her mouth but didn't speak for a few moments before replying.

"Well, it was originally about the Irish-American support for the Republican movement. You know, so much has been written and so much has happened. Very complicated. I'm not sure if the Americans knew what they were supporting. Even today, they tend to have kind of a—what's the word—romantic vision of things over here. Things weren't very romantic on the ground. There was so much blood and cruelty, horrific things."

"What do you mean, his *original* topic, Sarah? Did the focus of the project change?"

Sarah looked at Rosaria, her brows drawn together. *She didn't mean to tell me that.*

"Patrick didn't want to tell me. He said it was better for me not to know yet. He didn't even share with his faculty advisor at the end what he was working on. He kept postponing meetings at the department. The advisor was getting annoyed. He said that if he didn't know Patrick so well, he'd think he was slacking off on his independent study time."

Sarah gazed out the window. "But Patrick was very excited. He said he'd go to Boston for a few weeks' research. He'd have a good solid story when he got back, and it would blow everyone away. That's what he said. It would blow everyone away and be the makings of his career."

The girl pushed back her long black hair with nail-bitten fingers before she looked at Rosaria. "But it didn't and he didn't come back, did he?"

"Was there anything at all Patrick said that might have given a lead to what he was working on?" The girl looked at Rosaria and then away. Rosaria continued, "You know how important this is, Sarah. Do you think you might owe it to Patrick?"

There was only the sound of the busy cafe around them for a few moments before the girl spoke—the cash register ringing, the laughter at the table of students behind them.

Sarah started slowly. "He was excited about going to meet some man in Clifden. Patrick was in a pub there the night before—it might have been Manion's or maybe Lowry's—I can't remember—and was talking to a friend about his independent project for university. About how he was looking for a new perspective. He just felt he was going over the same old ground. He needed a new hook on sympathizers and what was going on up North in the seventies and eighties."

She shifted in her chair, closing her eyes, concentrating. "I guess after Patrick left the pub and was walking back to his car, he noticed an older man following him. Patrick stopped and asked the man if there was something he wanted. Patrick said the man acted all cautious and quiet-like, looking around like he didn't want anyone to see him." Rosaria was surprised to hear the girl chuckle. "Patrick said he wondered for a minute if the old guy was going to make a pass at him."

The smile left her face and Sarah sipped her latte, which Rosaria thought must have gone cold by now. The girl gazed out the window of the coffee shop again, looking as if her mind were somewhere in the distant past. Rosaria exercised patience—never her strong suit—with some difficulty and remained silent until the girl resumed talking.

"The man said he had something to tell Patrick. Something for his project. Something important. Patrick should come to pub the next night. The man would wait near the smoke shop across the street. When Patrick saw the man from the pub, he should come out, not speak to him but follow him at a distance to a safe place to talk."

Rosaria felt a tingling, like an electrical current under her skin. This could be it.

"And did Patrick go?"

"He did, though he was not sure about the man—Patrick said he seemed a little addled. Not drunk, mind you, but just a little—off, you know. Not really senile, but kind of disconnected when he talked." Sarah met Rosaria's eyes before lowering her own and, with her long, slim index finger, began to trace lines in the sugar scattered on the tabletop.

"Was it as important as the man said?" Rosaria pressed.

"More important than Patrick ever thought it could be. He said when he finally got the gist of what the old man was saying, it was more than important. It was explosive." She looked at Rosaria. "He wasn't sure how to weigh what the man told him at first because the guy seemed like his mind was starting to get a little muddled. But Patrick said when he talked about the story he had to tell, he was a clear as a bell."

"Can you tell me what he told Patrick, Sarah?"

A heavy sigh. "It's not mine to tell."

Rosaria struggle to restrain herself. So close.

"Patrick is dead, Sarah. This could be key."

"It's not mine to tell," the girl repeated and then said. "And, besides, Patrick told me it was too dangerous for me to know."

This was it. Rosaria knew this was it—whatever the man told Patrick was it. "He must have told you something, Sarah—about the man, the conversation. Anything?"

The girl seemed suddenly drained of interest and energy. None of this would bring Patrick back. What was the difference? "He told me the name of the man. He did tell me that."

"Yes?" Rosaria told herself not to be too eager, not to press to hard—she could feel the girl drifting away.

"Thomas Martin from Clifden."

Rosaria repeated the name and place. "Thomas Martin from Clifden."

"Patrick said that he was not well and that he had the beginnings of a dementia, I think. The man said he didn't have too long when he would be thinking straight, and he wanted to tell somebody what he knew."

"Do you know where he lived in Clifden, Sarah? Of course, I am sure I could find him anyway if I have his name." Rosaria was already planning a visit to Thomas Martin and had started to gather her things.

Yes, I do." Sarah leaned back heavily in her seat. "But you won't be able to talk to him."

"Why not?"

"He's dead."

"He died already? When did that happen?"

"Around the time that Patrick died." Sarah looked stricken again for a moment—Rosaria could see that it was so hard to say the words *Patrick died*—but the girl continued. "His family had to commit him to care home, for the dementia. And then, I guess he took a bad fall there, on a walk somewhere out on the grounds. He was with an orderly, but they said he slipped somehow and hit his head on a rock. Died instantly. "

She looked at Rosaria. "So, now the two people that knew whatever he had to tell are dead."

Chapter 24

Connemara, Ireland—1974

he boy watched the men load the heavy crates into the sheep transport from his hiding place behind the oak tree. One man handed a torch to another to leave his hands free to pick up a crate. It was then, as the light passed, that the boy's father glanced up. The man's face momentarily froze as he glimpsed his young son, watching from behind the oak near the stone wall. His father turned his eyes down hurriedly, but the bearded man did not miss the swift movement of his father's eyes. He turned to stare in the direction of the oak tree. Two of the other strangers, including the ginger-haired man, shifted their burden as they also turned to face the tree. The tip of a maroon-sweatered elbow stuck out from the side of the oak.

A matter of seconds. His father looked up again. His eyes moved to that of the men and finally to the tall, ginger-haired man. Pleading, desperate eyes. A moment of decision.

The boy held his breath, his cheek against the scratchy, rough bark of the tree. The damp night air chilled him through his pullover. Closing his eyes, he shivered.

He heard the ginger-haired man whisper, "Christ", then with a shake of the head, he breathed, "Let it go, man. He's just a bairn. He's the caretaker's bairn. He's been sound for us."

The bearded man stared back, then took a moment before acquiescing, if reluctantly. Without looking at the boy's father, he said, "You'll take care of that, man?"

"Yes, yes, I will. I will. It'll be all right. I will," his father whispered quickly.

Then, with a brief backward glance at the oak and the small elbow jutting out from it, the bearded man lifted his chin in the direction of the truck. "Carry on then. Let's get home."

His father closed his eyes for a moment and let out his breath as if he would faint. The men from the north started to carry crates to the truck. The ginger-haired man turned back to look toward the stonewall with a soft chuckle. "There's the wee Fenian, ready for the fight," he said. "You'll have your turn, lad. You'll have your turn."

————————

That night, his father didn't stop at the door when he walked into his son's bedroom. The blow to the boy came so fast, he lost all breath and dropped back against the wall on his bed. "You'll forget what you saw tonight. For pity's sake—for yours and for mine—understand?"

The boy nodded wordlessly.

"And, Jesus, don't let me ever, ever," his voice rose on the second *ever*, "see you near Saint Mary's again."

CHAPTER 25

fter a couple of pints and oyster stew at Quay's, Rosaria and Hugh
walked under the Spanish Arch and onto the quay that afternoon.
The walkway was busy but they were able to stroll quietly, catching
up on each other's lives over the years. Swans glided in languid patrol near the
River Corrib's granite wall by the harbor. Brilliant primary colors on the doors
of the row houses glowed in the early afternoon sun.

So much to cover for old friends, like Rosaria and Hugh, who hadn't seen
each other for years. They talked all through lunch and now couldn't seem to
stop, sometimes speaking over each other or interrupting to interject a comment or crude remark. *God, she had missed him.*

Both had made ill-fated, ill-advised first marriages that hadn't work out,
each union persisting much longer legally than in practice. "Her mother wanted
a doctor or a lawyer, not a seedy academic with empty pockets and too many
political passions. Over time, my wife agreed with her mother," Hugh said.
He shrugged. "You?"

"Bottom line—I was too independent for him and he slept around."

"More fool him." Hugh put his arm around her and kissed her hair.

Rosaria was surprised that her eyes moistened. Was she really that thirsty
for affection?

Each had professional successes—though in wildly different areas. Rosaria's
in a corporate life she had recently left behind. Hugh's as political activist, largely
supporting Cathal McKenna—the ex-IRA politician Patrick had mentioned
was running for Taosich. Hugh was also an instructor of Irish history and
politics at NUI Galway. Both pursuits ensured he still had empty pockets, he
commented wryly.

Rosaria had a relationship in her life now with Solly. Hugh was unencum-
bered, not having a romantic interest in his life at the moment.

He mentioned that last part several times during their walk. "Did I tell you
yet that I'm not romantically involved with anyone, Rosaria? Did I mention
that point yet?" he would laugh.

"Well, yes, in fact, you did mention that a few times, Hugh," she responded. "And once again, for my part, I am in a serious relationship."

"Uh-huh. Right." A brisk, late summer wind came up from the harbor. Hugh reached over to pull the hood of Rosaria's light jacket over her head. He cupped her head affectionately and smiled before putting his hand back in his own jacket pocket.

"So, tell me again. I'm thrilled to have you here, but tell me again what are you helping the Keenan family with? Long way to come to investigate a Boston murder."

"Oh, you know, just to see if maybe there's something that might shed some light on the murder over here."

"Seems like a long shot. Where would you start looking?"

"Not sure yet."

"Well, you'll be a help to the family, Rosaria. I hear you're a good detective." Rosaria was fleetingly puzzled as to where Hugh had heard about her detecting abilities, but let it go. Gossip traveled like the wind in Ireland. Too, the Irish were always up-to-date on U.S. news, especially in cities like Boston where so many friends and family had settled.

"I'm not surprised to know what you are doing with your life, Hugh. After how intense you were, how fierce you were about Irish history and politics." She glanced at him slyly. "And how you used to go on...and on...and on."

He chuckled. "Give it a rest, O'Reilly."

"Anyway, you were just so committed, I figured you'd be involved in politics somehow. Though I thought you'd be running yourself." She gave him a questioning glance.

"Oh no," he laughed, "that's not for me—all that speechifying and hand-shaking, God knows. But I can make a lot happen behind the scenes. That's where I work best."

"And I thought you might have ended up teaching—probably at a university, since you're so goddamed smart. And I was right."

"Thank you, dearie." He gave her a friendly nudge.

For a moment, Rosaria remembered other times, other days, hiking in Donegal around Malin Point. Days when they had been so close, so intimate, in every sense of the word. She felt her heart quicken just a little. She thought Hugh must have remembered those days too since next he asked, "When is your friend Sally coming over?"

"It's Solly, not Sally, Hugh."

"Just having you on. You never did have a good sense of humor, Rosie."

The only three people in the world that ever called her Rosie were her father, Hugh and Solly. *How interesting.* "He can't come. He's pretty locked into work in Boston right now," she responded. "And, you know, I'm almost afraid he'd be bored anyway. The cottage I'm in isn't all that far from Clifden. And it's a gorgeous place, but it feels in the middle of nowhere. Just the ocean, rocks and seaweed. Lots of seaweed. Solly's a city guy. He might go berserk. But," she sighed, "I think he would like to come if he could." Rosaria wondered why she added the word *think* to "he would like to come."

Hugh gave her a side glance, and they walked along in silence for a few minutes.

"I have Patrick's young black and white dog with me, that border collie at the car. The family has a hard time looking at the dog, reminds them of the boy. His name is Fergus."

Hugh broke out in his broad, high laugh that she remembered well. A joyous sound halfway between a man's laugh and a donkey's bray. She loved it. What a pleasure to hear that laugh again.

"Well, he must be a manly little fellow. That's what Fergus means, you know, manly." He chuckled again. "Fergus the manly dog. Why not?"

Rosaria turned serious as she continued. "Patrick was working on a project—about Irish-American support for the IRA in the North."

"Any particular aspect?"

"Not that I can determine."

"Too broad a subject. So many questions and issues."

"Yes, it does seem like a big, complicated project for a student. Apparently, his advisor was pressuring Patrick to narrow it down, but without success."

"Happens all the time. Even if you think you have an agreement on the area to be covered, a young and curious student finds an interesting scent leading away from the trail and off he goes. Certainly, rich pickings in the area he chose to work." Hugh stopped to pick up a white seagull feather. "Could be anything," he continued as he turned to look at her. He ran the seagull feather down the side of her face with his long, slender hand, lingering on the scar over her right eyebrow. Rosaria remembered his running that long, slender hand down the side of her face at Malin Point in Donegal and could almost feel the tenderness of it again.

The touch of the feather gave Rosaria chills. Neither of them spoke for a moment, after which Hugh put the feather in his pocket and continued.

"Could be anything," he repeated, "Still so many people with grievances. And rightly so. You just can't sign a piece of paper and have all that emotion and the history of injustice disappear. And there's the hope for a united Ireland, for one country again."

"I thought people were kind of moving beyond that now."

"Oh, maybe for some. So much of this generation is about waltzing around with new electronic devices, traveling to the Continent. Not Irish. European—whatever that means," he added with disgust. "But in others' minds—including my own—that hope of a united Ireland is not going to go away." Hugh paused and looked up the Corrib to the harbor. "In my estimation, I'd say that there'd only be one or two men that can keep pushing unification forward, making it happen."

"Like who?" Rosaria asked.

"Well, Cathal McKenna for one. He's got the guts and the drive."

"I've heard he has a history—I'm not sure what that means."

Hugh's face darkened. "Well, Christ, who doesn't? Anybody that had any guts in those days has a history. Where did you hear that? From that young Padraig Keenan?"

Rosaria noticed Hugh used Patrick's Irish name, and was surprised at the tone of the response. "Yes, that's where I heard it from."

"Foolish talk. Old gossip. Those newspaper rags have always had it in for McKenna. It's like a conspiracy. The kid didn't know what he was talking about—just trying to sound important, like he actually knew something."

He paused and turned to her. "It's others that are carrying the flag now. The Real IRA, the ones that split from the peace process. They have no patience for all the endless talking, all the compromises. Good God. When will it end?" His voice quickened. "And they get their man too. They know how to take care of things. Like back in the day when they picked off that turncoat Denis Donaldson—hiding in a decrepit little pre-famine cottage in Donegal, like a hermit. Did you never hear about that?"

Rosaria shook her head. How would she hear about that, or be alert to crimes by these old revolutionaries? It was like inside baseball. Somebody else's game. She was also troubled by a weird excitement she felt in Hugh's telling such a brutal story.

Hugh's voice continued to gather energy. "Nowhere to run, nowhere to hide, as the song goes. I hope the boy didn't get too close to something best left alone. Or get in the way of something bigger than he is."

Alarmed now, Rosaria stopped walking and asked, "Like what? What's bigger and more important than the life of a young student, Hugh?" She knew she sounded harsh. *Good.*

Hugh gazed out over the harbor before looking directly at Rosaria, his face more composed. "Ah, I'm talking shite, Rosie. I'm just a shabby, gabby old professor," he said dismissively. "But there are things an amateur shouldn't be wandering into. These are seriously hard people. Everyone says it's over. Believe me, it's not over." He touched her face softly and kissed her on the forehead. "People have to be careful. It's a dangerous game, darlin.'"

Rosaria felt a shiver of something. *Fear, or excitement, or both?* "Dangerous for who?"

Hugh didn't respond. "Come on, Rosie. I'll walk you down to the car."

CHAPTER 26

r. Burke's Sky Road cottage had ample electric heating to keep it snug against the raw, wet drizzle of the day. Still, Rosaria couldn't resist putting on a peat fire if only for the sweet, soft smell. The smell of Ireland—peat smoke and rain.

She sank, a glass of Cabernet in her hand, into Mr. Burke's great green chair, with its stack of books holding up the broken front leg. She placed her glass on the end table beside the chair, with its still fragrant pipe stand, ashtray and the silver-framed picture of a forever smiling, permed and coiffed Mrs. Burke in her blue fancy dress.

Fergus, exhausted from charging all over the wet rocks and thorny brush that surrounded the cottage, had collapsed at her feet—adding a pungent wet dog smell to the mix in the room. The dog's long legs and tail stretched across the floral carpet, the picture of contentment—snoring loudly.

Rosaria had discovered that Fergus was a heavy snorer. The deep noise had startled her the first night in the cottage and woken her up. Too sleepy and dazed to be afraid, she'd crept out of bed to look in the sitting room. Perhaps Mr. Burke had come back from Seattle and had crawled into the side bedroom. Perhaps a sleepy burglar was taking a break. Or, it was always possible that she'd taken up snoring—perhaps so loudly that she had woken herself up. Or maybe it was the wind from the sea finding its way into the cottage through a strange sort of little orifice in the roof or walls that made these rhythmic sounds. Or, maybe...She looked around the bedroom again and saw that it was none of these things. Just Fergus, sleeping at the foot of the bed, blissfully blaring away through his big black nose.

She'd noticed a vet clinic the other day down the Galway Road, near the Connemara Pony Sales barn and the Frank Acton Auto Repair Shop. Fergus seemed happy and healthy enough, but maybe she should have that snore checked out, she mused.

Fergus's wet doggy smell and the scent of the peat fire brought Rosaria into a meditative state. For the first time since she'd arrived, she could think.

And that brought her to thoughts of Solly and a number of the attendant complications around him.

Rosaria and Solly had talked several times since their Justine-as-an-acute-observer-of-people conversation. Their discussions now were disturbingly polite and distant. Also, although she had thought that Solly had come to terms with her being here, she knew it was hard for him. It got more difficult after Mrs. Keenan called Solly directly with the request that Rosaria represent the family in the information flow around the investigation of Patrick's death. He accepted Rosaria's role, but wasn't at all happy about it.

She knew all the reasons for this. Her intrusion—as he accurately predicted when she announced she was going to Ireland—into the official investigation, *his* investigation, *his* territory. Her decision to come here, when he specifically asked her not to. His—again accurate—reading that the Keenans thought his relationship with Rosaria would give them the inside track if she were their conduit.

On this last point, Rosaria had warned Mrs. Keenan that Solly would not share any more information with Rosaria representing the family. Perhaps, actually less, because he wouldn't want to give the appearance of any impropriety. Mrs. Keenan was undeterred. Rosaria remembered one of Bridie's descriptions of Patrick as sometimes "like a dog on a bone, he is". Rosaria thought she knew where he got that focus.

She was aware that her involvement was causing problems for Solly in his job. He had mentioned, in a terse report to her, that one old-timer had asked Solly what his girlfriend was doing in Ireland with the vic's family and had sneered, asking if she was over there "helping out her *Boston cop*". Referring, of course, to that infamous picture, shot by Justine, of Rosaria and Solly at a high profile social event. The picture which appeared in the Names section of the *Globe* with the caption "*heroine in nun murder scandal and her Boston cop*".

She took a sip of wine and shook her head. A terrible conflict. She didn't want to compete with Solly—at least she didn't think she did. Clearly, it was the Boston Police Department's job to find Patrick's killer, not hers. Still, she couldn't shake the feeling, growing on her more every day, that there was something to find here, in this rocky, boggy, mountainous place. Something to do with Patrick's research and perhaps even his death. She didn't know how to find that key. She sighed. Perhaps there wasn't one at all.

Maybe in the end, Solly and his colleagues would find Patrick had indeed had a disagreement with another patron at one of the bars down near the

Boston waterfront—a patron who'd followed him and, in a drunken rage, given him a savage blow to the head.

But still. But still she couldn't stop herself from searching for some answers here—not yet.

Besides, the prospect of the key to Patrick's murder being found on the remote western shores of Ireland was too far-fetched—*too fanciful*, as Nora Keenan put it—for the resource-constrained, pragmatic Boston Police Department to expend any energy on, or to ask the even more constrained local Garda in the Galway District to do so. So, if she wasn't on the hunt here, no one would be.

Rosaria ran her finger over the rim of her wine glass—Galway crystal, she saw. Must have been a Mrs. Burke extravagance. Didn't seem like Mr. Burke's style. Then, she found herself musing over other, larger personal questions.

Solly had been her best hope for the kind of stable, loving, equalitarian relationship she assumed she'd never find after the disappointing experience of her first marriage. Perhaps now she was blowing up that chance. But, if she gave in on this—distanced herself from the investigation and just went home now to Solly—what else would she give in on? What shell of herself would be left in such a stable, loving—but perhaps unequal—relationship? Rosaria started to get that old feeling when she was penned in too closely in a relationship—the walls closing in, her throat feeling constricted. She couldn't do it. She hoped the relationship would weather the storm but if it didn't—it wasn't meant to be.

She heard her cellphone, in her jacket pocket across the room. She was so comfortable, she briefly considered letting the call go to voicemail.

Ah, but it might be Solly—maybe Solly. It was afternoon in Boston, probably a convenient time to call. With his schedule, it was hard to play phone tag if she missed the call. Rousing herself from the big chair and a thicket of troubling thoughts, Rosaria got up to take the call, hoping for the best—maybe just a little of the old camaraderie and affection—but keeping her expectations low.

Rosaria didn't look at the screen before pushing the Talk button. She was surprised then not to hear Solly—tense, clipped, subdued, businesslike and resentful Solly Belkin. Instead, she felt Hugh Moran's booming, warm, and enthusiastic voice wash over her. "Rosaria, my Boston beauty—I'm coming to the wilds of Connemara to see you. What do you think of that?"

CHAPTER 27

Later that week, after some errands at the bank and the stationers, Mossie suggested a ride along the Bog Road to Roundstone. It was a sweet, clear day and Rosaria agreed—though in truth the name Bog Road as a destination didn't exactly inspire her. It did, however, apparently inspire Mossie.

"The bogs, the mountains, the sea, that's what makes us who we are here," he commented as he turned down the Ballyconneely Road toward the turnoff for the Bog Road. "You know, some might think the bog is a swamp. That's not what it is. It's poorly drained, peaty land—peatland, not a swamp. But it's filled with life. Wait till you see the birds."

As they pulled on to the narrow Bog Road, Rosaria found it hard to absorb the vastness of the bog, stretching to the horizon. From a distance, it might look like a flat plain or moor. In reality, it was rough with heathery hummocks, lakes and rock formations. People still laughed at the story of the first transatlantic flight in 1919 when the pilots Alcock and Brown thought the great Derrygimlah Bog was a smooth landing strip near the Marconi wireless station, and promptly sunk a good part of their plane in the rough bog when they landed.

And Mossie was right about the birds—cruising, swirling, and wheeling over the bog. Rosaria was mesmerized watching a merlin's low flight over the grasses to its nest in one of the rock islands. The colors of the bog itself were a patchwork of purple and gold with bell heather, low-growing western gorse, and the tall purple moor grass.

"There's a little yellow lily that grows out here too. I forget the name," Mossie said. "I think that's my favorite."

"You're an appreciator of nature, Mossie O'Toole."

"I am, I am. That's why I'm here."

The peat harvesters—or turf cutters—as they were sometimes called, had been busy earlier in the season. Cutting neat logs of earthy vegetation from squares in the peatland, as they had done for centuries. Now, the peat logs were stacked to dry for the winter season next to their tractors and old trucks along the peat harvesting side roads. Rosaria could see a couple of turf cutters out there, perhaps checking on things, with their dogs.

Fergus saw the dogs from his perch by the back window and barked a greeting, clearly wishing he were out racing around the uneven bog chasing hares with them.

"They'd better get the turf while they can," Mossie commented as they passed the side roads. "The EU is putting strict limits on the harvest."

"How come?"

"Oh, the environment. I guess the cutting releases some gases that pollute. And, you know, once you cut acres of peat out, it's gone. We're going through it fast. Of course, there's always the burning of it too. I suppose it's not so green."

"Oh, I love the smell of it."

"So do we all." Mossie turned for a moment to look at her. "You're a good girl, Miss O'Reilly. Good taste."

"I'd like to think so." She smiled back.

"Anyway," Mossie continued, "quite a few bogs been protected by the EU. Because of their unique ecology. Is that the right word—ecology?" he asked.

"That's the word," Rosaria responded as she watched a sleek fox slide through the long grass.

"There are some things that grow here that you don't see anywhere else."

"I believe it. I just saw a fox, too."

"Oh yes, lots of small animals for the foxes to feed on. Like a fox all-you-can-eat buffet." Mossie laughed.

Rosaria relaxed into her seat and inhaled the sweet fresh air coming straight across the bog in gentle gusts of wind. Somehow, she'd expected the bog to smell damp and fetid. Anything but, it smelled of life, long grass and wildflowers. And the musky smell of a large flock of sheep who now seemed to be wandering everywhere—snuffling and munching about the bog with bright markers on their long-haired coats, daintily navigating with ease the uneven surfaces on their tiny black feet.

All the windows of the van were open. Fergus hung his head out the back window, tongue lolling, in an ecstasy of smells with the wind blowing his black and white fur back.

"Good thing there's a nice breeze here today. On a bad day, the midgies—those damned little biting black bugs—can drive you wild," Mossie commented. He inhaled deeply. "Oh, but there's a lovely wind right now. Just right."

They rode in silence for a few moments. "There are stories, of course, out here," Mossie said.

"Like ghost stories? I can imagine it's eerie at night or in a fog or a storm."

"That's the truth," Mossie replied. "There is one story about a place called the Halfway House. The ruins are up here." Mossie pointed ahead at a pile of stones. Using her imagination, Rosaria could see the rough outline of a ruined cottage. "They say that in the days before the Famine, a murderous brother and sister used to live here—halfway across the Bog Road. When the packmen, the peddlers, passed by on their way to the fair at Ballinboy, the brother and sister would invite them in for food and drink, murder them, steal their wares and throw their bodies in the lake behind."

"That's pretty awful. Do you think it's true?"

"Oh, yes, it is a fact, a historical fact, as they say. And would you know what the family name of that brother and sister was?"

"I give up."

"People say they were Conneelys."

"Like Gerard Conneely? Brave, upstanding, basic good guy Sergeant Conneely?"

"The very same name. But don't ever say it to his face. He gets flaming." Mossie chortled. "Maybe they made that part up just to annoy him. Even our Gerard can get annoyed."

"All the same, it's pretty scary to think about."

"Well, Miss O'Reilly, don't spend too much time thinking about the old stories. Just enjoy the day."

On the way back from their excursion to the Bog Road, Rosaria mentioned to Mossie that Hugh was coming in for a talk at the Clifden Historical Society and they'd be having dinner afterwards.

Mossie scowled and blew out a long breath. "Oh, Jaysus. Shoot me now."

Rosaria laughed, "Now, Hugh's a perfectly nice guy."

"I think he needs to get over himself."

"No, he just says things to be funny, yank your chain a little."

"Well, I'll pull his chain right good if he says anything like that again." Mossie hit the steering wheel with his big hand.

"Anything like what?"

"A man who would insult your club before he even knows you is lacking in the social graces."

Rosaria leaned against the passenger side door so that she could face Mossie, to see if he was truly serious. "I knew it. It was the hurling comment. He was only teasing you, Mossie. You were supposed to tease him back and say something derogatory and outlandish about Kilkenny. Really, give it a rest."

"If you say so," he grunted in reply.

They rode on, an awkward pause between them.

"Would he be staying over with you?" he asked.

"And this concerns you, how?"

"I just don't like to see you mixed up with some people who might not be your type—of good character, I mean. A fine woman like you." He didn't say "with a shite like that" but Rosaria could feel it implied.

Mossie's jaw was tight as he pulled into a parking place and, without looking at her, said, "Hugh Moran reminds me of that statue in Galway at the university—that one of a graduate in his robes with no head. All show, no brains. And no character, I'll wager."

"Thanks for your input, Mossie. I'll take it under advisement."

Mossie stared straight ahead and didn't respond except to give Fergus, whose head was wedged between them from the back seat, a bitter glance. "And you. Dogs are supposed to be good judges of character. You're a disgrace. That man's done a big con job on the both of you."

Fergus gazed lovingly at Mossie and accepted the compliment.

"That will be enough, Mossie. Not your affair."

Mossie snorted and didn't speak as she got out of the car.

The next morning, as Rosaria was pouring coffee from the French press into two mugs, she looked out the back window of the kitchen to see Mossie's van driving slowly by, just like on the first day when she saw him scoping out who was moving into the Burke's cottage. Now Mossie was checking to see if Hugh's silver Mini was still parked in front of Mr. Burke's cottage after his speech at the Clifden Historical Society and dinner with Rosaria the night before. And it was.

———

She had almost forgotten about the guy in the black Bruins tee shirt that she'd told Solly about—the one who she thought was following Patrick Keenan. But Solly hadn't, and he was convinced it might be the construction worker he'd met on the stairs at Declan Twomey's offices.

"Want the lowdown?" he asked on one of their phone calls.

"Yeah, what did you find out?"

"Francis Xavier O'Brien aka Obie, originally from Charlestown. No paper as an adult, though he has a sealed juvy record. Nothing violent. Probably the extracurriculars kids there used to engage in—swinging baseball bats to smash the car windows of yuppies moving into the neighborhood, stealing equipment from the Boys' Club. Nothing big."

"Sounds like he could be useful to someone like Declan Twomey."

"Right. I'm pretty sure he is. But he's like his boss. A mixed bag. Ex-Marine, couple of kids, owns a two family over in Brighton. Active in the Disabled Vets, volunteers at Saint Martin's."

"Breaks into apartments."

"He could be our guy—you saw his picture."

"Right, I did."

"But I have nothing to hang on him. I can't pull in every guy in the city who wears a black Bruins tee shirt. I'd have half the city in here."

"Yeah," Rosaria agreed wearily. She closed her eyes and sank back in the green chair, ready to close the conversation.

"One more thing," Solly said.

"Uh-huh?" she asked absently.

"I got a voicemail from a guy named Moose—or Masse—he had a really thick accent. I couldn't understand him."

"Mossie?" *I'll kill him, the interfering brute,* thought Rosaria. "What did he have to say?"

"I wasn't sure, but something along the lines that I had better watch out for my girly."

"Did he really call me your *girly*? I don't believe it."

Solly went on, ignoring her objection. "...that I'd better watch out for my girly because a fox has been circling. A shite of a professor from the university putting on the charms."

"Jesus Christ."

"And he hated to say so, but for a fine lady, she wasn't showing good judgment. He wondered if I wouldn't think about coming over for a visit and straightening things out."

"I'll fire that guy. None of his business. And..."

"And true?"

"I have an old friend here."

"I see." Solly's voice was condensed, concentrated.

"I..."

"Listen, I've got to go."

"Solly..."

Solly had closed the call and was gone—again.

CHAPTER 28

osaria wondered if her hands were big enough and strong enough to wrap around Mossie's thick neck and to squeeze the life out of him. She was that angry.

"Just who the hell do you think you are?" she demanded as she got into the passenger seat when Mossie pulled up the next morning. Fergus jumped past her to get into the back seat, ruining her moment of towering rage by almost knocking her over in the process.

Mossie stared at the sea. A stoic, a martyr to the cause. "I had your best interests at heart."

"I'll decide what my best interests are, Mister O'Toole. You don't get to decide. You have no right."

Mossie didn't respond.

"Do you hear me?"

Still no response.

"I said did you hear me?" she shouted.

"It would be hard not to."

"Then answer me, for Chrissakes."

"I hear you, ma'am."

He stared out at the water, a curious amethyst shade on the blue gray day.

"I should goddamn fire you. Find someone else to drive me around. Someone who's not going to stick his nose in my personal business."

"That's your prerogative, ma'am."

"And stop calling me ma'am, dammit."

Fergus, who in his doggy wisdom was lying quietly—perhaps cringing—with his head on his paws in the back seat, emitted a low whimper.

Mossie turned to look in the back seat and said to Rosaria. "You're disturbing the dog."

"I don't care if I'm goddamned disturbing the goddamn dog," Rosaria hissed.

Fergus whimpered again.

"Oh, for Chrissakes," Rosaria stormed. And then she started to cry.

"My life is so complicated and you're not helping," she sobbed.

The big man's face fell, the stoic expression collapsing in a nanosecond. "Oh, Jesus. God, Rosaria. Please don't cry, please don't cry."

Fergus whimpered more loudly and put his head between the two front seats, worriedly nosing the side of Rosaria's head.

"I'm sorry, Rosaria. I was only trying to help. I thought you couldn't see."

"I can see. I can see." She knew she was blubbering and this enraged her more. She hit the dashboard with her hand. Fergus jumped back, this time emitting a sharp, high bark.

"I just didn't want you to get hurt. I..." Mossie started to say.

She thought he might start blubbering in a minute too. "Shut up." She brought herself under control and just then saw the shadow of a figure at the driver's side window.

"Everything all right here?" Sergeant Gerard Conneely asked, clearly seeing that everything was not all right at all.

"Yes, yes, Gerard. Just a little misunderstanding," Mossie stammered.

"Miss O'Reilly?"

"No problem, Officer Conneely. I was just upset about something." She almost shouted the *something* part of the sentence as she gave Mossie a resentful stare.

Garda Conneely didn't respond for a moment while he looked at them both carefully. Then, he stood back and directed himself to Mossie.

"Mossie, you know your car is not registered this year?"

"Oh no, Gerard. Did I forget that?" Flustered, Mossie reached for the glove compartment and rustled around among his papers until he found what was indeed an outdated registration for the car. "You're not going to pull me off the road, are you, Gerard?" he pleaded. "I can go get my insurance papers, my inspection from Frank Acton and everything I need to just fix this right up."

Conneely didn't respond immediately, but then said, "I won't pull you off right now, Mossie, but I will if next time I see you, you haven't fixed this up." He leaned down in the window close to Mossie's face. "Jesus, man, you earn your living with your car—whatever kind of a living that might be—at least keep the old thing legal."

"I will, Gerard, I will."

After Gerard Conneely had driven away, giving one last warning look at Mossie, Rosaria said, "Okay, that's enough. Pick me up after you've done all that. I need to calm down."

"Okay," Mossie said, his voice pained now. "Okay, Rosaria."

She pushed to open the door.

"Wait, Rosaria," Mossie said. "Would you ever want to take a ride back to my cabin with me while I get my insurance papers and the like?"

"Why would I want to do that?"

"My little place is up in the Inagh Pass—between the Bens and the Maanturk Mountains. Very pretty. It might make you feel better." When she didn't respond immediately, he said, "It would be a mercy to me, Rosaria. It would make me feel better."

When she still didn't respond, he added, "I won't say a word the whole way. You can just look out the window at the beauty and calm down."

Rosaria nodded wordlessly and closed the door.

The van was infinitesimal against the landscape as they rode along Loch Inagh through the Pass. Like a small insect, it inched along the lonesome road through the hugeness, the vastness of uninhabited moorlands, bogs, lakes, and mountains. The mountains lay resting around them like gigantic tawny creatures reclined against an endless sky. Rosaria had never felt so inconsequential, such a small part of the natural world.

Mossie's cabin was a speck on the side of one of those tawny creature mountains. The road up to it was one step above a sheep path. The old van gamely took on its familiar and challenging route up the rutted, rocky path to the cabin. After much jostling and bumping of its passengers, it pulled beside a small shack.

"My humble abode," Mossie said. "Come in for a cup of tea, while I look for my damned insurance papers."

Rosaria stood for a moment beside the van and took in the immenseness around them before walking to Mossie's front door. She craned her neck to see if it was really possible to see the Atlantic beyond the mountains. Her confrontation with Solly and her argument with Mossie seemed suddenly trivial against this expanse.

Mossie led the way into his cabin—more of well-worn shepherd's hut—but apparently sufficient to Mossie O'Toole's needs. A crusted kettle sat atop of a small peat-fired stove in the center of the single room, a sleeping cot in one side. On the other side, a table with two mismatched chairs next to the stove.

"What was it your Henry David Thoreau said about chairs?" Mossie asked. "One chair for solitude, two for friendship and three for company?

Or something like that." He chuckled. "I don't get much company." Mossie started the peat fire and poured water into the kettle from a plastic water jug near a wash basin. No running water, of course, and no electricity. A long way from Adams corner in Dorchester back in Boston.

From the cupboard, he took down a box of Barry's tea and a tin of Boland's fig rolls. "There, we'll be set in no time," he said. With a flourish, he flicked a worn flowered tea towel in the air and watched it drift softly onto the table. "Just be a moment now."

While the water for tea boiled, Mossie knelt beside his sleeping cot and pulled out a plastic storage container. Rosaria could see in it sheaves of paper—all the documents of Mossie O'Toole's unique life. He sat on the cot, opened the lid of the box and then looked up. "Will you ever forgive me, Rosaria? I was out of line." His face looked stricken, his eyes wet.

"Yes, you were out of line, Mossie."

Rosaria wanted to continue being furious, but her heart wasn't in it anymore. Maybe she'd been furious because Mossie was right about Hugh. Mossie was *way* out of line in calling Solly. But. Maybe he was just...right. *Dammit.*

She looked at the peat fire in full sweet smolder and glanced out the crude window over the vast, untreed, and lonely landscape. This land had seen so much hardship—like the lonely and good-hearted man before her now.

Rosaria sighed and looked over at Mossie. "But I forgive you."

CHAPTER 29

he next day, Rosaria was to have lunch with Bridie and Nora Keenan, but called to cancel so that Mossie could drive her to the home of the late Thomas Martin. Rosaria explained to Nora that Thomas Martin was a man who'd shared a long-ago secret with Patrick one night in a Clifden pub.

"Now, I can't tell you if this is related to Patrick's murder, Nora," Rosaria said. "But I feel a need to follow up on it. It may be nothing, not connected at all."

"I don't know what's connected to anything anymore," Nora commented, "but you'll tell me about it afterward?" Rosaria was amused at the way Nora gave orders. As if one had a choice.

"Yes, when I get a sense of things, I'll fill you in, Nora," Rosaria promised.

The Martin cottage nestled on a side street in Clifden, across from the Owenglin River running to Clifden Bay. Window boxes were filled with trailing geraniums and busy lizzies. The iron gate in a privet hedge stood open.

Rosaria had called ahead to introduce herself as a friend of the Keenan family. The family wanted to know more about Patrick's activities in Ireland before he went to Boston. They were trying to put pieces of the puzzle together. Perhaps the Martin family had a moment to talk to Rosaria since the Keenans knew that Patrick had met with Thomas Martin some weeks before going to Boston.

"I know this is such a hard time for you, Mrs. Martin, with Thomas having died so recently, but the Keenans would be very grateful if you could spare the time to let me ask you a few questions."

After listening to Rosaria's introduction and explanation on the phone, Thomas Martin's wife Eleanor had hesitated. "One moment, please," she said, and seemed to put her hand over the phone while she consulted with someone in the kitchen, as Rosaria could hear muffled conversation.

Sarah had mentioned a daughter named Theresa, so perhaps that was who she was talking to. Mrs. Martin was saying something like, "It's that American woman. What would she be wanting now at such a time?" and then a plaintive, tear-filled, "I can't. I just can't, Theresa."

Rosaria could feel her stomach clench in disappointment. Then, Theresa got on the phone, calmly authoritative.

"Yes, this is Thomas Martin's daughter, Theresa."

Rosaria explained her mission again, praying the daughter would be willing to talk.

Theresa listened. A long pause and then said in a kindly voice that Rosaria suspected may have come from her father, "How are the Keenans doing now? Such a loss for them. So young."

"Not well, Theresa. They're devastated, of course, but it's made the worse to have so many questions about what happened and why."

"We're in the same place here, Ms. O'Reilly. We're in the same place here. Though, of course, my father had a long life and Patrick Keenan didn't. Yes, certainly, you can come over and we can talk."

Now, Rosaria rang the small ship's bell beside a blue door, bright against the white of the Martin's cottage. Theresa came to the door. Young, slim, and tall, with soft brown eyes and a mass of dark curls. Behind Theresa, her mother—smaller, rounder—stood by a dormant electric fireplace, holding her elbows as if making a tight defensive package of herself. Rosaria thought she saw the shadow of a scapular under the woman's rose-colored polyester blouse. She didn't realize that they made scapulars anymore—the small rectangular pieces of cloth with religious images worn around the neck. She hadn't seen one since she was a child in Catholic school with the nuns. But then, this was Ireland and Mrs. Martin was apparently devout. Perhaps of a different personality profile than her daughter.

When she spoke, Mrs. Martin's was the hard voice of a shy person who'd gathered the courage to confront and say her piece. "Now, I'm sorry, Miss O'Reilly, but I can't talk about anything related to Thomas. It's too much for me." She took a breath. "And I'm not sure what you think you'd be finding out anyway going into all that with my poor Thomas. He had nothing to do with any of that."

With this, she started to cry softly. Theresa came to her mother and leaned down to put her arm around the smaller woman. "It's okay, Ma. You don't have to talk about anything. I'll talk to Ms. O'Reilly." Her mother nodded, staring ahead and taking a tissue from her skirt pocket. "For the Keenans. For their loss," said Theresa. Her mother nodded again.

"Well," Mrs. Martin straightened her back and turned to the hallway door, looking back over her shoulder at the two of them. "I'll leave you to it then, Theresa. Forgive me, Miss O'Reilly, I am having a hard time."

And then she was gone even as Rosaria was responding, "Oh, I really do understand, Mrs. Martin."

Theresa stood gazing after her mother for a few moments, then pressed her hands together and looked at Rosaria. "Well, then, a cup of tea to start?"

"Yes, that would be lovely, thanks." Rosaria had never said *lovely* until recently. She had picked it up here, usually in connection with accepting the required cup of tea and some biscuits in a small parlor like this one. Parlors filled with a breath-taking collection of china knick-knacks and holy pictures.

The tea arrived with a plate of cream biscuits. Another habit Rosaria was picking up—how had she lived without these afternoon breaks of properly-made tea and sweet biscuits? Replenishing for the spirit and, unfortunately, also for the waistline.

"So," said Theresa, after preparing the tea and refreshments and making small talk with Rosaria from the kitchen. She took a sip of tea before putting her cup down. Rosaria was not surprised to see Theresa Martin get directly to the point. "So, you be wanting to know about a conversation with this young man my father might have had before he died? The student from the University at Galway?"

"Yes, he may not have mentioned this to you or your mother, but I thought I'd see if you might have some idea." Rosaria could hear Mrs. Martin moving about in the kitchen, no doubt listening closely.

"No, I don't recall his saying anything like that. What do you suppose they would have been talking about?"

"Patrick was a journalism student working on an independent project about the ties between American sympathizers and the activities in the North in the seventies."

Theresa Martin sat very still and Rosaria could hear the movements in the kitchen freeze.

"I see," Theresa said carefully. "Has he published this study?"

"Sadly, no. Patrick was murdered in Boston shortly before your father died."

"Mother of God. I knew he died, but murdered, you say?"

Rosaria nodded.

"How old was he now?"

"Just turned twenty."

Theresa glanced toward the kitchen and ran her fingers through her hair. "You know, we wonder about my father's death, too."

"No, I didn't know that."

A long silence followed, broken only by the ticking of a china clock on the mantel above the electric fire. Theresa got up slowly and closed the door to the kitchen. She walked to one of the windows looking over the Owenglin and pulled back the laced curtain. "My father had a secret in him."

Rosaria did not respond. *Secrets. Always the secrets. They never stay buried.*

Still looking out at the river, Theresa spoke now in a quiet, flat voice. "Maybe with his mind going, he felt that he had to let it out." Her eyes were filled when she sat again and faced Rosaria. "And, so, I expect he did and maybe he died for it."

"I thought he died from a fall in the care home, Theresa."

Theresa let out a long, wet sigh. "Well, yes. He did. A fall in the garden there. Hit his head on a rock. 'He slipped' they said." She smoothed the tea cloth in her hands before speaking again. "But the orderly with him was new and disappeared right after my father died." She looked at Rosaria and with a hardness to her voice said, "Me, I think there's a good chance it was not an accident, no matter what they say at the home. But I haven't said anything—that would just be too much for my mother. She's not that strong."

Theresa bowed her head and rubbed her forehead with her hand before raising her eyes. "He started to do the odd thing or two, letting the water run in the kitchen till the floor was covered and things like that. Then, he'd get up at two o'clock in the morning and get dressed for church. He went up to Saint Joe's for Mass every day, you know. But getting up in the middle of the night for it? My mother would say, 'Where are you going, Thomas?' and he'd say, 'To church.' She started locking the door on him, but he got out sometimes and they would find him wandering up the Market Street in the dark toward the church."

She lowered her hands to her lap and straightened her back. "We felt we had no choice but to put him in the care home, you know. My mother's old. It was hard for her, always watching, always on edge. He was starting to be a danger to himself and others."

"How did he feel about going to the care home, Theresa?"

"Well, we told him he had to be there for some time while they adjusted his blood pressure to a healthy level. He had very high blood pressure, you see. And once he was there, he was content."

Rosaria marveled at the Irish way of making things happen sometimes. Thomas Martin's family misrepresented to him both the why and the how long parts of moving into a care home so that he would go without complaint—and with some pride. Rosaria was sure Mr. Martin was well aware of the why and the how long of the situation, and accepted it with dignity.

Her thought process was interrupted when she heard Theresa speaking. "But, you know, perhaps they did him a mercy. He had other health problems besides the dementia—the bad cancer—and he didn't have that much longer. It would have been awful toward the end. Yes, perhaps they did him a mercy. I just didn't know why they couldn't wait."

"Who's *they*, Theresa?"

"Oh, I can't say who I mean or even if I know—never mind—I don't know what I'm saying." Theresa waved her hand in the air as if hitting away a small bird.

Rosaria didn't respond, waiting Theresa out. Finally, Theresa spoke.

"There was something—something big and dark—that my father knew. He told me a little about it. Not all about it, but enough. It was dangerous to know. It's why he never told anyone before. And I still don't know how it all fits together."

She sat quietly for a few moments, staring at the patterned rug as if it might offer an answer, a way forward. Rosaria let the silence do its work.

"But what I do know from what my father told me is this." There was long pause. The clock still ticking on the mantel, the sounds of the river and the occasional car outside. What she said then came out in a rush. "A man was murdered out here by the IRA."

"You mean here in Connemara?"

Theresa nodded. "It was by the old famine burial vault at the Mother and Baby Home—Saint Mary of Egypt. Derrygimlah on the way to Ballyconneely. They used the vault to bury the babies that didn't make it. Such a terribly sad place." She shook her head. "Anyway, the home's closed now."

"Really? At the mother and baby home that the nuns ran?"

"Right, that very one," Theresa answered. "An IRA sympathizer, a local man, worked there and he had some kind of operation going on with them. I don't know what it was, way down here." She stopped again to take a few deep breaths, "A man was executed during the operation. He was not a local man. One of theirs from the north. This sympathizer helped them drop the body in one of the bogs." Theresa embraced herself and stroked her upper arms as she continued. "My father said to never tell anyone."

"But he told you."

"Yes, he did. It was on the way back from the University Hospital in Galway, the day the doctor told him how bad the cancer was. I went with him. My mother couldn't handle taking him, you know. It was just him and me."

"Yes," Rosaria responded. "I can understand."

Theresa looked to the side at the curtained windows again, perhaps wishing she were outside standing by the river instead of in this small parlor talking about hard things. "He said he had to talk about it. I think my mother knew more than she let on, but she wouldn't talk about it. Still won't." She turned her eyes to Rosaria. "I'm thinking now that my father must have told Patrick the story. Perhaps after he heard about Patrick's special project. Maybe my father thought this was a way to bring the truth forward."

"Would that have still been dangerous? It's an old story."

"It's still sensitive to talk about secrets from the North. People think everything's come out. I think there's much more that we don't know about. But my father was beyond thinking about danger or ramifications. He already knew he was going to die." She looked down at her hands. "But perhaps he didn't think about the danger to Patrick."

They both let that awful thought settle between them before Rosaria asked, "But how did your father find out about this in the first place, Theresa?"

"The workman at the Home had a son who witnessed the murder, not really understanding who or what he was seeing. The boy used to wander up to the Home sometimes in the evening if his father was working, and just watch his father from behind a stone wall. Only for something to do and to see his dad, you know."

Rosaria nodded.

"They boy had to tell someone what he'd seen, though his father had threatened him against it. Eventually, the boy told his teenaged cousin he was close to, my own father—much older than he was, but close, you know. They made a blood pact never to tell anyone else. As time went on, when they were older, and read the news and saw pictures in the paper, they understood who and what Liam had witnessed that night."

Rosaria almost stopped breathing. "Liam?"

"Yes, that was my father's cousin's name. The workman's boy was Liam Joyce."

CHAPTER 30

ossie had been walking Fergus up and down the Market Street while Rosaria made her visit to the Martins. The big man and the dog, who now sported a kerchief around his neck in the maroon and white colors of the Galway Tribesmen hurling club, were on the stone bridge over the Owenglin when she came outside. She joined Mossie in silence for a few moments—as they both looked over the bridge wall at the river rushing down to the salmon weir.

"I'd like you to drive me down to the old Saint Mary of Egypt Mother and Baby Home."

Mossie frowned. "What would you be wanting to go there for? You know, when I first signed up for this job, I thought you'd be wanting to do things like go to the super for food or the hairdresser or even to Mass." At this last he gave a derisive snort, since Rosaria didn't go to Mass.

She smiled back at him. "Maybe another time. Right now, it's Saint Mary of Egypt."

He stared at her and said slowly, "Now, you know I like you, Rosaria, but you wouldn't be one of those nosy reporters or writers now too, would you? Digging up half-cocked old tales about the Mother and Baby Home and dragging the place down?" He didn't say it, but Rosaria could hear the unspoken end of the sentence *"just to make a buck"*. She recalled Declan Twomey asking her the same kind of question.

"I'm not a reporter or a writer, Mossie, but I do need an answer to some questions about what happened back in Boston. It's possible that answer may involve Saint Mary of Egypt. You know Patrick Keenan was murdered, and that I'm here to help the family."

The big man nodded.

"Patrick was just twenty, Mossie."

"A terrible thing, a terrible thing." He closed his eyes briefly. "But that was some guy in Boston that did that, am I right?"

"Maybe, but the answer to why it happened may be over here."

Mossie cocked his head and looked at her skeptically. "At the old Mother and Baby Home? That's hard to believe."

"Maybe. I can't tell you more than that, but if you knew the story, you would want to help me find an answer."

A long silence as Mossie gazed at Rosaria from under his bushy black brows and thought about the situation. A heavy sigh followed. "Okay, you're the boss, Miss O'Reilly. Saint Mary of Egypt it is."

He gave Fergus another head rub and started for the car.

"Thanks, Mossie."

Mossie nodded. "We'll go straight out from here to the Ballyconneely Road and Errislannan."

While they rode on the winding road out of Clifden, Rosaria asked, "Mossie, did you ever know of a man named Joyce who worked at the Mother and Baby Home?"

"Joyce, is it?"

Rosaria nodded.

He rubbed his face with his hand. "Well, there was a man there by the name of Joyce. I think it may have been Brendan, who used to work at the home. Kept it going for the nuns for a long time—with all the work and upkeep around the place. Of course, that was years ago. He's gone now."

"Do you remember if he had a son, Liam?"

"Yes, I am thinking I've heard of him. Liam Joyce. Is he the one went to Boston and they call Saint Liam sometimes?"

"Right. Quite likely they're related," Rosaria mused. "That's interesting, if it's true, father and son running charity homes, like a family tradition."

Mossie reflected on this for some time before speaking again. He laid a heavy forearm on the bottom of the car's open window frame and stared out at the road ahead. "Well, maybe not all the family traditions." Rosaria shifted in her seat to face him, but Mossie continued to stare ahead. "They say there was some other business that went on here."

"What do you mean *other business?*" Rosaria asked. "Do you mean something other than separating young mothers from their babies? All the illegal adoptions, trafficking in the babies—selling them to America?"

Rosaria knew the sad history of the mother and baby homes. Pregnant, unwed young mothers sent to the nuns at the homes where they worked for their keep, only to have their babies swept away in adoptions, often to America, and often arranged by parish priests on both sides of the Atlantic. Aching holes in the hearts of the young mothers, most never healing even after they had families of their own. Aching holes in the hearts of the adopted children who may have tried to trace their birth mothers through the obstruction and stonewalling of Church bureaucracy.

"Well, that was a dark business. But I'm talking about something else."

"Yes?" Rosaria asked. "What would that be, Mossie?"

Mossie continued at a thoughtful pace as if Rosaria had not spoken. "You know, many people in the South, in the Republic, have always been sympathetic to the resistance in the North. Not active really, but sympathetic in many ways, if you know what I mean."

Rosaria nodded, thinking of the adoptive father she loved who was not only sympathetic, but apparently active.

"Liam Joyce's father, if it was him, would have been no different, but there were whispers that he was active."

That word again. "What does *active* look like?"

"Oh, helping the Cause in different ways." They both allowed a prolonged silence before Mossie continued. "You know that New York, Boston, Philly used to send money for Derry up north."

Rosaria nodded again.

"But, they sent arms. Weapons."

"Really?"

Mossie looked at her as he would a child. "Yes, really, Rosaria. This was a war, you know. That's what happens in a war."

Rosaria thought by then that she could be pretty sure where Mossie's sympathies lay.

"Sent over on ships in crates labeled something else—in one local case, they say maybe as fishing supplies. I think they used those big long rubber waders from some factory around Boston to hide the guns. No one would have looked at those. You know how big the salmon fishing is for visitors here. Anyway, guns and rounds of ammunition in the waders."

Mossie's comments settled like a stone in Rosaria's stomach. She thought back on Declan Twomey's sly comment when she'd visited him. A comment that had nagged her ever since her visit to the construction magnate. How useful her adoptive father, Jim O'Reilly, had been with his job in the rubber footwear factory. Of course, the factory made, among other things, fishing waders. Long, rubber fishing waders shipped in long crates.

She remembered her father as a sentimental Irishman, nothing more. The workers in his department in the factory who were not Irish American suffered under endless corny Irish songs on the loudspeaker system. He might occasionally intersperse the Irish singer Carmel Quinn's songs about Galway Bay, the Green Glens of Antrim and The Old Bog Road with Frank Sinatra or Perry Como songs about moons like big pizza pies in the sky—or maybe Julius LaRosa for the rest of the population—but mostly it was an endless procession of smaltzy Irish tunes. She was not sure how the workers felt about this cruel and unusual punishment, but her father was well-loved and they seemed good-humored about it.

Still—this sweet, sentimental man a *gunrunner for the IRA?* The thought took her breath away. *How well do we know anybody? Even our parents.* She felt her world shifting. She was in one of those time-out-of-time chapters of life. Anxious about what she might learn, perhaps even about her own father.

Mossie hadn't noticed her momentary freezing and continued. "They'd be picked up from the larger ship by a fishing boat, ferried to the shore here, hidden for a while, then collected and brought up north along back roads in farm trucks with false bottoms and the like."

Rosaria stared at him. "Where are you going with this, Mossie?"

"They say that the grounds of the Home might have been used as a collection point. There's a nice little old granite wharf there right in front of the Home. Never really used much. It was built during famine times as a work relief project." Mossie took a deep breath. "Now, I'm not saying what the nuns really knew about all this. They trusted Joyce. As I say, he kept the place going for them. They relied on him."

Mossie took a glance at Rosaria. "Of course, the nuns were only human—though some weren't so sure about that, the way they treated those young girls. But all the nuns were Irish and may have been sympathizers too. Jaysus." He turned the steering wheel suddenly to avoid a large stone on the road.

Rosaria thought for a moment they were sure to get lodged in one of the thick hedgerows, but—thank God—Mossie righted the car in a matter of seconds and they proceeded along the road. Not for the first time, she congratulated herself on hiring Mossie O'Toole as a driver.

"How did the people in the South feel about the events up North?" she asked.

"Oh, sympathetic. Not necessarily the government—I think they were afraid of the violence, the complications and maybe their own relationship with the UK—but the people, yes. Mostly armchair Republicans, as they say—not active, but supportive." He nodded as if agreeing with himself. "I saw a clip about the big march in Dublin during the eighties in support of the IRA hunger strikers up in Her Majesty's Maze prison in Belfast. You'd know about that, would you?"

"Yes, terrible. How many? Ten?"

"Right. Ten. They wanted to be held as political prisoners, not common criminals and to wear their own clothes, not prison uniforms—that kind of thing."

"Seems reasonable. But then, I don't know that much about it."

Mossie laughed. "Would I be riding along here with an incipient sympathizer now—a fellow traveler, so to say, Ms. O'Reilly?"

"Oh, perhaps," she smiled. "It always helps to know a little bit more, though, before you sympathize, don't you think? Anyway, they never got those demands met, did they?"

"From that heartless Maggie Thatcher? Not a chance. No, they didn't get those specific demands met, but in the long term it had a big effect." He glanced over at her. "Have you never heard of the 'King's Threshold' hunger strike tradition in Ireland?"

"No—what's that?"

"Legend has it that in olden times—like really olden—maybe seventh century, a travelling bard was not paid after he'd entertained a king and his household for some time. Maybe the king didn't like the bard's verses or maybe he was just a cheap bastard. Anyway, the bard pleaded with the king for payment to no avail. Finally, the bard was so desperate that he made a decision to starve himself to death at the gate of the king's castle—the King's Threshold—for all to see."

"That's a dramatic way to deal with it," Rosaria commented.

"Yes, indeed. Now, I'm not sure that the poor bard ever got paid, any more than the Belfast boys got their demands met, but the King's Threshold hunger strike is an old tradition here. A way of bringing an injustice into the public eye. They used it during the fight for Irish independence."

"Sounds like it would have a big emotional impact."

"Oh yes, an effective tool—if you don't mind giving your life for a cause. During the strike at the Maze prison, someone put up the name of Bobby Sands—the lead hunger striker who was dying in the Maze—for Parliament and he was soundly elected by the people. They say that is when the IRA realized how much power they could have at the ballot box."

"A turning point."

"Of a sort, I'd say. Then, when he died from starvation, a hundred thousand people attended his funeral. He often quoted the famous line of an Irish independence hunger striker who said, 'It is not those who inflict the most, but those who suffer the most who will conquer.'"

"Powerful."

"Yes, it is."

They were quiet for some time with only the sound of the car, the wind in the hedgerows and the grass and the occasional lowing of the cattle.

"So, these nuns might have been sympathetic."

"Oh, I'd say they were. Putting on the black veil and rattling a rosary around your waist doesn't always mean you leave your political passions behind."

Mossie stopped again, speaking even more slowly this time. "And then—practically speaking—they were always in need of funds to keep such a big place going. They got money from the government for the care of the young women and babies and, of course, from the adoption fees, but I imagine finances were strained. Joyce was very devoted and I expect would have found a way to take care of them. In his fashion, if you know what I mean."

It took some time for the meaning and the weight of these words to settle in Rosaria's mind. It all felt so strangely foreign. So *other*. Her ancestors were sons and daughters of this place, but she was not part of this world. With its desperate, complicated history and long grievances, no more desperate and complicated than her own country's, but unique. Her ancestry gave her no special insight. In fact, a journalist had commented that the chasm between Irish America and Ireland was as deep as the Atlantic. She felt that now. She didn't understand it at all. *Nuns and guns.* It couldn't be.

"Of course, the house has been closed for years now, thank God. Terrible place. It's all shut up, but still standing. I don't know why they haven't sold it. Maybe the history holds back a sale. I heard another developer is looking at the land now. He'll tear it down, you know, for holiday cottages. It's a beautiful spot."

Rosaria gazed at her hands thoughtfully. "What order of nuns would have run the place?"

Mossie snorted. "The Sisters of the Compassionate Heart—as if they ever had one. They were known as the Compassionates."

"Irish order?"

"Oh yes, based in Dublin, I think. I don't know if they're still around or if the order died out. I'd say the publicity about the mother and baby homes didn't help with vocations, you think? Though as some say, no nuns broke into our homes to steal our daughters and their babies—we were the ones who drove them away. And we knew what that would mean for the mothers and the babies. But still people blamed the nuns and the Church."

Beware of bull said the sign on the metal gate of one rocky pasture. Rosaria's stomach was tight in anticipation of what she could soon learn at the sad place they were about to visit. Still, she had to smile thinking of the many corporate meetings she'd been part of in her life that could have used such a sign. *Beware of bull.*

"There's no real bull around here," Mossie commented. "Farmers put those signs up all the time against the hikers, the trekkers." He glanced at her as they turned a tight corner. "Hikers forget to close the gates and the sheep or the cows get out. Or they hike with those dogs who chase the animals. Better to keep them out in the first place."

Rosaria sat in the passenger seat of Mossie's antiquated Renault van. It was a little too strange for her to sit in the rear seat while Mossie drove. Sitting in the front seat also softened her ride, as the old car's well-worn shock system was clearly unequal to its present challenges. Still, Rosaria felt every bump and rock on the narrow road descending from the hills outside Clifden down to the shuttered Saint Mary of Egypt Mother and Baby Home near one of many small harbors on a jagged coastline.

Outside, close by her window, the bramble and fuchsia hedges occasionally brushed her arm. Then, they'd suddenly make way to wide vistas of rough green fields—an endless mosaic filigreed by stone walls—rocks, hills and valleys, lakes and bogs, all the way to the Bens, the mountains in the hazy distance. Gentle white Connemara ponies—blessed creatures say the poets—and cattle watched the old Renault bump along the road with uncurious eyes. The occasional pre-famine cottage, nestled beside a modern farm house, held an assortment of farm equipment and garden tools or perhaps a cow or two. Ancient memories not quite crowded out by the beasts and workaday debris of a new generation.

"Well, they certainly chose a remote location for Saint Mary's," commented Rosaria.

"Oh, yes. Well, they couldn't look a gift horse in the mouth, could they?" Mossie replied. "Someone gifted the place to the order of nuns—shortly after our Civil War, maybe in the nineteen-twenties." He swerved quickly to avoid a particularly impressive boulder in the road. "The place originally belonged to one of the old Anglo-Irish families." Mossie paused to chuckle. "You can bet the road would have been better maintained in those days, what with summer guests coming from the train station in Clifden and all. Different times."

A high bump on the road lifted them both momentarily from their seats.

"Jesus, Mary, and Joseph," Rosaria gasped.

"Now you sound like my ma," Mossie laughed.

After she had settled down, at least for the moment, Rosaria asked Mossie, "When did the Home close?"

"Oh, I don't know. Might have been in the late seventies. Times change, you know. Girls who found themselves in that way now might go over to England to take care of things. Or, if they decided to keep the baby, their families might not be happy, but they wouldn't abandon their daughters or those poor babies the way they did before. Ireland took some time to grow up like that. Out of the dark time with the old priests calling the shots on everything."

Mossie sighed heavily. "There may be a referendum soon on reproductive rights. That might bring us into the modern world on that kind of thing. We'll see."

"I never heard of Saint Mary of Egypt."

"No, you wouldn't have unless you were of a certain mindset like the nuns were. Saint Mary of Egypt was a prostitute who found the Lord—very old times—maybe seventh century."

Rosaria could just see their destination, the roof and chimneys of a large stone building, as the van continued its descent down the long, narrow road. "Well, that would certainly put a name to how the Church felt about those girls," commented Rosaria.

Mossie murmured his assent as they pulled to the end of the road and got out of the van. In front of them, a small harbor with a heavy, deserted granite pier, gulls wheeling overhead in a dense gray sky. *If this pier was a famine relief project,* Rosaria thought, *where in God's name did men, even with horses, ever get the energy to maneuver those heavy granite blocks with so little available food to fuel them?* She guessed food must have been part of their compensation.

On the other side of them stood the Saint Mary of Egypt Mother and Baby Home. A high stone wall, a good foot taller than even Mossie O'Toole, surrounded the main building. In the center of the wall, on an entrance wide enough to allow a vehicle to pass, a heavy wooden door stood with a rusted chain and lock dangling from its handle. Rosaria looked at Mossie with a question in her eyes.

He nodded and picked up a good sized rock with a sharp edge. Two quick blows and the rusty lock surrendered.

Mossie went first, Rosaria following close behind.

The house was designed by someone from another place. A place where a big house was expected to have a curving driveway where a car could pull up and dislodge its visitors under a welcoming portico. A place where graceful lines softened stonework.

They had used long, generous windows to view the sea. That must have been before someone built a tall stone wall to stop people from getting in, or perhaps from getting out. Now, the first floor windows looked only at the gray stone enclosure at the end of the driveway, maybe with a glimpse of the sea from the top floors.

The order of nuns had not been able to keep the house up to its previous standards, and it clearly showed the damage of having been abandoned for many years. But the old owners—"the strangers who tried to teach us their ways"—had left their mark and a vestigial grace in the old building.

In her mind's eye, Rosaria couldn't help but see the faces of young women in the windows, in the overgrown gardens, on that driveway. Seeing a girl clumsy with pregnancy being dropped off under that portico with only a cardboard suitcase. Perhaps by a tasca or taxi from the train station. Perhaps by one member of the family she likely wouldn't ever see again—maybe her heartsick older brother.

Here to work and earn her keep until the baby came, only to have the child taken from her—if it survived—often given to Irish-Americans who pulled up that long circular driveway in big cars. Americans rich with hope and cheer and money and a future she couldn't offer her own flesh and blood.

Prevented from coming downstairs by the nuns, the agony of watching through these long windows as her child is taken away—leaving an open wound in a young mother's being that would never heal.

———

Rosaria and Mossie walked to the cemetery beside the Home, where the Home's high enclosure gave way to the loose rubble of a low stone wall. A wide gate stood open just beyond an old oak tree. They could see beside the Home itself a small lot of white gravestones within a wrought iron enclosure. A Celtic cross stood in the center. "For the nuns," Mossie murmured.

They climbed the road up a gentle incline until they came to a flat grove of stubby, windswept trees that led to a large burial vault.

"This one was originally from the famine years," Mossie said. "Before so many died that there was no one left to bury the bodies. They'd be left by the side of the road covered by some dirt with a few stones beside them to mark the site. For a long time you could find those little piles of stone all over the back paths, the unimproved roads and lanes."

The door to the vault was a heavy concrete slab with its iron hinges hanging loose, long since rusted and useless. Rosaria leaned closer to the door to read the blackened Latin inscription on it. *De profundis clamavi ad te, Domine: Domine, exaudi vocum meum.* "Out of the depths have I cried to thee, O Lord: Lord, hear my voice."

"Let's go, Mossie. I think I've seen enough." Rosaria turned and walked to the van, her arms folded and her head down.

CHAPTER 31

olly and Marguerite sat on one of the benches on Northeastern University's Centennial Common—just across the street from the Tremont Street police station. They ate their takeout Asian stir-fry in companionable silence and watched Archie join a student game of Ultimate Frisbee.

"So," he said as he delicately mixed his stir-fried vegetables, "you didn't really have to drive all the way from Maudsley to Boston—with the dog—for an appointment in Jamaica Plain today, did you, Mother Superior?"

"Oh, stop calling me that, Solly. It's Marguerite. And yes, it was a nice-to-do, but not a necessity, I guess." Marguerite smiled.

"And you really didn't have to bring his nibs." Solly lifted his chin to indicate Archie, a study in canine joy, his short legs pumping wildly as he ran back and forth among the Frisbee players.

"No, I didn't. I just thought you might miss him and I know your schedule wouldn't allow you to drive up to Maudsley."

"Yeah, I do miss the little guy."

"I could tell from the way he greeted you that the feeling was mutual." Marguerite laughed. "I think you miss his mistress too."

"That's the truth." Solly leaned his elbows on his knees and concentrated on the Frisbee game. He nodded. "That's the truth."

"She's been an independent woman for a long time, Solly."

He nodded and listened as Marguerite continued. "But you're good for each other. I hope nothing gets in the way."

"Yeah." Solly looked across the campus for a long time before slapping his knee. "Buy you an ice cream, Mother Superior?"

"Marguerite. And I'd be delighted, Detective Belkin," Marguerite replied.

"Let's go, Archie," Solly hollered. "Let's go, big guy."

Archie came galloping across the grass. Solly caught him up in his arms, and turned his grinning face against a frenzy of doggy licks. Then, he looked at the little dog. "We need our Rosie back. Right, Archie?"

CHAPTER 32

he Marian Manor Care Home where Thomas Martin had spent his last days sat atop a hill behind Saint Joseph's Church. A statue of the Blessed Mother, surrounded by colorful autumn plants, anchored a circular driveway in front of the red brick building. Rosaria caught a glimpse of the back garden where Thomas Martin had taken his deadly fall, just below a small granite cliff that bordered the property.

Theresa Martin had called ahead to speak to the nursing supervisor, asking her to take Rosaria's appointment and to feel comfortable about relaying information on her father's death. She assured the supervisor that the family had no interest in pursuing legal action against the care home because of her father's death in a fall.

Rosaria didn't think that very American, litigious thought had ever occurred to the care home. With some hesitation, but with the certain trust that one finds in small communities, the supervisor agreed to talk with Rosaria. They met in her small office. The supervisor had a round, efficient face, wireless glasses, and frank brown eyes. The badge on her flowered smock said Sheila Early.

"Well, you know, Mr. Martin had a number of issues cognitively and physically. Pity. He was a wonderful man. Lovely family. I went to school with his daughter Theresa. "

"Did he have balance issues?"

"Yes, he did. Not all the time, mind you, but he could be shaky. That's why we were so sorry, but not entirely surprised, when he took a fall in the garden." Sheila Early paused for a moment and, looking away, shook her head.

"It seems odd that Mr. Martin took a fall when he had an aide with him," Rosaria said, reading the woman's mind.

"Indeed. It seemed that way to us, too." She leaned forward, elbows on her desk. "We thought Joseph Mulvaney was a fine aide too. New, but showed so much promise. He was good with the patients. And he was strong. He could lift them with no trouble from the wheelchairs and the beds. I thought he had a gift for working with the elderly and the infirm. It's not always easy, you know."

"No, it isn't," Rosaria agreed. "Do you think I might talk to this aide?" she asked, knowing the answer.

"I wish you could, but he left the day Mr. Martin died." Sheila Early looked down and then raised her face to Rosaria's. "There was a big hullabaloo when someone looked out the window and saw Mr. Martin on the ground. We rushed to tend to Mr. Martin. Then," she paused, "then afterwards no one knew where Joseph Mulvaney had gone to."

"That's curious."

"Yes, at first we thought that maybe he was just so upset, or..." She waved her hand. "We didn't know what to think."

"Would you happen to have a picture of Joseph Mulvaney, a staff photo, Ms. Early?"

"Call me Sheila, please. We gave the employee picture to Gerard Conneely, but I may have another one here." She rustled through her desk drawer and handed a photo to Rosaria. The face that looked out of the picture was square-jawed and pleasant, with dark eyes and a distinctive pug nose.

"Sergeant Conneely is investigating?"

"Yes, he is now. We just spoke to him again this morning." Sheila Early dropped back in her chair. "The staff has been talking. See, the rock garden arrangements out back deliberately include only smooth, round stones – smaller ones. Mr. Martin had a deep gash on the back of his head." She moved her hand to the back of her own head. "From a sharp rock."

"What do you make of that?" Rosaria asked. She certainly knew what she would make of it.

"Well, you know, there are some stray sharp rocks on that stony face in the back of the building. One of the staff had the idea to search in the bramble bushes in that area."

"And?"

"And she found a sharp stone with blood and hair and tissue on it."

"And you called Sergeant Conneely."

"I did. He came right up. We told him the story and gave him the rock and the photo. The first thing the guards did was do a search for Joseph Mulvaney in all the civic databases."

Rosaria waited.

"Joseph Mulvaney died up in Sligo five years ago."

"Stolen identity."

Sheila Early nodded.

"Do Theresa and her mother know this?"

"They should now. Gerard was going to sit down with them this afternoon."

On her way out of the care home, Rosaria decided to drop in on Father Roche, pastor of Saint Joseph's, who had said Patrick Keenan's funeral Mass. She thought perhaps he might be able to shed some light on the history of the Saint Mary of Egypt Mother and Baby Home.

Father Roche was putting up a notice in the back of the church, which was empty on this quiet weekday afternoon.

"Why would that be of interest to you now, Ms. O'Reilly?" he asked when she told him her purpose in talking to him. "But come, come, sit down," he invited her as he led her to one of the back pews.

"I'm just checking out details about some activities there in the seventies for an interested party."

Father Roche looked perplexed. Though he apparently decided to take this vague explanation at face value, it didn't seem to be of much use as he knew nothing about the Home.

"Oh, I can't tell you anything about that. I can tell you that one of my predecessors used to say Mass and hear confessions at the Home while it was open." He looked at his hands. "A sad place, by all reports. I would have had difficulty supporting it in any way. But I suppose Father Dolan thought he was giving some comfort and hope, both to the nuns and the young women."

"Is Father Dolan still practicing as a priest?"

"Oh, Father Dolan died a long time ago and the Home has been closed for years." He shrugged. "And, as for me, I was transferred out here from County Waterford four or five years ago. So, I'm not a very good source on local history. I couldn't even tell you what order of nuns ran the place or even, honestly, tell you where it was."

"I see. Well, Father, thank you for your time. I appreciate it." Rosaria rose from the pew. "It was worth a try."

"I'm sorry I couldn't help, Ms. O'Reilly. I didn't know the place, but apparently, it's a dark memory around here."

Rosaria nodded. "Good afternoon, Father." As she turned to leave, she heard an apparent afterthought from Father Roche. "You know, now that I think of it, when I first came here to Saint Joseph's, I did bury the old caretaker from the Home. I think he spent the last few months of his life at the care home."

Rosaria resumed her seat. "Really."

"Yes, he was quite old. Not too many people came to the service. When they get that old, you know, that happens. Anyway, I think his son came from Boston – I hear he does wonderful work with the poor there. A big man from Boston came with him. He's the one that bought the cemetery plot and tombstone. Seemed to have money. I think he's in construction."

CHAPTER 33

ugh had called several times since they'd spent the night together when he'd visited Clifden. Rosaria let the calls go to voicemail and hadn't listened to or returned them, hoping he would get the message. Rosaria was usually direct. She'd always disdained as cowards people who "ghosted" in a relationship. People who just stopped responding without explanation. And here she was doing it herself.

The night that she and Hugh had spent together in James Burke's cottage on the Sky Road had been beautiful. It would have been a very sweet memory if it hadn't been so darkly shadowed by her betrayal of Solly.

Mossie O'Toole was being a good friend—though she could have killed him at the time—in his dogged intrusion into her romantic life. She knew he was right. It had all become clear to her the day they rode along Loch Ingah to Mossie's cabin. Hugh was the past, and she had to admit that some parts of his personality had not aged well. Perhaps he might say the same of her.

In any case, he was not a good fit for her anymore. Solly was the right partner for her. She would explain this to Hugh, not in a letter or email, but in person or by phone. They were different people now than they were then. They had some rich memories. And they should leave it there.

Yes, she would explain all that, but not right now. She couldn't handle it right now. Instead, Rosaria called Marguerite at the Motherhouse in Maudlsey with a question.

"I'm not familiar with that order, the Compassionates," Marguerite responded. "I do remember we had some Bon Secours Sisters who did good work at home in Quebec. I know the Bon Secours ran hospitals in Ireland, too—and I believe, much to their shame now, mother and baby homes. From what I read, the philosophies of these orders back then were quite different from our order. How shall I say it? More punitive with a streak of—perhaps this is too strong a word—cruelty. And I think they were under the thumb of the church hierarchy and the priests far more than our order was. You have to remember that Ireland was a theocracy for centuries."

Rosaria thought back to her own birth mother's experience of real compassion from Marguerite's order—the Sisters of Jeanne d'Arc. If they'd been in Ireland, Rosaria's and her mother's story might have been quite different.

"Do you want me to take this for you, Rosaria? To find out if any of the sisters who were at Saint Mary of Egypt back then are still alive—and would be willing to talk about those days?

Rosaria didn't respond.

"Your own history might make that line of inquiry a complicated experience for you,"

"I'm a big girl."

"A big girl always asking for trouble, it seems. And one who always has to do everything herself." Marguerite paused for a few moments. "Loosen your grip, Rosaria. Let me clear the way for you first. If the order still exists, and there is a nun willing to talk about those days, it will be easier for me to initiate contact and a discussion."

Rosaria gazed out at the rocks and seaweed outside Mr. Burke's cottage and the sea beyond. "Okay, okay. You win, Miss Bossy." She could hear the nun chuckle at the other end of the call. "You know, you're not *my* Mother Superior, Marguerite. Okay. Let me know," Rosaria said.

When Rosaria hung up from the call with Marguerite, she was surprised at her level of relief and gratitude. As she got older, she was experiencing how good it felt to share the burden sometimes. It was true—she didn't have to do everything herself. Still learning.

Rosaria wasn't sure that she had the strength to call Solly that night. He should really know about her conversation with Theresa Martin and the Mother and Baby Home and the mystery surrounding Thomas Martin's death. She really should, but the thought of telling him, it all gave her the beginnings of a headache.

Professionally, Solly would feel he had to do something with this new information about what happened in the Saint Mary of Egypt cemetery those many years ago. He'd want to call the Galway Garda, or insist that she do so.

The authorities would also want to talk about the old events in the cemetery with Thomas Martin's family, to see what else he had told them. Theresa and her mother were still in the throes of grieving not only about the death of a father and husband, but now trying to absorb the fact that Thomas Martin was likely murdered. Maybe there would be a leak to the press. The Irish could be so chatty, and the press would descend on the Martins' little cottage. It would be awful. A nightmare.

Yes, it could wait. She'd give Solly an abbreviated, watered-down version for now. Some old IRA political thing. Not too much information. She'd let him know when she knew more. No need to stir things up prematurely. She wouldn't even mention the new suspicions about Thomas Martin's death.

As for her own father's illegal activities—she'd wait until she got home for that. Rosaria envisioned telling Solly when they were sitting on the couch at her place with a glass of wine, his arm around her shoulder. She hoped things would work out and that indeed they would sit that way again in the not too distant future. Her heart sank when she thought about their last conversation.

But she didn't have to worry about a conversation with Solly when she called. She got his voicemail with its brusque, businesslike greeting. "Belkin here, Homicide Boston PD. Leave a message."

She left him her water-downed report of events. He'd know she was withholding. He knew her so well. Maybe it would be wise to avoid his calls for a while until he calmed down, and until she knew more on the ground here.

Right now, she was exhausted from the events and emotions of the day. Time for the horizontal solution, time to flop into bed and hope her mind would let her sleep.

She was more open with Nora Keenan during their regular update at Cullen's Coffee Shop. She shared in full her conversation with Theresa Martin and her visit to the care home where Thomas Martin had been a patient. A visit that Theresa had helped arrange.

Nora frowned and shook her head. "A horrible business, Rosaria. But how would that involve our Patrick?"

"I don't know yet. It may have been part of what he was researching."

Nora looked down at her hands, which she was turning over in her lap thoughtfully. "Did I not tell you that the answer might lie over here, not in Boston?"

"You did, and you may be right, but we don't know yet, Nora."

"Should we be telling Gerard?"

The last thing Rosaria felt she needed right now was a hundred questions from Gerard Conneely that she had no answers to.

"Could we wait on that? I just have wisps of an old story. There's nothing he could dig into. I'd worry that it would just waste his time."

She was afraid Nora would reply that perhaps they should let Gerard and the guards decide that. But she didn't.

After some thought, she looked at Rosaria.

"I understand, Rosaria. For now."

CHAPTER 34

osaria had walked the path down the low cliff from the Burke cottage to stroll along the rocky beach below when Marguerite called. Rosaria had been missing Fergus, who spent a good deal of time with Mossie now. The stony coast somehow seemed less interesting without the noisy, hyperactive young dog racing all over the rocks around her. But still, this stroll was a welcome break from all the unanswered questions and half-truths that seemed to be floating around her.

"Hi," she picked up Marguerite's call, grateful for the steady cell signal. With low tide, the noise from the lapping waves was a pleasant background. "Find anything out?"

Rosaria picked up an unusual shell—or unusual to her—and wondered if it were a dog whelk shell. She knew there were still middens of dog whelks down near Ballyconneely. Apparently, just inside the creature sat a precious gland which emitted a tiny spot of deep indigo when pressed. Through a highly labor-intensive process, the coastal people had, according to legend, dyed special fabrics a gorgeous color purple, unsurpassed in brilliance, from this little shellfish.

"Well, your friend Mossie was right. The Bon Secours order of nuns may have survived the Mother and Baby Home scandals for now, though I feel sure that they will have to answer for that history as more and more comes to light. The Compassionates did not survive as an order. Their recruitments dried up and so did their philanthropic support. If what you heard about the payoffs they received from the IRA for collusion on gunrunning is true, they really must have struggled when that stopped—even with the fees they received from adoptions and from the Irish government for housing the young mothers in their care."

"So, the order doesn't still exist?"

"No, it doesn't. Its members were subsumed into another order—the Sisters of the Immaculate Heart."

"Were you able to find any of the former Compassionates?"

"I was. In one of the Sisters of Nazareth care homes. A Sister Finbar."

"And?"

"And bedridden with a deteriorated hip, but still sharp. And pretty combative. She wanted to know who put such ideas and wild stories about gunrunning at the Home in my head. I told her it had to do with an investigation into the murder of a young student who was exploring the story. She was very taken aback with this—she couldn't really talk for a minute."

"Pretty shocking. She probably thought too that these old stories were all in the past and would never come out."

"Right. To that point, I did tell her it would indeed all be coming out and that it would be easier to talk to me—a fellow religious—than it would be to talk to the Garda and the journalists."

"You're good at this."

"You're not the only one with the gift, Rosaria," she chuckled. "Anyway, I explained again about Patrick and the story he'd been told."

"Did she confirm the gunrunning?"

"Oh, to my mind she did, if not directly."

"Like how?"

"Like going on too much about how they knew nothing about such a thing as illegal gunrunning on the property. She couldn't imagine such a thing. In any case, Mr. Joyce took care of anything that happened on the property. That would have been his business. They left everything to him."

"I bet they did."

"She talked a good deal about how strained the Sisters' finances were in taking care of the girls and the babies. It sounded like a litany of excuses. As she continued talking, I was sure the nuns were aware of what Mr. Joyce was up to and where this stream of extra income came from."

"Those poor girls and their godforsaken babies in that cruel place with those unkind women."

"Right you are. And, you know, she made a telling comment at the end."

"Yes?"

"She said that those were complicated times and that the struggle for freedom was always hard. '*It's the long game, you know,*' is how she framed it."

When she and Marguerite were about to end their call, Rosaria said, "So, I've found something else out in this investigation, something personal."

"Yes. What would that be?"

"It's about my father."

"And?"

Rosaria told Marguerite about her adoptive father Jimmy O'Reilly's likely involvement in the gun-running organization.

"Ah, I'm so sorry, Rosaria. You've had many complications in your family history. Another shock for you."

"How many more secrets will I uncover about my family, Marguerite?"

"We can't know that, but no more, I hope," Marguerite responded. "But just remember one thing about Jimmy O'Reilly, Rosaria."

"What?"

"How much he loved his daughter. *Over the moon*. Isn't that how the Irish say it? He was *over the moon and back* about you. With everything else, you have to remember that."

Rosaria had prepared herself when she took a call from Solly two days after avoiding all his phone messages. Their last conversation had ended badly on the subject of an *old friend* of hers in Ireland, after the unforgiveable interference of Mossie who'd left a message for Solly about her seeing Hugh Moran.

She was enraged anew every time she thought of Mossie taking it on himself to tell Solly about her reconnection with Hugh Moran. Solly would also certainly want to dig deeper into her abbreviated report on illegal activities at the Mother and Baby Home decades ago. She wasn't ready to go into all that yet and was contemplating how to do a little defensive verbal meandering and blocking to avoid a direct response.

Rosaria was not surprised at Solly's brief, chilly greeting. She was surprised when he asked only perfunctory questions about the subject of the Mother and Baby Home and commented, "Well, let me know if there's more that comes out."

She had to admit that she was just a little annoyed at the last comment. Things didn't just *come out*. She found information by actively tracking it down, for crying out loud, not just passively waiting for things to *come out* magically.

While she was distracted with being annoyed, Solly moved onto another sore subject. She should have been prepared, but she wasn't when Solly then said. "So, Rosie, I guess we'll have to talk about old friends and what it means for us."

A beat of silence.

"You have an old friend, Solly." The issue of his ex-wife Justine had been there all along. It was only a matter of time before it came out. "Have you been seeing Justine?"

"Ah, so that's it," was Solly's dry response. "Yes, I have been seeing her."

Did she hear defiance in that response? *Jesus.* Rosaria's stomach churned. Her eyes watered. She looked out to the sea for some solace. None there. Gray sea. Gray Clouds. *Oh please, don't cry. Don't cry. Don't cry.*

"I helped her and a friend take some of her photographs up to the North Shore Art Association on Rocky Neck in Gloucester yesterday," Solly continued. "She has a show there."

"How sweet. Is our picture from the Globe in the show?"

"Very funny. No, it's not. She'd got some nice work, though."

"I'm sure she does," Rosaria responded flatly.

"She has a book coming out—black and white shots of some Boston neighborhoods."

Why was he telling her these things—turning the knife?

"Independently published. Her fiancé—her friend that helped out with the photo show yesterday—is funding it."

"Lovely. Why are you telling me this?" She was rubbing her eyes hard now, pressing on them not to cry and snivel. She had to maintain some dignity here... *wait...* "Wait, her *fiancé*?" A gulp. "That wouldn't be you, would it, Solly?" Okay, now she was going to cry.

"No, no, not me. Somebody else. Nice guy, for a Waspy artist, another trust fund kid. A good match—sure better for her than a Boston Jewish cop with an attitude. He lives down in Lanesville, Gloucester. She's moving there next month."

"Good." Rosaria's voice wavered. "Good, I'm happy for her, for them. Really happy."

"Love you, Rosie."

"Love you, Solly." And then she did burst into tears.

CHAPTER 35

either the name nor the voice on her phone messaging system was familiar to Rosaria. Michael Cahill? She searched her mind for any reference to a Michael Cahill. And came up empty.

"Hello, Miss O'Reilly. My name is Michael Cahill. You don't know me but I have information for you that I think you will want. It regards the murder of Patrick Keenan." Rosaria's breath quickened.

"I don't feel comfortable going to the Garda with this information and I'd rather not be seen talking to you in Clifden. You'll understand why when we meet. If you can meet me in Roundstone at the Roundstone House Pub this evening, I'll wait for you there from eight o'clock. If you don't show up tonight, I won't call again. I'm not sure I should be involved in this at all."

And the message ended.

"What the…?" So many data points coming out. Patrick's research project tipping into long ago IRA gunrunning and a murder at Saint Mary of Egypt Mother and Baby Home. Patrick killed in Boston—why Boston? Liam Joyce, Saint Liam, son of the caretaker at the Mother and Baby Home during the gunrunning operation and probable IRA execution—how is he involved? And Thomas Martin—also likely murdered after telling Patrick his secret— who could have done that? All pieces of the puzzle, but she couldn't quite fit them together.

Maybe this was the key. Rosaria was getting impatient to put together the full narrative. She didn't know what this message was about, but she was going to follow it. Should she call the guards? Tell Gerard Conneely? No, she'd spook Michael Cahill. He wouldn't talk to her. And she'd never tell Solly—he would make such a goddamn fuss.

Rosaria knew Roundstone was up the coast to the east, on the other side of the gigantic bog between it and Clifden. There was an old Franciscan school and monastery there, long closed and now home to a craft workshop making bohdans, the mesmerizing goat-skinned Irish hand drums. The village was also home to a summer regatta of Galway hookers—the red-sailed traditional

Galway fishing boats named for the way they hooked the wind. That was all she knew about Roundstone, just another charming and picturesque village on the coast. And apparently where a Michael Cahill was waiting for her to tell her how this whole disjointed story fit together.

She wished Mossie were available to drive her to Roundstone but he was on his way to Dublin, for the Galway match against Kilkenny the next day in Croke Park. He'd been talking about the match for weeks on end. She knew Mossie was saying a novena that Galway would trounce Kilkenny, giving him an opportunity to triumph over that annoying Kilkenny man, Hugh Moran. Oh how would he relish that. For her part, Rosaria mused at how the heavens might have time to answer novenas about sporting matches with all the troubles in the world, though best to leave that subject be.

She was happy for Mossie, but here she was without a ride to Roundstone where a mysterious voicemail had told her critical information was waiting. And where was Mossie when she needed him? At a hurling match. Figures.

And Bridie had taken Nora Keenan to Kenmare for a getaway near the Killarney National Forest. "To walk, talk together, you know," Bridie had said. "Whatever I can do to help her. Poor woman." It's what Bridie should have been doing for her sister. All the same, Rosaria wished selfishly that Bridie had been here to drive to Roundstone with her.

So, here she was, stuck for a ride. The hell with it. She'd go herself. She'd long ago returned her rental car, but Mr. Burke's little blue Ford Fiesta sat at the end of the driveway, its key on a hook by the back door. She hadn't driven a manual shift since high school. Still, she thought she could remember and could manage. Muscle memory and all that.

Rosaria looked at the map. The R341 would bring her along the coast to Roundstone. The bog road was straight through that endless blanket of peatland. It would be a straight shot, save her precious time. There were no lights along the bog road and she didn't think anyone really drove it at night. During the day, there was something magical about the bog—the larks and the merlins, the smell of the wildflowers and the heather. The sweet, fresh winds and wide open sky. Quite lovely in its own way. But at night—no way.

There was also that creepy Halfway House site at the midpoint of the bog road with stories of a murderous brother and sister preying on travelers in the old days. Nothing but a pile of stones in a small clearing there now, yet still with an aura, if she were to be honest. But Halfway House was the last thing on her mind at the moment. She had to get going. She could drive on the Ballyconnelly Road, the R34, and take it slow. She was getting entirely too timid. She'd borrow Mr. Burke's car, leave Mossie a text so that someone would know where she was. Then, she'd put the car on the wrong side of the road and get on with it. *Best laid plans*, she thought to herself ruefully a short time later. She'd had terrible problems shifting with the manual system, gotten flustered and now taken a wrong turn and ended up on what indeed appeared to be the bog road. *Dammit. Dammit. Dammit.*

But perhaps not entirely a disaster. Not a great road, no lights except her own, but certainly the fastest route and she didn't have much time. Right—not optimum—lonely and just one lane with the bog on each side. All the same, she could manage it if she focused. Just drive straight ahead for around six miles. She didn't even have to change gears.

Rosaria berated herself for being so incompetent to end up on this road at night. Incompetent and reckless. *Jesus, it was dark.* She could barely make out the narrow road ahead. There was no place to turn around and she'd make a mess of it anyway, not being able to see with her bad right eye.

She didn't know what she would do if a car came the opposite way. She'd just to have the hope that the other driver would pull over and let her pass. *Oh God. I wish Mossie were driving. Damned hurling.*

Fortunately, she saw the headlights of a car some distance behind her, so she wasn't totally alone. Her shoulders started to relax a little. The sweet smell of the bog wafted through her window. Rosaria breathed the dense, musky air in deeply and felt refreshed and a little bit calmer. *Just keep on going. Slow and steady.*

She opened her palms on the wheel to stretch her fingers, which had started to tingle from her tightened grip. *Breathe in, breathe out. It's just a road. Other people drive on it without a problem. Roundstone's only nine kilometers, about six miles away at the end. And besides—I'm not alone. There's another car on the road behind me, with people who could help me if I had a problem.*

She started to think about who might be waiting to meet her at the pub in Roundstone. Michael Cahill. Where did he hear of her, and how was he connected in this shadowy, complicated story?

A picture was starting to emerge of what young Patrick Keenan had found out. Somewhere at the heart of the story, the mystery of a man murdered during an IRA operation at the Mother and Baby Home. Murdered outside a burial vault where the bodies of sick little babies and their exhausted, young unwed mothers lay in uneasy eternity. A dismal story.

Rosaria almost forgot for a moment that she'd made a grave navigational error which left her now, with her impaired vision, inching along a lonely bog road in the dark. She glanced in the rear view mirror, into the glare of the headlights. She saw that the car behind was getting very close. Rosaria sped up a little, but then so did the car. The other car got so close that it bumped her rear fender, lightly at first and then aggressively several times. *What was he doing?*

Rosaria put her arms out the driver's side window and waved to the car to pass—not being sure how it could on this narrow road and where she could ever pull over to make more room. The other car ignored her wave. She looked in the rear view mirror, seeing her worried frown reflected back at her along with the headlights on the other car and two dark shapes inside. She could tell they were men. They started to bump her car fender again—this time at an angle. What were they doing? *Jesus, Mary and Joseph—they're pushing me off the road!*

She looked around frantically and fruitlessly—nothing around but miles and miles of bog. No people, no lights—just a car behind her trying to push her off the road into the bog. *Jesus Christ*. Rosaria did the only thing she could think to do. She floored the gas pedal—hurtling down the road, seeing only as far as her headlights allowed. Her hands were frozen to the steering wheel.

The other car followed. She could hear the driver gunning his engine, but he responded just a hair too late. She had a small distance advantage and increased it as much as she could with a heavy foot on the pedal. *Somebody, anybody—even a broken down peat truck with a dog in the passenger seat. Wouldn't anyone come?*

Then, a sudden moment of awful clarity. *She wouldn't meet another car on this road. No one would be stupid enough to take this road at night except a reckless Yank with a bad eye who didn't know how to drive in Ireland.*

And who else? Who else would take this road? Men who were following this reckless Yank. Men who meant this reckless Yank no good. There was no Michael Cahill. Jesus. I'm such a chump. That blow on my head last winter didn't impact just my eye. My brains are turning to mush. Christ.

She drove head-on—not seeing where she was going. Mr. Burke's toy-like Fiesta bumped along wildly—not equal to the challenges of a rough bog road. She'd ruin it, but that was the least of her troubles right now.

Rosaria could hear herself crying and gasping when she missed a switch and ran the Fiesta off the road into the bog. *Jesus God*. Her heart ceased beating for a moment.

She could hear the spray of gravel and loose dirt hit the boulders beside the road as the car behind her braked to a fast, full stop. Then, she could hear the hurried movements of the two men rushing to get out of their car.

Shaking, Rosaria crawled as fast as she could across the seat to the passenger side and half fell out the door. Staying low, protected by the car, she inched toward an outcropping of boulders, stumbling on the grassy hillocks, rough ground and rocks. She didn't think the men could see her.

"Where is she? You take that side." Sharp, rough voices.

Rosaria's mind was swirling, her senses on some kind of disoriented alert. *What was going on?* Her animal instincts screamed—*danger, danger, run, run!*

"Jaysus. I can't see a thing," responded another voice. "Get the damned torch." A clipped, angular northern accent.

Rosaria could feel the comforting rough surface of the large stone between her and the men, whoever they were. *Who were these people?*

There was a rustling on the other side of the road. "Over there," she heard the first man call. The lights from the Fiesta were still on. She peeked around the corner of the boulder and saw the men heading across the road away from her. Her heart stopped. Both men were carrying handguns. *Handguns. For her?*

The face of one man looked dimly familiar. A broad pug nose, square jaw. *The man who called himself Joseph Mulvaney—the missing aide from the care home? Was that possible?* Her head was whirling. This must be a weird, horrible nightmare.

"Watch for the stream here," the first man called to the other. "Ach, why isn't Moran taking care of his own job?"

Rosaria covered her mouth to stifle a gasp. *Moran?* That couldn't be *her* Moran. Hugh Moran connected with these men searching for her with guns in their hands? *Impossible.*

"She's an old flame. Doesn't have the stomach to do it himself," the sham Joseph Mulvaney responded. No northern accent there. Dublin?

Old flame? Do what to his old flame? thought Rosaria, trying to keep herself under control.

"Piece of luck though, that he had that connection when we got the word."

Got the word. What word? Even in her disoriented state, Rosaria knew what they meant. She just couldn't absorb it.

"Well, not the time for hearts and flowers. He's the one who's always saying that hard things have to be done and...Oh, Jesus Christ." The man apparently had stumbled on yet another rocky hillock. "And now, suddenly," he said as he recovered, "he has one goddamned assignment, to off an old girlfriend from years ago and he hasn't the *stomach*. Big talker. That's all he is."

She wasn't sure she could move from the shock. *Off an old girlfriend?* Suddenly there wasn't enough air to breathe. Her breath was ragged. So loud, Rosaria was sure the men would hear her. She desperately held the sobs in by covering her mouth with both hands. Her body shook from the effort.

"You know, he should have done the old guy in the care home—the one who was going a little soft and got talkative. He should have done him too. You notice how he never gets his hands dirty?"

"Shut up, for Chrissakes. She'll hear us coming, if she hasn't. This whole thing already looks like one big fuckup. Let's get this done."

Poor Thomas Martin. And now they want to get this done. Shoot her. Get the job done. *Hugh's job.* A great wave of fear and shock and grief washed over her all at once.

Another, quieter rustle nearby. Rosaria was shaking almost uncontrollably, terror clawed at her heart and her movements were clumsy, but she willed herself to crawl to the side of the boulder, away from the rustle. A musky smell. A sheep. God bless the sheep. Now she could hear other small rustles around the bog. The sheep were out here tonight. Some sleeping, a few moving about, alerted by people intruding on their territory. Those men seemed like city men—they would certainly never know about sheep.

Rosaria hoped the random noises from the sheep would keep the men off kilter. She had to get out of here. The prospect of spending the night in a cold bog was not pleasant, but the bog was vast. If she could find a place to hide, some small bolt hole, they would have a hard time finding her. She thought of the old saints and hermits who lived in holes in the ground or caves. To crawl into a hermit hole and hide from men who were roaming the bog looking to kill her. Men that *Hugh* sent to kill her—*for what? For what?*

She could see the men's flashlights in the distance, moving diagonally toward her. They would cross back to where she was hiding soon, having finally figured out that the rustling noises were from a flock of sheep. Rosaria looked around wildly—where could she go in this vast space when she could see so little? And then she glimpsed the outline of a pile of rocks on a small knoll. *Christ*—the Halfway House. Is that where she would meet her end?

She gave a crazy snicker. She was losing it. The long hand of a grisly history reaching out for her tonight. No time for old tales. There might be something near there to hide in. She would try.

Running low and as fast as she could, Rosaria stumbled over the uneven ground and fell once on a rock, bruising her leg painfully. She turned to see the flashlights coming in her direction. Limping, flooded with adrenaline, she pushed forward. Her leg shrieked from the pain. Nowhere to hide. When they saw the rock piles, they would know where she would head. Maybe she was better out on the wildness of the bog.

She stopped and looked around, breathing heavily. Then, she saw a tall stack of something—wood. No, peat. *The peat harvesters had been here. Oh God, she wished they were still here with their dogs, tractors and trucks. Trucks. Oh, she could never be so lucky. Never.*

Should she keep going in hopes of a truck, knowing that the men would know where she was or should she just forge ahead into the vastness of the bog? Rosaria went for the possibility of a truck.

There were a number of peat piles. The first one had no conveyance around it, nor did the second. Oh, Jesus, behind the third there was an ancient harvesting truck piled high with peat logs. She ran, crying, with her leg collapsing on her several times. She lost a shoe and ran lopsided, the rocks maiming her feet.

Rosaria reached the fender of the old truck and hung to the side until she reached the door. The door opened with a loud creak. "There!" she heard behind her. Breathless, she climbed in and peered at the dashboard in the darkness. A key in the ignition.

But. *Oh shit. Of course.* Another manual shift. She was inept at driving a manual shift in the best of times. Now her hands were shaking, her mind buzzing with a terrified confusion. Rosaria could hear the men running toward her, but closed her eyes for a nanosecond. *I can do this. I can do this.*

Opening her eyes again, she whispered a Hail Mary as she pushed in the clutch and turned the key. *Hail Mary, full of grace. Blessed art thou among women...*It started. It started rough, but it started.

She heard a shout again. "Over there!"

No hiding now. She put the truck in gear and...it stalled. It stalled and it made a lot of noise stalling.

Rosaria's hands were shaking. *Blessed is the fruit of thy womb Jesus...*, she stuttered as she pumped the gas. *Pray for us sinners now and at the hour of our death...Please. Please. Don't flood.* An endless few seconds and...it started again. She heard the crack of a gun behind her and was unable to stifle a scream.

Somehow, trembling and weeping, Rosaria turned on the headlights and maneuvered the truck onto the narrow lane. It started slowly, but she floored the gas, struggling to stay on the narrow road with the bog on either side. The old truck bumped and jostled her on the seat. In the cracked rearview mirror, she could see the dark outlines of the two men joining the road behind her and running. Ordinary-looking men—she would have passed them on Market Street without a second glance. Maybe she already had. No, they were not from Clifden with those accents. She had no time to think about it. *Hugh's men wanting to kill her. She had to get away.*

The workaday truck was not built for speed, and the men were gaining on her. She floored the gas, and then in the dim light—saw a wide lever to the side. *"Release".* Was that what she thought it was? Oh God, she hoped it was.

She pushed down hard on the lever. It stuck. The truck veered to the side of the road when she'd taken her eyes away. She turned her eyes back to the road—she couldn't go off the road. *I can't go off the road.* She pushed the lever again. Again. And then. It popped.

The rear gate on the truck bed flew open with a rush and a clatter. The truck's speed and the bumpy road surface quickly loosened the peat logs piled high in the back of the truck. Heavy, water-soaked logs of earth and vegetation began cascading onto the road before the two men.

"Shite!" she heard behind her. "Shite, shite, shite." They had to jump off the road out of the way of the heavy logs—into the bog where walking, never mind running, was difficult. But, while they were slowed, the two men kept coming.

Rosaria could see the metal road gate ahead at the exit of the peat harvesting site. She had no time to get out and lift the rope securing the gate. The men were making up time, running behind her. She had to smash the gate and break the rope.

The first time didn't work—she backed up, with one long-legged man in the lead getting closer and his partner not far behind. Rosaria floored the gas again and this time the rope snapped. In the dim light, she saw the shadows of the men as they stopped running when the truck broke through the metal gate. Winded, the first man slapped his hands on his knees as he watched the truck move away, the outline of his body an agony of disappointment.

A long ago image of Hugh flashed across Rosaria's mind, Hugh panting from one of those strenuous Donegal hikes when they were students. Hugh, laughing with his hands on his knees like that. Hugh before time, before—for some reason—he wanted to kill her.

Within minutes, Rosaria was on the Ballyconnelly Road again. Here, she knew the way. Hands glued to the wheel, she leaned over—peering out the windshield to stay on the road—past the beach, past the hedgerows. She didn't stop until she got to Keough's Pub across from the Holy Family Church.

With the gas pedal on the old truck still floored, Rosaria roared into the parking lot. She threw the shift into Park, stalled the truck out and hurled herself out the driver's side door. Her leg was collapsing, but she made it to the front stairway of the pub, where she hung onto to the railing and crawled up the steps. She was able to stand by hanging on to the door jamb.

The door to the pub was sticky and wouldn't open. *Dammit. Is there no mercy?* With an exhausted grunt, she pushed hard against the door one more time and fell through when it opened. The pub was crowded and noisy. No one noticed her falling through the door. Everyone was facing the television over the bar where Rosaria could see the images of what looked like last week's football match—apparently a very exciting one as not a soul turned to see her on the floor near a back table. Until a barmaid looked over.

"Mother of God. Someone see to that poor woman."

CHAPTER 36

f there were budget cuts at the Galway Garda and emergency services, it would have been hard to tell from the number of vehicles that descended on Keough's Pub after the barmaid called. Rosaria sat in the midst of a swarm of guards and medical personnel, her leg propped on a chair while an EMT bandaged her up. No breaks from her fall in the bog—just painful bruising and cuts, especially to one leg and her feet. She'd be fine. Physically, she would be fine. Emotionally, maybe not so.

Sergeant Conneely pulled the story of the chase in the bog from her, as Rosaria sipped a hot coffee with a generous shot of Jay. The coffee and the Jameson smelled and felt good going down—warm, comforting. She needed it. She was a wreck—wanting to cry, but too numb. She let the magnitude of Hugh's betrayal sink into her. Into her very being. Into her guts. A tear escaped. She didn't bother to wipe it away.

Hugh Moran sending men after her with guns. What in the world? Everything was upside down. His deep hazel eyes gazing lovingly into hers these past weeks, his caressing her face with a seagull feather on the quay, bringing back old memories at a time when her very soul needed the solace of those old memories.

But now she knew that it was all so that he could pump her for information and then send someone to get rid of her. It was all a farce, his attention, the way he'd looked, the words he spoke.

Her Hugh. Using her, offering her up.

Pushing those thoughts away, she told Sergeant Conneely the story in a hoarse, halting voice, her body buzzing with pain and relief and betrayal. A false old friend named Hugh Moran and two accomplices had tricked her into driving to Roundstone. She'd gotten lost on the Bog Road, and two men had driven her car off the road, then chased her with guns through the bog.

No, she didn't know why. Wait, maybe she might. But she was so confused, so tired, so shocked. She couldn't really talk to it right now. The guards had already called in an alert for a car with two men, probably driving on the Galway

Road. And another call to the Galway City station to pull Hugh Moran in for questioning.

Rosaria had become an attraction in the pub, which had started to fill with curious locals. News had spread about a murderous chase out in the bog involving the American woman—"just like in the movies". No one knew why. Word was that the mob from Dublin was involved. Probably drugs. You'd never think that, would you? She looked like such a nice lady to be involved with that kind of thing.

A Mr. O'Malley in heavy work clothes and a flat hat arrived at the pub with his collie looking for his peat-hauling truck and a crew to help him recover his logs in the morning. They were all over the bleeding road, half of them broken. Rosaria saw in her mind the moment when she'd released the logs in a frantic attempt to impede the two men. She felt again how frightened she was. She started to tremble. A woman nearby put a sweater over Rosaria's shoulders and cooed. "That's all right, dear. It's all over. They're gone. You're in a safe place now."

Suddenly, there was a roar at the front entrance to the pub and what looked like a very angry, very large bull seal burst through the door. A bull seal holding a hurley stick. All conversation ceased.

Mossie had seen her text. And, *sweet Jesus,* thought Rosaria, he had turned around on the road to the hurling match because he was worried about her driving. Along the way back, someone had called him to tell him about the assault on the bog road.

"Where are they? Where are the bastards?" roared Mossie, "They'll be eating dandelions by the roots when I'm done with them." Alarmed, people jumped to the side, out of the way of the lethal ash stick Mossie was holding. Two guards in the pub started toward Mossie, but not before he confronted Rosaria. "Did I not tell you he was a lowlife son of a bitch, not to be trusted? Jaysus. Did I not tell you that?"

Rosaria looked at Mossie blankly. The woman who'd put the sweater around her shoulders stepped between them protectively. Rosaria held a hand up to the woman, "It's okay." To Mossie, she said, "Yes, you did, Mossie. Yes, you did. I should have listened. You were a better judge of character."

"Oh, he was a smooth one now. The Professor," he spat in contempt. "A professor of shite, that's what he's a professor of..."

Gerard Conneely took Mossie by the arm. "Walk with me now, man. Over here. Calm down and talk to me about what you know."

Mossie turned to the guard, "Oh, I'll tell you what I know all right." Then, as he walked to a nearby table with Conneely, he called to the barmaid, "Give us a pint now, Claire. My nerves are shattered. I have a savage thirst." He turned to the guard. "The first time I met him—without even a how do you do—he insulted the club. I knew he was no good after that."

Rosaria saw the guard's jaw tighten with a look that said, *Oh, did he now? As good as convicted,* she thought.

Mossie shared his impressions of Hugh Moran, including some dramatic embellishment, with Sergeant Conneely and his colleagues. When Mossie touched once again on the subject of Hugh's gratuitous insult on the Galway hurlers, Rosaria wondered if that insult would be part of the written criminal complaint.

CHAPTER 37

olly was scheduled to catch the flight over to Shannon the next night. He was beside himself with worry, rage and frustration after Bridie called him to tell him about the events on the bog road.

"Now, I want you to just stay where you are, Rosie," he said when he called. "Are you okay?"

"Yes, I'm okay," she lied.

"Is Bridie with you?"

"Yes, yes. She's staying over and Nora Keenan will be here this afternoon. The Garda have a car outside and Mossie is camped out in the driveway in his van and won't move. Please come, Solly, and send all these good people home."

Rosaria hadn't had nightmares since her arrival in Ireland. But that night, she slept fitfully, dreaming of shadowy figures chasing her over a landscape that wouldn't hold her weight, ground that kept collapsing under her. She regretted dismissing the doctor who had wanted to give her a couple of strong sleeping pills.

Marguerite, who called constantly, was furious with her for not getting prescription help. "Why do you always have to pretend to be so strong? False pride. That's what it is. False pride. And that's a sin, you know. A big sin." Rosaria closed the call without saying goodbye.

She woke early to Fergus at her feet and Bridie making coffee, eggs and brown bread toast in the kitchen. Rosaria had just limped to the big green chair, refusing Bridie's offer of help, and taken a grateful sip of her friend's good coffee when her cell rang.

"I'll get that for you. Don't answer," Bridie called from the kitchen.

"No, I've got it," Rosaria responded when she saw the name on the phone. Thomas Martin. Was Theresa Martin calling? Maybe she'd heard about last night on the bog road. She answered and found it wasn't Theresa Martin calling. It was her mother Eleanor Martin.

"Ms. O'Reilly, Eleanor Martin here," Thomas Martin's widow announced in her flat, affectless and shy voice. Rosaria could picture Mrs. Martin in her tidy kitchen with her wool skirt, the shadow of a scapula beneath a pastel polyester blouse. "I heard about your trouble last night. Are you all right now?"

"I am, Mrs. Martin. Good of you to phone."

"It's important that I see you, Ms. O'Reilly, if you're free. I know this is not a good time, but I need to tell you some things. Important things. Things that need to be told."

"I see."

"Do you have anyone who can drive you to Saint Joseph's Church this morning? I would like to meet you there with Father Roche. Are you well enough to take the ride into town?"

Rosaria didn't respond immediately, looking at her bruised leg which throbbed in complaint even at the thought of getting up to move around.

"I wouldn't ask you but I need to tell you some important things before I lose my courage. It would be easier for me to do that in the church with Father Roche there."

Rosaria recalled uncomfortably that just the day before someone else had persuaded her to drive to Roundstone so that he could tell her some important information, and she'd almost died for it. Still, this was Eleanor Martin and Father Roche. Rosaria was intrigued. Mossie could drive her.

"Yes, I'll be there, Mrs. Martin. Forty minutes?"

"Good. The small chapel at the back of the church. I'll be there with Father Roche."

Rosaria closed the phone and looked up to see Bridie with her arms folded across her chest. "You'll be where, missy?" she demanded.

"Saint Joseph's. To pray for your soul, Ms. Callahan. Would you ask Mossie to come in? I need him to drive me to church."

There were one or two people in the main body of the church when Rosaria arrived, holding on to Mossie's arm. She saw Eleanor Martin and Father Roche sitting side by side in a back chapel. Banks of votive candles flickered before a statue of Saint Theresa.

"You can deposit me here, Mossie." Rosaria pointed to a pew in front of Eleanor Martin and the priest. She sat and stretched her leg to the side to support it and turned to face them, her elbow over the back of the pew. "Good morning. Forgive me, I have to keep this leg up."

"God, yes," said the priest. He rose to get a pillow from a side kneeler and placed it under her leg.

"How're you getting on, Ms. O'Reilly? I've never heard of such thing as you had happen to you last night."

"And I hope you never do again, Father," Rosaria smiled and turned to Eleanor Martin. "It's good to see you again, Mrs. Martin."

"I wish it were under other circumstances," Eleanor replied, fingering a crystal rosary in her lap.

"Yes, I do too," said Rosaria. And then she waited for Eleanor Martin to give her a clue as to the important information she had to tell her. But there was nothing forthcoming. Instead, Mrs. Martin stared at Rosaria and counted the beads of her rosary, murmuring the prayers and mysteries.

Finally, the priest intervened. "Thomas told Eleanor about something that happened here many years ago. Her daughter Theresa knows the core of the story, but, Eleanor would like to share the rest of the story that she knows with you now." He put his hand on the widow's shoulder for encouragement.

"Thank you, Mrs. Martin," said Rosaria looking at the woman who seemed about to collapse in on herself.

Then, in a burst of energy, Eleanor Martin straightened her back, folded the rosary into an embroidered purse and started to talk. To Rosaria, she looked for all the world like a brave little sparrow.

"Theresa told you about the IRA murder at the Saint Mary of Egypt Mother and Baby Home forty-five years ago."

"She did," Rosaria replied.

"It was an IRA man from the north. He was executed for being an informer."

"Did Thomas know who murdered him?"

She shook her head. "Liam never told Thomas that part or told him any names. So, Thomas never knew. But I knew." She looked at Rosaria with what might have been old pride in keeping her long-held secret. "The man who was murdered was a Johnny Powers and it was a Belfast man named Declan Twomey that did the deed."

Rosaria couldn't speak for a few moments. Momentarily disoriented, she put her hand to her mouth and shook her head slowly. *Declan Twomey.* How could that be and how in the world did Eleanor Martin know this?

Rosaria took her hand from her mouth, about to ask this very question when Eleanor spoke again. "You see, Thomas thought he was keeping secrets from me, but I was the one that knew the real story." She let out a deep breath. "I told no one, not even Thomas. There would be nothing but trouble for us if anyone found out what we knew."

Rosaria recognized the ingrained survival habits of an island long occupied by oppressors. "Whatever you say, say nothin'" was a mantra that had carried through the generations even into the old Irish neighborhoods of South Boston and Charlestown.

"But, how did you come to know that full story, Mrs. Martin?"

Eleanor settled in her seat and started to talk. Her eyes were slightly unfocused. Rosaria could see the woman was in another place and time now.

"It was when Thomas and I were courting. One night near the lane when it was quite dark but for the moon, Thomas and I were sitting under an old tree where we liked to meet. We'd talk for hours there," Eleanor said, with a gentle, long-ago smile. "One night, almost before we were each about to go home to our families, Thomas fell asleep. He worked so hard at the farm for his father, you see, he'd get exhausted. I sat there with Thomas's head on my lap. The night was sweet with the moon above. And the sounds of the fields all around. We were so in love, you know." She paused for a moment, a soft expression on her face, still back in time forty-five years. Rosaria could see the lush, pretty young countrywoman Eleanor must have been then.

After some time, she continued, "I heard voices then coming up the lane. Two men coming along and talking quiet-like. I recognized one voice as Mr. Joyce, Liam's father. The other voice had a hard accent. I thought it was from the North, but I had never heard that voice before."

Eleanor took a deep breath and crossed herself. "They were talking about guns—the guns they were bringing onto the shore at the Mother and Baby Home. None of us in the village were supposed to know about that, but there were always whispers about.

"The man from the North was saying to Mr. Joyce that you had to take care of touts—I didn't know what that word meant then—touts. But he said you had to take care of informers right away or everyone was in danger. And he for one was not afraid to do what needed to be done. No one would ever think that Declan Twomey was afraid of doing the hard things to take care of business."

They were all quiet for a few moments. "And you never told anyone this, Eleanor?"

"No, I didn't. Not even Thomas. It was as I told you, better for him not to know." She looked at Rosaria and at the priest. "Those were dangerous times. And now, I can see that these are dangerous times too, Father. Young Patrick Keenan killed. Murderers with guns chasing an innocent woman across the bog at night. And my own Thomas. Do you think I didn't know that he died wrong too?" She started to cry, as the priest patted her shoulder. "A fall in the garden, never," she said with disdain. "I'm not a fool. It's enough. And him not even knowing the name of the killer. They thought he did, but I was the one that knew. Not Thomas. If they come for me, I'm ready to go. The bastards. It's enough."

Turning to the priest, she added, "Sorry, Father."

The priest smiled. "You're forgiven, Eleanor."

Rosaria reached her arm now over the back of the pew and placed her hand on Eleanor's, still folded in her lap. "You're very brave, Eleanor. Would you be willing to share your story with the Garda?"

"Yes, I would." The little pointed jaw on her heart-shaped face moved outward slightly in resolution.

"Sergeant Conneely should be back at the station now. May I ask him to come here to talk to you or would you like to call him yourself?"

"You can call him. I'll wait here with Father. Is that all right with you, Father?" she asked the priest.

He nodded and then asked Rosaria, "Shall I ask Mossie to come in and help you to your car, Ms. O'Reilly? Or would you want to stay?"

"Thank you, Father. Perhaps I will stay, but I think I should go out now for a bit and call Sergeant Conneely first. And I probably should move my leg around some. Yes, Mossie can help me."

The priest walked out the door to the chapel and the room became very quiet. The votive candles flickered, each sending up someone's prayer to Saint Theresa in thin, continuous streams of smoke and supplication. Immersed in the silence for a moment, Rosaria was allowing herself a brief sliver of time to digest what she'd heard. It was then that Eleanor Martin said in a quiet, determined voice behind her, "Cathal McKenna murdered that man."

It felt as if time had stopped in the little chapel. Rosaria was aware of Father Roche and Mossie frozen at the door.

"Say that again, Eleanor?" the priest asked.

"The Declan Twomeys of this world do a job. They *take care of business.* But someone else was the murderer that night just as if he had pulled the trigger himself."

Rosaria heard a sharp intake of breath from Father Roche. "Cathal McKenna, Eleanor? Are you sure?"

She gave the priest a grave look. "Cathal McKenna was at the site—at the Mother and Baby Home cemetery and ordered the murder. That's what

Declan Twomey said that night. He said that Cathal McKenna was there and had ordered him to take care of Johnny Powers that night."

"Cathal McKenna." Rosaria repeated.

"The big man himself. Mr. bloody Peace Process himself."

CHAPTER 38

olly picked up Rosaria's call just as he was leaving his office to wrap up a few things before flying over to Ireland that night. "You okay?" he asked.

"I'm okay. Everything's okay. Cancel your flight tonight."

"What the hell?"

Then, Rosaria told him Eleanor's story.

"So, it's the story of knowing too much," Solly said after a long, thoughtful pause. "Patrick knew too much. Someone had to take care of him."

"Yes, and it would never be Liam Joyce who could take care of Patrick, but he might be pretty sure who did. I think that's really devastating him, not the old story coming out. You'd better stay home and go talk to Liam Joyce and Declan Twomey."

"I guess. Jesus. This is rich. The police there involved?"

"They are now. Gerard Conneely has your card. He'll call with details and follow-up."

"And I'll head off to see Saint Liam. Are you okay? This is all making me crazy with worry about you."

"I'm good, Solly. Don't worry."

"And you were right about the answer being in Ireland."

"It was a long shot."

"Yeah, but you still called it."

"Solly, the answers were on both sides of the Atlantic. We're a good team."

"Miss you."

"Love you, sweetheart. I've been scared to death."

"Me too on both counts."

It all hit her physically when she arrived back at the cottage from Saint Joseph's. Ready to fall into bed, she took one last call from Solly.

"You resting?"

"About to collapse into bed."

"Who's there?"

"Everybody, but they're all in the kitchen. Where are you? Did you talk to Joyce or Twomey yet?"

"Chatham Police are going to pull Twomey in—he's down at his Cape house. Irish security police are on the next flight from Dublin to talk to him. I'm on my way to Vermont."

"Vermont? What for?"

"I'm going to the monastery to see Brother Liam."

"What the hell?"

"Our Liam has joined the Trappists."

"Jesus." Rosaria thought she remembered that Trappists were a contemplative order. "Will they let you talk to him?"

"Apparently, and he sounds like he's ready."

CHAPTER 39

he guards had picked up both men who'd chased Rosaria in the bog, but Hugh Moran was not to be found in either his apartment or his university offices. A teaching assistant covered his classes for the moment while the University tried to locate him.

Before the guards could cordon off Hugh Moran's office, sometime in the wee early morning hours, an intruder had broken into the department offices. Nothing was taken but Hugh Moran's office was ravaged. The computer monitor was smashed, and the computer itself was damaged—though not enough that the guards could not scrutinize it for the investigation. A broken hurley stick, left on the desk atop Professor Moran's shattered office name plate, was used to wreak this havoc. Framed memorabilia, photographs, certifications, honors were thrown to the floor and ground under heavy boots. A flag from the County Kilkenny hurling team was torn to shreds and burned. The University was just glad that the fire did not spread, that Dr. Moran's research and paper files were not destroyed and that the damage was confined to his office.

"Had a busy night last night, did you, O'Toole?" Sergeant Conneely pulled his police car up next to Mossie's Renault van on Market Street the next day. "You're looking peaked, I'd say."

"I'm never better," responded Mossie, jaw out, staring straight ahead.

Conneely nodded and regarded the big man before pulling away. "You take care of yourself now, Mossie. Good men are hard to find."

CHAPTER 40

he leaves hadn't begun to turn yet, but the air was cool and crisp and autumnal. Solly and the soon-to-be-Brother Liam Joyce walked along a clear, flat path in the woods behind Saint Benedict's Monastery in the Vermont hills. Liam's walk, with his hands clasped behind his back and his head down, struck Solly. A penitential walk.

"I'm not really a brother yet," Liam told Solly. "Still in my probationary period. Ordinarily I would not have been able to talk to an outsider during this time, but they could hardly refuse police business." He looked at Solly with a gentle smile. "I certainly hope you have not undermined my chances for a delayed vocation by casting suspicion on my moral character, Detective."

"That depends, Mr. Joyce." Solly returned the smile.

Joyce straightened the dark brown fabric around his legs. "Can't get used to all this cloth around my legs. Gets in your way, especially when you're working."

"Where are you working, Liam?"

Joyce gave Solly a sideward glance and shy grin. "I've been assigned to the brewery."

"Not a bad gig."

"Got lucky. I could have gotten jam-making or—God forbid—managing inventory for the gift shop."

The future Brother Liam seemed at peace. A different man from the one Solly had interviewed in his offices at Saint Martin's.

"Tell me about the story we heard from Eleanor Martin, Liam."

Joyce walked, head down, in silence for a few moments before looking up. He straightened his shoulders, took a deep breath and responded.

"The story your friend Ms. O'Reilly heard from Thomas Martin's widow was essentially correct."

"Go on. Fill me in."

"My father—God rest his soul—was an IRA sympathizer—no, I'd have to say that he was an IRA operative, part of a gunrunning operation at the Saint Mary of Egypt's Mother and Baby Home. What the nuns knew or didn't know,

I can't say. I've always thought they were reconciled to seeing nothing and to hearing nothing—a special Irish talent. The Compassionates were compensated for their complicity with special Irish-American financial contributions to the Home, but perhaps also compensated in another way by satisfying some ancient Republican sentiments of their own."

Liam began to finger a heavy rosary at his waist and took a moment before continuing. "I was just a small boy and understood none of this, of course. When I saw what I did that night at Saint Mary's, all I knew was that there were a group of men with strange accents and my father was helping them.

"I did remember a tall, bearded man to the side, leaning on a car. He didn't say much but seemed to be running things. As I got older and saw the news on the telly and the pictures in the paper, I recognized him, of course, as Cathal McKenna—the TD, the parliament member who's now running for Taoiseach, our prime minister."

Solly found it interesting that Joyce referred to the Taoiseach as *our* prime minister. "Are you a United States citizen, Liam?"

Joyce smiled, "Ah yes, I'm both, Detective. Dual citizenship, God save me. Perhaps I should have made the hard choice, but I was never good at making hard choices. Which is, I guess, the root of all my trouble today."

"How so?"

"That night was not the last time I saw Declan Twomey as a child. There were more operations moving arms through the cemetery. Each time, he'd ask after me, maybe bring me something from a shop in the north—a sporting ball or maybe a kite. Once he brought two pairs of binoculars—one for my father to watch for the boats carrying the arms and another small pair for me for watching the birds.

"He came to our cottage regularly—always at night, though my father didn't encourage that—concerned about security and what people might see. At first I was afraid of Declan. I had seen him kill a man. Even at that age, I sensed he had taken other men's lives, perhaps many other men. And he was big with that reddish hair and those godawful eyebrows." Here Joyce paused to give a sad chuckle. "And by then, he'd had that mark on his face from when the murdered man had thrown a big rock at him.

"But over time I warmed to him. He often came to our cottage, would ruffle my hair and call me the "wee Fenian" and the "young soldier." I liked to think he came just to see me. Perhaps he thought I would grow up to be a militant like he was." Liam laughed softly, "but he sorely overestimated me there."

"How did Declan end up here? How did *you* end up here?"

"I never really knew precisely why Declan left Belfast, but as best I understand it, there was some dissension in the ranks of the organization. For some reason, Declan had fallen out of favor and was on the outs. Not enough to be eliminated, but it would be wiser to for him to move on. And he could be useful in Boston."

"How so?"

"He'd come to Boston a number of times before to make different arrangements on the gun shipments. And there was still work to be done to keep the level of support in the Irish-American community up."

Liam stopped and pointed to a small bench by a rocky stream. "There's a little resting place here that I like. It's very peaceful. Would you mind if we took a break while we talk?"

Solly sat with Joyce on the wooden bench, watching the water in the stream flowing over smooth gray stones. Lost in time. The air was cool. He turned up the collar on his light jacket.

"I could never get over that night at Saint Mary's. It was always with me. I would wake from sleep with nightmares, terrified." Solly thought he heard a light sob but saw no sign on Joyce's face when he looked over. "I still do." He shook his head as if to throw off dark thoughts and memories.

"Later, when I was older, I applied to Trinity in Dublin. I did poorly on the admissions test, but got in anyway—only to find out later Declan had pulled strings to get me in. In school I struggled—both academically and emotionally. I was more sensitive, weaker in so many ways than my father and certainly than Declan Twomey. I was just not equal to it all. I wanted to drop out to save my father the tuition. That's when I learned Declan was paying it." Joyce picked up a small stone, rolled it around in his palms and threw it into the stream. He let out a wet breath and Solly could see tears on the man's cheeks now. "If they were disappointed that I was such a weakling, they never let me know."

Joyce took a deep breath and straightened his back. "My mother had died by then and my father was getting older. My father contacted Twomey, to my great embarrassment."

A small bird landed in the bushes near the bench and two squirrels rustled in the leaves across the stream. Life proceeds. Life goes on.

"Then one day, I got a letter from Declan. He was doing well in Boston, had his own construction firm now. Would I consider coming over to join him? He could use the help."

The small bird in the bush had started to chirp. Solly wished he knew his birds. Gray—what kind of gray bird? Didn't matter. Peaceful here. Listening to an old story. This was the real heart of his job—listening to stories. The reasons why things happen. He had to get this down formally later—written, recorded. For now, listening without interruption to the story of why an innocent young student was murdered.

"The letter came at the right time and I decided to take the shot. Declan had this...this life force, you know. It felt as if someone had thrown me a life preserver. Turned out I was not the best fit with the construction trade. So when there was a staff opening at Saint Martin's, Declan suggested I apply for it, even though I felt I was unqualified. Needless to say, I got it.

"But I did have a talent for dealing with the damaged, the lost—feeling so damaged, so lost myself. I worked my way up the administration ranks and when the executive director job opened, I got that, too. Only later did I realize that every promotion I got coincided with a generous donation by Declan. Declan was beyond generous to the House—and to me."

Two monks walked on the path behind Joyce and Solly. Seeing the weight of the conversation taking place on the bench, they gazed tactfully forward and did not acknowledge the occupants.

Without looking at the bush beside him or at Solly, Liam commented, "Lovely little dark-eyed junco. They have that sweet, sort of tinkling sound to their song." And then Liam mimicked the bird's song perfectly. It was a beautiful moment. Solly almost hated to ruin it. But he had a job to do.

"And Patrick Keenan?" Solly asked.

"I didn't know what to do when he called wanting to talk about an event at the Mother and Baby Home in the '70s. When he came to my office that day, it was clear he had the whole story you have except for Declan's name—he didn't have that. But, he was a smart kid. With a little research, it was only a matter of time. I...I didn't know what to do. And it all came back to me, stronger and darker than ever. That night in the cemetery at the Home with my father and those men. A man weeping and pleading for his life, for his children without a father, Cathal McKenna's cold words—and Declan's laughing before he shot him. That was the worst." He covered his eyes.

"You told Declan about Patrick's visit?"

Joyce said nothing, lost in thought. The small bird in the bush had flown away and the squirrels were busy elsewhere. Solly looked up to see a red-tail hawk cruising in the sky.

Joyce dropped his hands to his lap. "I told him, right after Patrick first called. I told him the boy was coming to see me. I felt I had to—after all Declan's done for me." Joyce stopped talking briefly, and when he spoke again his words came out choppy through small sobs. "Declan came to my office after Patrick left. He wanted to be clear about what Patrick knew. He was enraged.

"I left the office and went to the training area where we were to have our picture taken with the graduates. I was trying to keep to some normal routine, even if I was falling apart. But Declan was white hot. You saw the picture. In the end I couldn't take part in the graduation ceremony—though it turned out that we were in a picture, if not the formal one." Here Joyce gave a wet laugh. "I was a mess and he was—what? He was volcanic."

"Volcanic like what?" Solly asked.

"Volcanic like murderous."

"Do you know if he killed Patrick, Liam?"

"I don't know that, but I think that. I asked him outright."

"What did he say?"

"He said, 'Don't ask me a question that you don't want an answer to, Liam. I'm not afraid to do things that need to be done. But don't ask me what you don't want me to tell you, lad.'"

"Mr. Joyce, did you think that Declan Twomey would harm Patrick if you told him about what the boy knew?"

Joyce gave a strangled sob. "God help me."

"Did you tell Mr. Twomey that you were going to talk to me?"

"I did. I did. I told him. I had to. After all this time. I had to." Joyce put his face in his hands and wept.

CHAPTER 41

osaria listened on the phone as Solly told her about Liam's story that night. "My God, what a tale, Solly. The IRA killer and construction magnate who loved a little boy, tried to take care of him in his fashion, and ends up killing someone else's boy. I wonder what Liam Joyce's life would have been like without Declan Twomey."

"I guess we'll never know," Solly replied.

"Have you picked up Twomey yet?"

"In a fashion, as you say."

"What's that mean?"

"Chatham Police went to Twomey's house on the Cape. Out on the porch, they found Twomey in a rocker facing the ocean, with a half a bottle of Bushmill's and an old IRA revolver, a Webley, in his hand. He had used the gun on himself."

"Good God."

"Mrs. Twomey was at the kitchen table, saying the rosary. She wouldn't talk except to say over and over, "He was a good man. No matter what, a good man. Heart of gold.""

"What would Nora Keenan say to that?" Rosaria commented sharply. "A cold-blooded killer."

"Right."

"Do you think he was still IRA? Such a long time ago. Do they even do things like this anymore?"

"I'm told by a couple of experts here that only a small number of extremists are active that way these days. Everyone else has moved on to the political process. Twomey was not an extremist. I think he was protecting Liam from it all coming out. It would have destroyed Liam's life completely. For Patrick's death, I could see Saint Liam as an accessory to murder, but that depends on the prosecutor."

"You know, Solly. Liam knew Declan and what he would do with that information. Joyce might as well have hit Patrick with that oar himself. And he might as well have killed Thomas Martin—his own cousin, for God's sake—after telling Declan where Patrick got his information. Liam Joyce has blood on his hands."

"I'm with you on that."

"How do you think Patrick's murder happened?" Rosaria asked.

"Best we can figure out, Patrick learned that he should be talking to Declan Twomey, who looked like an old-line IRA operative. So he set up a meeting. Declan said he had work on the Long Wharf and could Patrick meet him there? Completely naive. Kid had no idea who he was dealing with. Those days are so far removed from this generation. They think it was all like a movie or a TV special or something. Anyway, he unwittingly set up a meeting with a seasoned killer with a long history."

"It's painful to think about it..." Rosaria said. "What people will do for love. Twomey loved Liam, didn't he? Like a son, I mean."

"That looks like the heart of the story. Of course he wanted to protect himself, but Declan was always very fond of Liam and had high hopes for the boy. Aspirations Liam couldn't live up to as tortured as he was by the crime he witnessed. Now, Declan just wanted to protect him from more pain. One last favor for Liam that went so terribly wrong."

"What a favor. It's all so tragic. A little boy sees something no child should see and it defines his life."

"Yeah."

"Liam wasn't a child anymore. He should have stepped forward. He didn't, and he sacrificed not only Patrick but Thomas Martin, his own cousin."

They settled into a sad silence for a few moments.

"When are you coming home?" Solly asked.

"End of this week."

"Thank God for that."

"You sound almost Irish."

"Sounds like a dangerous thing to be. Save this nice Jewish boy from that."

"Hey, Solly?"

"What?"

"I'm signing papers for this house."

Solly was very quiet. She could hear only his breathing.

"You're shitting me. You're not moving there, are you?"

"No, no. It's just a good buy. Mossie's going to rent it. Move out of the mountain hut he lives in. He's taking the dog too. What a pair. I'll miss them both."

"I miss you more."

"And I miss you more," she murmured.

In her hand, Rosaria was rolling some flecked gray stones from the beach in front of the house. She'd taken to picking up stones she liked, perhaps the odd interesting piece of driftwood or seaweed, some shells and a feather or two. They lined the window sills of the house. She'd taken down all of Mrs. Burke's fussy curtains and had put up some light, sheer ones which she kept open to the view.

"He's already bought a big Galway hurling flag he's going to hang outside." She placed the stones on the side table beside Mr. Burke's pipe stand. His daughter had bought him a new one for Christmas, probably sitting on another end table now in his new Seattle apartment. She hoped he'd be happy there. Perhaps she'd keep this old pipe stand here—kind of a shrine to an old man she'd never really met, but felt she knew.

"I thought maybe I could ask Mossie to move back to his little cabin up in the Ingah Pass every once in a while so that you and I could come over in the summer for a vacation. The scenery is gorgeous, the people are great and the days are so long and magical in the summer."

"I hope I don't have to go to a hurling match."

"You will, and I think you are going to become an addict, Mr. Belkin. Just like Mossie. You might even forget your Bruins."

"Now, that's just crazy talk, Rosie."

CHAPTER 42

he last thing Rosaria wanted to do was take another phone call. It was all so tiring and sad. She only hoped that what she'd found out and what the police investigation uncovered would bring some comfort to the Keenans, though she honestly didn't think it would bring much comfort to her if she'd lost a son. But then, she'd done the best she could.

She saw it was Sarah on the phone. She picked up. Maybe there was some follow-up.

"Ms. O'Reilly?"

"Yes, Sarah. How are you?"

"Good. Good. I'm good, Ms. O'Reilly. I'm calling because I got something in the mail from Patrick."

"From Patrick? How could that be?"

"He must have sent it before..." she paused, "Before, you know. Before it happened. He sent it to our old place, the Corrib Village, where we were staying before."

"And no one ever forwarded it to your new place?"

"No, it's a little packet—too big to fit into the letter slot, so it was thrown onto a hall table with all the circulars and the other junk. You know what a mess it is when so many students live in one place—coming and going. Just lucky it didn't get tossed. Now and then the caretaker just dumps it all. But one of our old neighbors picked it up and called me. I just opened it."

"Yes?"

"It's a flash drive. There was a little note. Shall I read it to you?"

"Please."

"Sarah—yours for safe-keeping. Pulled an all-nighter to get this done after my meeting with Joyce yesterday. Tell no one. It's big. Home soon. Always, always, yours alone. — P."

The girl's voice broke on the last words.

"Not easy, Sarah."

"Yeah. Not easy." The girl let some moments pass. "Yeah. Well. So I took a look at it. I figured what harm could it do now?"

"Should I come?"

"Yes, I think that would be a good idea—as soon as you can."

Mossie picked Rosaria up for the drive to Galway City within the hour, dropping her off at Sarah's new apartment on Seamus Quirke Road after morning classes. Sarah opened her laptop on the kitchen table. She brushed away the crumbs and debris of a rushed early morning tea. Neither woman spoke as she loaded the drive.

Rosaria had a sharp intake of breath as Patrick's words came up on the screen. A newspaper article ready for submission. The headline was sensational:

Nuns and Guns—Murder and the Taoscich Candidate
1970's IRA Murder and Gun-Running Uncovered at
Connemara Mother and Baby Home

Patrick's prose was florid, yellow journalism at its best, but flowed well—skillfully capturing a dangerous and complicated time in Irish history. The story was compelling, well-researched and, Rosaria believed, all true. The key source was Thomas Martin. But Patrick's report of his meeting with Liam Joyce, in which he'd ambushed the shelter director with his knowledge of the murder at Saint Mary of Egypt Mother and Baby Home, locked the narrative down.

It was all there.

An IRA execution at the Mother and Baby Home by a high-level IRA operative, most likely Declan Twomey of West Belfast, on orders of Cathal McKenna, who was present the night of the murder and led the operation. The arms shipments from America, the nuns' implicit knowledge of the Home as a waystation for arms transport through their general factotum.

Brendan Joyce. The story of Brendan's son, wracked with remorse and conflicted loyalty, escaping to Boston for a life of penance and service. Always under the protection of Declan Twomey, the man who pulled the trigger that night at the Home—devoted to protecting the "wee Fenian," the young boy who saw what he shouldn't have. The young boy now a man who kept his secret for the sake of his father, for the sake of Declan Twomey—like another father to him.

Rosaria and Sarah were lost in their own thoughts for a few minutes. Sarah stared into space, mindlessly stroking the handle of a blue teapot. Rosaria dropped back in her chair and turned to look out a nearby window at the students walking by.

There had always been stories. Maybe the stories were true, or only in part. Before the IRA contracted with Libya for arms shipments, guns destined for Belfast were said to arrive off the west coast of Ireland from Boston, Philadelphia, and New York. Perhaps the crates were marked as maritime supplies or fishing gear or other innocuous cargos. Ferried to the mainland by local fishing boats and then perhaps stashed in abandoned farm outbuildings or buried in the local rocky fields near the border until picked up for transport to the North.

One moonless night, a fishing boat, motors muted, glides into a seldom-used little harbor at the end of a long, bumpy, and overgrown road through the Derrygimla commonage. It pulls silently alongside a granite wharf just big enough to handle one Connemara fishing boat at full tide. A granite wharf which fronts the Saint Mary of Egypt Mother and Baby Home.

On the rise beside the Home sits a cemetery. Built into a small hill there an old burial vault from famine times, filled with victims of the Great Hunger—victims perhaps early in the famine years—before so many, so many skeletal, ghostly figures began dropping like flies on the sides of the roads. Before the communal spirit became utterly overwhelmed and lost the capacity to absorb, to give decent burials, decent rituals.

Years later, there was room to hold the remains of babies and small children—bits of humanity perhaps too weak or malnourished to withstand the frequent epidemics or the damp Connemara cold. Joined too, by some of their despairing young mothers in this final resting place. Those who didn't make it lay here by a small, dark harbor in the wilds of western Ireland, after lives perhaps punctuated with brief, youthful moments of forbidden ecstasy. A steep price—theirs alone to pay—for those moments. Or perhaps, there was no ecstasy involved. Perhaps some had been violated through no fault of their own, and were punished for becoming victims.

But then, maybe this burial vault was still not entirely filled. There was clearly room enough for crates on their way North, with another, later stop at an arms dump in a Munster farm outbuilding. Crates bound for the gray, crowded streets of Derry. For the callused, experienced hands of hard men, for the softer hands of young men filled with rage and excitement, reaching for manhood.

And outside the vault one night, a murder. A big man who'd been alive just the day before, who'd kissed his wife and children goodbye when he left his row house on a side street in West Belfast. A big man who'd stopped afterwards to buy his tickets for the GAA All-Ireland football match-up between Tyrone and Mayo. Now, dropped by his former colleagues like a piece of meat off the back of a sheep trailer with a false bottom. A short, emotionless errand for these men on their way North. To the North with their cargo of death into the cauldron of The Troubles and the warring streets.

Behind them, a man's body—still warm—sinks into the oblivion of the bog. A bog keeps its secrets and preserves them. Bog bodies from thousands of years in the past are frequently recovered, amazingly well preserved. It would be no great thing to find a leathery, preserved victim from the time of The Troubles— perhaps an informer or just a generally inconvenient person. Happens all the time. The years of The Troubles or even the Great Hunger are such tiny slivers of time in the life of the vast, boggy prehistoric moors. They will hold their secrets—until the day they decide to tell.

Rosaria straightened her shoulders and turned to Sarah, speaking softly. "Where do you think Patrick would have sent this article if he'd been able, Sarah?"

"Oh, right to *The Independent.*"

"Then that's exactly what we'll do right now."

Together, Rosaria and Sarah composed an email to the editor of *The Independent,* explaining the background of the article, including Patrick's murder. By mid-morning, they'd attached Patrick's article and it was ready to go. Rosaria let Sarah press the Send button, after which she wrapped the girl in a long embrace.

"Well done, Sarah. Well done."

Patrick's story was indeed as explosive as he thought it would be when it appeared in *The Independent*. After the article appeared, *The Independent* did more research, and a follow-up article reported on a small group of activists, including Professor Hugh Moran of the National University at Galway and his accomplices.

While this group was not involved in the earlier arms smuggling operation, its members were passionately devoted to protecting the ambitions of men like Cathal McKenna, who promised to speed up unification of the two Irelands. These men became aware through communications from Boston that a woman named Rosaria O'Reilly would be asking questions about Patrick Keenan's research—questions that might lead her to learn about an IRA execution in the seventies ordered by Cathal McKenna at the Saint Mary of Egypt Mother and Baby Home.

The article went on to comment that to have been active during The Troubles was forgiven and even understood—within limits. But for a politician with national ambitions in the Republic to have blood on his own hands— that was another matter. A Taoiseach who had murdered or who had ordered murders was not the image of a modern, European, forward-looking Republic. Too dark. Too violent. Too much reality.

The article finished:

How could one not draw conclusions now about the connections between the murder of Patrick Keenan—who was researching the story of an IRA execution ordered by Cathal McKenna—and the claims of Mrs. Eleanor Martin of Clifden that her husband Thomas, who gave the young student the story, was murdered in the care home where he was living?

CHAPTER 43

efore Justine's ill-advised photo of Rosaria and Solly at a local fund-raiser appeared in the social pages several months ago, Rosaria had never really had her picture in the *Boston Globe*. Unless you counted a couple of group photos in the business pages from her former corporate life.

"You're famous again. Check out the *Globe* on-line," Solly said in his next call. "Cute picture but you're not going to like it any better than the last one."

"Hmm. Great. Okay. I'll call you back later."

Rosaria searched for the iPad which she'd stashed away on arriving in Ireland, and had never missed. She found it behind Mrs. Burke's fussy settee in the corner, fortunately plugged in and fully charged.

While the cottage did have WiFi, no one had promised that it would be fast. The little blue "working on it" circle seemed to rotate for a maddeningly long time. In the meantime, she went to the kitchen to refresh her coffee and let the little blue circle do its thing. She'd just sat down in the green chair again when the front page of the *Globe* appeared.

Solly had told her that the papers were full of the Declan Twomey and Liam Joyce story. The public couldn't get enough of it—a high profile philanthropist and the saintly director of a Boston homeless shelter—with this kind of history. It was unbelievable. Reporters were hungry for as much information as they could uncover for their readers.

For her part, Rosaria did not have the heart to go to the *Globe* website and read about Patrick's murder, Saint Liam Joyce's long-held secret, and his new vocation in a Trappist monastery. Nor did she wish to hear more about Declan Twomey's dual life as a successful and upstanding citizen of Boston as well as a violent IRA operative. A life lived by a hard code that ended in suicide. She'd been isolating herself in the Burke cottage to get away from all this—with only Fergus, Mossie, and Bridie for company.

Now, she steeled herself to see the photo Solly told her about. She did not have to scroll down very far to find it. The picture was part of the front page news, accompanying the story of Declan Twomey's death and the investigation into Patrick's murder. And she did indeed look cute in the old black and white photo. But then, she was probably about six years old at the time, and who doesn't look cute then?

Her dark hair was in thick braids, with plaid sateen ribbons that matched her plaid dress with a white bodice. Smiling happily, she was holding up a doll with dark braids like her own. Two men sat on either side of her, each grinning and each with an arm around her shoulders.

Each with an arm around the shoulders of a sweet girly. Jimmy O'Reilly's sweet girly daughter. Her proud father on the one side of her and, on the other side, a younger version of Declan Twomey.

Rosaria knew the restaurant in the picture—O'Keefe's in Malford Square. The wood-paneled wall in the background, covered with photos of groups and mementos—including crossed Irish and American flags and a large brass shamrock. O'Keefe's—where they'd often celebrated special family occasions and events and entertained visitors.

Looking at her father's wide open and smiling face, Rosaria called to memory the visitors he'd meet and receive with his family at O'Keefe's restaurant over the years. There were so many occasions and so many visitors in Jimmy O'Reilly's exuberant life. They were all a blur to her. Mostly business related, but perhaps not always to do with the shoe factory's commercial business. Maybe, she couldn't deny now, some had to do with the gunrunning business.

She had a wisp of a memory of Declan Twomey. One of any number of big men who came to socialize with Jimmy O'Reilly and his family over a pot roast at O'Keefe's. Some had odd accents, but were kindly to her and, like her father's other business associates—the real ones in the shoe business—they often brought small gifts to Jimmy O'Reilly's daughter. After dinner, they would repair to the long wooden bar in O'Keefe's and talk about—what?—talk about arrangements.

Rosaria gazed at the doll in the picture again. How she'd loved that doll. Brought by one of those big men she'd somehow forgotten. Brought by Declan Twomey for *Jimmy's wee girly*.

She touched Declan Twomey's image through the screen. A full mass of hair which must have been a deep red brown then, those thick black eyebrows and lively eyes. This picture was before those eyes deadened over the years from having seen too much, done too much. Deadened with all the killings, all the betrayals, all the revenges. And there was no ragged scar on his right cheek. This was before he murdered a man at the Saint Mary of Egypt Mother and

Baby Home. Before the man he murdered had thrown a jagged rock at him and left a memento of that violent night.

Two hands around her shoulders in the picture. Her father's long, slim hand on one shoulder, dwarfed by the heavy hand and blunt fingers of Declan Twomey on the other.

Declan Twomey's hands. She saw them in her mind's eye pulling the trigger on the man called Johnny Powers. Those hands wielding an oar on the Long Wharf when he smashed Patrick Keenan's head and left him to die in Boston Harbor.

How many others? How many other John Powers? How many other Patrick Keenans?

And her father. Her gentle, generous, naive father. Did he know any of these horrors? Was he caught in some romantic old story of songs and brave republican martyrs? Could he ever have imagined the agony of endless violence and cold brutality—the ceaseless deaths of innocents? She had to believe, for her own sanity, that he couldn't.

Solly called a few minutes later. "You see it?"

"Yeah."

"It was mailed from Chatham. We figured Twomey dropped it in the mailbox just before he did himself."

"I see. Why do you think he did that?"

"For you, I think."

"Nice."

"You know, honey, I don't know if it was meant maliciously—outing your dad and all. That's kind of ancient history and plenty of guys around Boston could be held accountable in different ways during those years."

"Give me another reason he sent it."

"In a funny way, I think maybe he wanted you to remember him differently."

She didn't respond.

"Complicated," said Solly.

"I guess."

"Will you come home now, sweetheart?"

"Yeah, I'll come home."

CHAPTER 44

all was in the air when Sergeant Gerard Conneely called Solly one morning a few weeks later. The leaves on the hardy urban chestnut trees that the Boston Park Department planted on Tremont Street had started to turn. Students at Northeastern, across the street from Boston Police headquarters, now wore sweaters and jackets as they rushed to classes, and had switched to hot coffee takeout from Peet's instead of the warm weather iced coffee.

"Well, Solly, my friend. Looks like we've found our man. Looks like we found Johnny Powers."

"No kidding. Where'd you find him?"

"Well, we didn't find him, exactly. One of the turf-cutters' dogs did. The men were out collecting the dried peat stacked in the bog when—wouldn't you know it—one of the dogs came prancing up the road with an arm bone in his month."

"You're shitting me."

"No, I am not. The bone was partly deteriorated. The acidity in the bog does that, but the skin—the skin, you know, it gets tanned like leather. All brown and tough—it's almost like a shroud for the bones."

"Got it. Don't need to hear the rest about the bones and the skin and the bog."

Conneely laughed, "Wimp."

"Yeah, I am," Solly agreed. "How do you know it wasn't an animal bone?"

"Well, now, the animal would have to have been wearing a navy sweater and a bitch of an expensive watch."

"Find the rest of the body?"

"Yeah, the dog led us right to it. All fits together. You know, he even had the remnants of tickets to that year's GAA football match between Tyrone and Mayo in his leather wallet, along with his identification. The leather must have given some protection to the contents."

"Who won?"

"Which game? The football game? Probably Mayo."

"What other game would we be talking about?"

"This other republican game that this case was all about, Solly—no winners yet in that long game. The Long War. May go into overtime. My money's on the Republicans. In the end."

"Figures."

CHAPTER 45

ust before Thanksgiving that year, Rosaria was in her kitchen experimenting with a new curried pumpkin soup recipe that she intended to serve for dinner on the day with Solly, Bridie, and a couple of guys Solly worked with.

Archie slept in an afternoon patch of sunlight near the long window facing the harbor. Favorite grubby tennis ball beside him, content that all was as it should be again in his little doggy world.

Rosaria had brought up the mail earlier and dumped it on the hall table without looking through the pile. It was that time of year when catalogs and circulars seemed to mate and procreate in the mail box. Even as she tried to get her name off of various mailing lists, she had to work hard to stay ahead of the catalog flow before the pile got overwhelming.

Now, while the soup simmered—*this recipe is a keeper,* she thought, *if only for the smell*—she brought the pile of mail over to the recycling container to do a quick sort and discard the day's collection of catalogs. In the process, she almost threw away a letter tucked in among the brochures and circulars. A small white envelope with an unusual stamp. She peered at the stamp closely— Gibraltar? Who would be sending her a letter from Gibraltar?

But it was the handwriting on the front that took her breath away. Painfully familiar and blocky—the a's almost like Celtic script. She had to sit down quickly on the hall chair before she stumbled from the dizziness, the tingling throughout her body. Inside, a few lines in that once-loved script floated on a hard white card:

> *I won't ask for forgiveness—beyond forgivable. Remember Malin Point and pray for me. — H.M.*

Rosaria's Curried Pumpkin Soup

 clipped this recipe from the "Home" pages of a local paper in Madison, Wisconsin many years ago when two of our kids were at UW Madison. If I knew the original author of this delicious soup, I would gladly give credit.

We have served this soup at Thanksgiving and fall dinners for decades. I thought the smell of a curried pumpkin soup on the stove in Rosaria's apartment would enrich the last scene of *Buried Troubles*. I hope you enjoyed the book and perhaps will also enjoy her pumpkin soup!

Ingredients (Serves 7):

½ pound fresh mushrooms, sliced
½ cup chopped onion
2 tablespoons butter
2 tablespoons all-purpose flour
½ to 1 teaspoon curry powder
3 cups vegetable broth
1 can (15 ounces) solid-pack pumpkin
1 can (15 ounces) evaporated milk
1 tablespoon honey
½ teaspoon salt
¼ teaspoon pepper
¼ teaspoon ground nutmeg
minced chives

Directions:

1. Sautee mushrooms and onion in butter until tender in a large skillet or cast iron frying pan.

2. Stir in flour and curry powder until blended. Continuing to stir, gradually add broth. Bring to a boil, continue to stir until thickened—for two or three minutes.

3. Add pumpkin, milk, honey, salt, pepper and nutmeg. Heat for several more minutes. Use chives for garnish (optional).

ACKNOWLEDGMENTS

I'm very pleased that Barking Rain Press picked up *Buried Troubles,* my second *Rosaria O'Reilly* mystery. Many thanks to editor Barbara Bailey and proofreader Hannah Martine for making it a better book. As with the first *Rosaria O'Reilly* mystery, *The Immaculate,* I've been in capable hands throughout the process.

Heartfelt thanks go to my writing teachers—now too numerous to mention—who have been the gifts that keep on giving with each story I write. To the writers and teachers who edited or critiqued this book—Ramona DeFelice Long—author, editor, and teacher, and Greg Fallis—Gotham Writers Workshop author and teacher. During my writing journey, I've been blessed with talented teachers, all skilled writers themselves.

My thanks to Sisters in Crime and Mystery Writers of America for their support. Writing is a solitary activity, in my case scribbling or tapping away in the early morning before the rest of the world gets up, hoping to create a story that will resonate with readers. But you never know. It's a long road. The warm camaraderie of fellow mystery writers can make the difference between keeping one committed to telling the tale or deciding to hang it up and go back to bed or out to Dunkin' for coffee and a glazed doughnut.

I can't say enough about the loyal support of my family and friends who will patiently read half-cooked manuscripts, faithfully attend bookstore readings on cold and sleety winter nights, write reviews, buy too many copies of my book for other relatives and friends, and arrange for book club discussions. I'm not sure what I've done to be gifted with such a rich reservoir of kindness and support, but I am beyond grateful.

My husband Bill and our children—Maggie, Nick, Katherine, and Mary and their partners—have always been there with loving support and encouragement in my aspirations (as has Archie, my loyal canine companion, who follows me from room to room and sleeps on the footstool of the Big Green Chair or under my desk when I am working). They and our grandchildren, to whom *Buried* is dedicated, are all the world to me.

And thanks especially to you, dear reader, who takes the time to read my story and even the acknowledgments. You are, after all, the one I write these stories for.

MARIAN McMAHON STANLEY

ALSO FROM
MARIAN MCMAHON STANLEY

The Immaculate: A Rosaria O'Reilly Mystery

———

COMING SOON FROM
MARIAN MCMAHON STANLEY

The Mariposa Circle: A Rosaria O'Reilly Mystery

———

WWW.MARIANMCMAHONSTANLEY.COM

About Marian McMahon Stanley

Marian McMahon Stanley enjoyed a long international career with a Fortune 500 company and a senior position at a large urban university before turning to writing mysteries. A dual citizen of the United States and Ireland, she is the proud mother of four adult children and a growing number of grandchildren. Marian writes in a small, bookish town outside Boston where she lives with her husband Bill and—just like in the book—a Westie named Archie. She is the author of another *Rosaria O'Reilly* mystery, *The Immaculate*, and is now hard at work on her next book in the series, *The Mariposa Circle*. You can find out more about Marian on her website, Facebook, Linked In and Twitter.

WWW.MARIANMCMAHONSTANLEY.COM

About Barking Rain Press

id you know that five media conglomerates publish eighty percent of the books in the United States? As the publishing industry continues to contract, opportunities for emerging and mid-career authors are drying up. Who will write the literature of the twenty-first century if just a handful of profit-focused corporations are left to decide who—and what—is worthy of publication?

Barking Rain Press is dedicated to the creation and promotion of thoughtful and imaginative contemporary literature, which we believe is essential to a vital and diverse culture. As a nonprofit organization, Barking Rain Press is an independent publisher that seeks to cultivate relationships with new and mid-career writers over time, to be thorough in the editorial process, and to make the publishing process an experience that will add to an author's development—and ultimately enhance our literary heritage.

In selecting new titles for publication, Barking Rain Press considers authors at all points in their careers. Our goal is to support the development of emerging and mid-career authors—not just single books—as we know from experience that a writer's audience is cultivated over the course of several books.

Support for these efforts comes primarily from the sale of our publications; we also hope to attract grant funding and private donations. Whether you are a reader or a writer, we invite you to take a stand for independent publishing and become more involved with Barking Rain Press. With your support, we can make sure that talented writers thrive, and that their books reach the hands of spirited, curious readers. Find out more at our website.

WWW.BARKINGRAINPRESS.ORG

Barking Rain Press

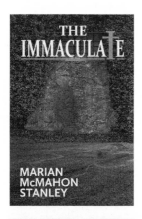

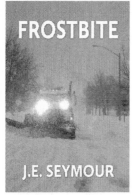
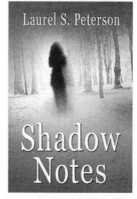